RAFFY'S SHAPES

TAMAR HODES

Published by Accent Press Ltd – 2006
ISBN 1905170173
Copyright © Tamar Hodes 2006

Printed and bound in the UK by
Cox and Wyman Ltd Reading, Berkshire

Cover Design by Emma Barnes

The publisher acknowledges the financial support
of the Welsh Books Council

For Rhoda, my mother and my friend

Acknowledgements

Thank you to all my family, especially to Dave, Ben and Daisy, and Aubrey; to my late cousin David Novitz, whose book *The Boundaries of Art* was an inspiration to me; to Paul and Sue Machlin for taking me to Lake Messalanskee, where I saw the lemon-slatted cottage; To Hazel Cushion and all at Accent press for their support; to Sharon Tregenza for her excellent copy editing; and to West Midlands Arts for a grant that allowed me time to work on this novel. Finally, Raffy's Shapes is also in memory of my late uncle Mayer, with whom I had a long correspondence about writing.

Chapter
I

Raphaella is a bird tonight.

The angles of her arms have rounded into soft wings, blue-feathered and gleaming. Her legs have tucked beneath her; her feet become claws. Her head tucks into her neck as she preens herself proudly. The beak is bright and sharp, her eyes alert and shiny. Full and plump, she perches on the sand beside the lake. Self-contained, contented. The slight waves which rise and flatten on the water lift her feathers slightly. Her chest juts out, a purple-blue sheen in the evening light. Her claws dig into the sand, her body rounded, nestled into its own imprint. Sometimes she takes flight, widens her wings, creates an image of herself upon the lake, but tonight she is still and thoughtful, a glimmering shape at the water's edge.

Later, and uncurled to human shape again, Raphaella returns to the cottage, throws a maroon velvet wrap around her bare shoulders, hangs blue beads in swathes around her neck, pours wine, lights the many fat candles that stand on the floor in this serene, white room. Flames leap and dance, create pools of wax inside themselves.

She takes the glass jars, which she keeps in a row on the shelf, and empties them, one at a time. Spreads the contents on her table. All the objects are white. From the first jar tumble shells, which she's collected. She rubs a finger along the serrated edge of one, feels its sharpness. Each is different – some are large and open out, offer, their bodies. Others are shy and small and their pink lips curl inwards. But each shell has been found by her. This is important, she thinks, as she places each shell back in the jar. Everything needs to be initiated by her.

Next, the jar of feathers, soft, with frayed tips. As she squeezes each fringed edge between thumb and forefinger, she recalls the birds she has plucked those feathers from – sometimes when she has been herself, at others when she, too, has been a bird. Some of those feathers are her own. From her back. Her breast.

And in the next jar, buttons. White and cool. Shiny counters. They spill on to the table and rattle like rice. She runs her finger along the smooth outer circle of each disc. Then each is replaced. Raphaella's jars and shapes go back on to the shelf, gleaming, rearranged.

She hears a car on the path. The front door opens. Oliver enters, holding white lilies, long-stemmed. She takes the lilies, lets him kiss her on the mouth, knows from the flowers and his lips and even from the well-prepared smell of him that he wants something from her tonight.

Raphaella puts the lilies in a tall glass vase. They drink, talk, or rather Oliver talks. He, after all, discovered her, or as he prefers to say, created her. He wants to know what she is painting, tells her there is to be another exhibition in New York, another opening night which he knows she won't agree to fly over for. She never does.

Raphaella brings them a black fig salad, luscious grainy fruits on a bed of rocket leaves with olive oil threading a snail trail over the greens. They eat and it is then that he tells her:

"I've decided to write a biography of you: The Life and Works of Raphaella Turner."

She laughs disdainfully. "Who said you could do that?"

"Who said I couldn't?"

"How would you know what my life or work are about? I'm not sure that I know myself."

"Your usual arrogance," says Oliver. "You assume your life belongs to you. I know you, or part of you. I know your body, know your paintings, can interview your family, friends, gallery owners, those who collect your work. Lucius is keen to get involved, too. I know – or will know – you. I'm sure you'll help me, answer my questions."

"I won't speak to you for your stupid bloody biography. I have spoken little to you about my work in the past. The paintings should speak for themselves."

"Your paintings do speak to me."

Raphaella laughs again, lifts a whole fig greedily to her mouth, wipes the drips of olive oil from her chin. Drains her wine glass. Oliver looks away, tries again:

"I'll look at the influences on you, where you're coming from."

"I have no influences. I do what no one else has done – and in a different way. There's absolutely no point in painting if you merely repeat what someone else has done. Or even if you use others as a starting point. I'm not coming from anywhere. You're not as bright as you wish you were."

"Maybe not. Maybe you're right. You very kindly reinforce what my mother always said. But I shall write the book anyway."

"Write it then. I hate books about art, with their reduced colour reproductions. They are mere failures, attempts to understand and articulate what can never be understood and articulated. They are acts of jealousy, of inadequacy."

"Then painting is mere vanity, done to show what you can do that I can't do."

"You're right," she says. "People pay me for doing what others can't."

They make love. Raphaella never knows why she sleeps with him. It seems more out of habit than anything else. It is satisfying but nothing more than that. His body, it is true, is beautiful, superior to his disappointing mind, she thinks. His fingers run over her thighs, trace her breasts firmly, sensuously. She thinks, however, I am not merely a shape. I am a creator of shapes. Afterwards, they lie, moist and warm for a while on white cotton sheets, aware of each other: her legs, his shoulder, the sharp edge of his chin, her breasts upon his chest, his soft dark hair.

Oliver drives away and Raphaella slips into her studio to paint.

Huge canvases rest their shoulders against the wall. Her current one, perched on a wide double easel, holds three rough blocks of colour – white, yellow, blue. It reminds her of that day when she was in the lake and looked from the water to the sky as from morning to night. She was the blue that day. Now she takes white and frays the edges of the painting – they were too hard. A white line runs from top to bottom, thin oil lines – a fracture, a division. The oil on the figs slips briefly into her mind. Paint trickles, runs down the canvas. She must not let the painting be too much like a Rothko. It must be a Raphaella Turner. For at this moment, only she exists. Her in her white room, with the blue beads tapping her chest lightly as she paints. She steps back to look critically at her canvas, forward again to paint. It is everything.

At home, Oliver sits down at the computer and calls a white page on to the screen. Drinks his coffee. Begins.

The Life and Work of Raphaella Turner

Chapter One: The Present Day

A lemon-slatted cottage beside a lake is the home of painter Raphaella Turner. Thirty-seven years old, she lives without

4

any companions – human or animal. She spends most of her time alone, painting, swimming, rearranging her possessions. Inside, everything is white – the sofa, the candles on the floor, the walls, the curtains. It is a sparse world where the only colours are Raphaella's huge canvases and her own exotic clothes.

Although she admits no influences on her, there are clearly painters whose work she admires. Many have compared her painting to those of Rothko, Klee, even at times Kandinsky, but she denies this. She insists that her creating starts with her, not with anyone else, that she does not come from any kind of tradition, but that she has emerged alone and not from any kind of artistic or historical backdrop.

Oliver stops, peers into his empty cup. Maybe he doesn't know her, after all. This is not the way to start. He will begin chronologically. Maybe that is unadventurous, but that is how he'll begin.

Raphaella is not pleased with her painting. It is too timid, not bold enough. The trickle of paint has been ineffectual. She takes her thickest, fattest brush. Emphasises the edges, repeats what she has done before, like a nightly prayer. She strives to be more emphatic, clear, more purposeful. Blue, yellow, white again. And again. And again.

Oliver deletes his writing, clears the screen. The white makes him think of Raphaella and her white home. Her white sheets. Her white body. The lilies. Maybe he loves her. Maybe he does not. He has slept with many men but few women. There is something sacred about Raphaella. Even when he talks to her about her earnings (surely, as her agent, he should do so?) she is far removed. When he makes love to

5

her, she is elsewhere. Somehow, she is never really there. Only in her paintings, and in her absence, is she really there. He will begin his chapter again.

Chapter One: 1961

Raphaella Turner was born on 1st May, 1961, in a large north London house. Her interest in painting began with her mother, a keen amateur painter. They lived, later with another sister, Charlotte, in elegant surroundings. Holidays were spent at the lemon-slatted cottage beside a lake, where Raphaella now lives. Her parents

Oliver breaks off. Her parents? What of them? He stares into his cup. It's empty.

Chapter
II

Oliver accepts the glass of melon juice and settles on the sofa. They are in Mrs Turner's studio, which Oliver thinks is more like a museum than a working space. He wonders when a brush was last dipped into paint in this room. He looks around him at dark red walls, crammed with watercolours, a tiny landscape with a single cow on a cliff edge, gold-framed sepia portraits. He wonders where Raphaella's style and aesthetics have come from. Canvas and paint, yes. Taste, no.

"So, Mrs Turner. Are you ready?"

The stony-eyed woman, trim and neat before him, nods.

"Good." He turns his tape recorder on. "Tell me, was Raphaella always keen on painting?"

"Oh yes, always. Even when the girls were young, I encouraged them to paint."

Mrs Turner is dressed in a grey woollen trouser suit. She sits back on the settee, looking nervous, Oliver thinks. He pushes the tape recorder slightly away from her. Maybe it is inhibiting her. She seems defensive. Her hair is formal, set. A pink azalea in a glazed grey pot is on a table beside her.

"And I believe you also paint. Did you fuel Raphaella's interest?"

"Oh yes. I felt that it was very important. And with Charlotte too. She is a very fine painter as well. Attention has gone to Raphaella, but Charlotte has been glossed over. I want that known."

"I see."

Oliver admires Mrs Turner's watercolours (she has not said, "Please, call me Gertrude") and notes the vast formal

7

garden from the bay window. None of Raphaella's paintings hang in this house.

"Wouldn't go with our style," says Mrs Turner curtly, in answer to Oliver's query. Several of Charlotte's are around the home. They are insipid, pale, of flowers, of the sea. Undistinguished.

Oliver looks at the mother. Her eyes are hard. "Tell me about Raphaella," he says. "What kind of child was she?"

"Not always very easy," says Mrs Turner, averting her eyes, "but painting bound us into a kind of friendship, you might say. I remember many happy occasions in this studio, painting together, the three of us. There was something very serene about that."

"No! I don't want to!"

Raphaella squirms as Gertrude squeezes her hand over her daughter's, tries to guide the brush. But brush and child are equally hard and stubborn. Gertrude releases her throbbing hand.

"Have your own way then, you little fool. But can't you see? Are you blind?"

Raphaella's cheeks are burning. Battles with her mother have become daily, hourly almost. Yet something in her drives her on, to resist. Her mother is evil, repugnant. A monster.

"Look at Charlotte's painting. Look!"

Gertrude places her hands hard on Raphaella's head and forces her to look, first at the arrangement of oranges and apples on an oval plate in the centre of the table, then twists it to look at Charlotte's painting. Charlotte, smug, all seven years of her, says nothing, thinks more than nothing, hair tied back with a velvet ribbon. Raphaella sees on her sister's canvas, small globes of pale yellow and green. Oranges and apples? What an insult. What a joke. But she says nothing.

"Look." Gertrude does her hands-on-the-head trick again and directs her daughter's gaze. "Look at the fruit. Round, shaped. Now look at yours."

Raphaella flicks her hair back defiantly, looks at her own canvas where she sees the oranges and apples as if transferred.

"Do you see?" spits Gertrude. "Yours are square. The real fruit is rounded. I think we'll have to take you to the opticians and see if you need glasses. Charlotte's eyesight is obviously perfect."

Still Raphaella says nothing. Silence is her only weapon against her mother's frequent assaults. But she feels pleased with herself and with her painting. The fruit, yes – she sees it as round and curved – is alive on her canvas – a solid, square representation of the real thing. Too young at nine to articulate the reason, she knows, absolutely knows that she is right and that her way of representing the fruit is more accurate than to draw it curved. Does not know why. Feels triumphant. Vows to continue to paint what she feels is there, not what she sees is there.

Piano practice fills another half hour of her mother poking her in the back with manicured nails.

"Do that bit again. It says *legato*, doesn't it? Doesn't it? Can you read?"

Tears prick Raphaella's eyes but she will not cry. This iron bitch will not make her cry. Then homework and dinner. Daddy is home by this time. Raphaella sees him entering the large tiled hall, hanging his coat and hat up, greeting his wife coolly, coming in to join them at dinner. Even though she despises her father at times, Raphaella cannot help but notice how good-looking he is, how smooth his hair, how immaculate his clothing – the silver cufflinks, the shiny buttons on his navy jacket.

She recalls how, the night before, he had come into her bed and stroked her thighs with his hands. How he had placed his large lips on hers, pulled her knickers down, stretched his tongue into her mouth and rubbed her with his rigid fingers. Entered her. And how she felt torn between enjoyment and repulsion. And how he had lain beside her afterwards, his face upon hers, his breathing heavy, and she had felt his tears slip down her neck.

Now they eat together. Donna, the newest maid (none of them lasts long) serves soup from a tureen, then roast lamb, shiny vegetables, potatoes. Trifle afterwards. Bed.

The next morning, Raphaella skips down the stairs. Outside the window, the sun is bright and alive. Summer holidays. Five more weeks of her mother trying to mould her into the kind of daughter she wants her to be. To be more like Charlotte. Compliant. Dull.

Raphaella goes into the studio, wants to see her fruit again. To her horror, on the canvas, her mother has painted over her solid shapes, made each line curved, round balls of colour, which have no gravity, no weight.

Raphaella screams, "She's shit! I loathe her! I hate her!" Howling, feels the betrayal as a pain in her body, the disgrace of it, the injustice, flings her easel and canvas to the floor with a huge thud, knocks the fruit off its oval platform, smashes the plate, throws Charlotte's painting on to the floor. Wrecks much of the studio.

"Bitch! Bitch! Nasty witch!"

For two days after that, Raphaella locks herself in her room and accepts no food. Her mother's voice slips under the gap at the bottom of the door.

"You have behaved disgustingly. You are evil. I rue the day I – you came into my life."

And you are a lump of shit, thinks Raphaella. I despise you, every bit of you. One day I shall escape you and Daddy and Charlotte and be free. Me.

And although Raphaella's eyes sting and her cheeks burn, she will not cry. She will not answer her. She will not allow that demon to make her cry.

And it is then that Raphaella is a bird. Feels her body sprout feathers, clawed feet. A beak emerges where her lips were. Her blue wings expand and stretch. She flies, circles the room, then out of the window and is liberated. The sky is large behind her, the blue endless. And nothing will contain or suppress what she is. Her father's rubbing his body against hers; her mother's nastiness; Charlotte's unfounded superiority – nothing will damage Raphaella. She soars the clouds and her wings are huge, wide, strong enough to take her where she wants to go.

Nearly thirty years later, Raphaella is a bird again. But tonight the air is warm and moist. And she is free to fly wherever she wants. And the flying becomes easier, more natural. Second nature. On the other side of the lake, she notices another bird. It looks strangely like her, blue as well, but smaller, the feathers slightly less bright, maybe an older bird. It is not the first time she has seen this bird or rock or tree and known that there is a woman within that shape. They have never spoken or touched but one day they will. They will.

"And were you able, because of your knowledge of painting, to give Raphaella advice?"

Oliver finds Mrs Turner hard and distant. Raphaella is distant too but in a different way. Oliver notices that Mrs Turner's cheeks are burning. Her eyes won't meet his. She takes the glass jug and pours him more juice.

11

"Oh yes, but, of course, no child likes to take help from her mother."

"No," says Oliver. "Of course not."

Outside, he stands on the pavement and looks up at the Georgian house. Its proportions are elegant, cold, the curtains at each window tied tightly back. He catches Mrs Turner staring at him from the edge of a window, then she slips away.

Oliver walks back to the tube station, feels exhilarated. This book will not just be an account of an artist's life. It will be a solution to a mystery. He feels there is much to be uncovered. He will not only be a biographer and art historian but also archaeologist, anthropologist, psychologist, sleuth.

Inside a large bookshop, Oliver senses a mixture of panic and excitement. Can he write the book? Will he be able to discover what he wants to? Will his book, one day, sit in the art department of this beautiful shop? He is haunted by his mother's sneers at his early attempts at writing. He tries to forget her wicked face, her disdain. He goes to the art section, runs his finger over the shelf, weighty tomes, art biography, Paula Rego, Picasso. He forces open a gap among the books. He recalls how Raphaella's legs parted for him. Slots his hand where the opening in the books is. An empty bit of shelf. There, his *Life and Work of Raphaella Turner*, will sit.

Inside the cottage, Raphaella showers and dresses. She unlocks the bottom drawer of her white cabinet and takes out her art books. How many times she has thumbed through these – Klee, Kandinsky, Rothko, Turner even. Hockney, Hodgkin, Heron. Paula Rego. Looking through, she notes the strokes of one painting, the edges of another. Holds a page with a Rothko up close to her face. Yes, that edge is jagged. Just slightly. She will try to replicate that. After an hour of looking, she puts back the books. Locks the drawer. Pours herself wine. Sees her shapes neat on the shelf. They are all hers. The shapes her body makes when she is a tree, a bird; the canvases and what she puts upon them; her jars and their contents; the movement of her body as she walks, stretches, sleeps. They are all, all of them, her shapes.

Chapter
III

"And what does he want? This Oliver Slatton." Julian Turner's face is grave, his tone sneering.

"He's writing a biography of Raphaella. All we bloody needed."

Gertrude passes her husband the salt. "This new cook's useless, Julian. And as for Mandy!"

Julian thinks of the previous night when he fucked Mandy, the maid. How smooth her skin; how soft her mouth. How much more delicious than Donna, the previous one. How delighted she looked when he paid her afterwards.

"Never mind the cook. What are you going to tell this Oliver man? About Raphaella?"

"Well, not the truth, obviously. Have you ever read a biography which tells the truth?"

"How would one know?"

Gertrude looks at her husband. He still looks good now, greying hair, back more curved than it used to be, but still that elegance, that poise.

"Anyway, he says it will be more about her painting than her life. I'll just speak to him about her childhood, if I can face it. He's not going to want to know details of her birth, for God's sake, is he?"

Julian falls silent. Looks troubled. Mandy enters, clears the table. In the drawing room, the couple sip coffee from tiny gold-rimmed cups, nibble chocolate mints.

"If I were you, I would refuse to speak to him."

"Then that will look as if we're hiding something. And if we annoy Raphaella, she'll say spiteful things about us. You know what she can be like. How would I face people? I'd rather go along with it. He looked like a real wimp. I doubt whether he'll ever even write the damn book. He didn't look capable of writing his own shopping list, frankly." Pause. "How was work today?"

"Another day of people telling lies and me trying to wring from them some sort of legal truth," he says, stirring his coffee. Too vigorously, too anxiously, Gertrude thinks. "The truth is so over-rated," he says.

In the kitchen, Mandy scrapes and washes the plates. She hates the Turners. They are cold and hard. They never speak to her in a pleasant way or ask about her life. No wonder none of the other maids have stayed. But she is determined to sit it out. For years even. Besides, she has to support her mother. Who else has she got?

Years earlier, Betty stands in the cold kitchen, scraping plates into the bin. She thinks of Nick. He comes first. She will do anything she can for Nick. She can never earn enough for she pours money into him which he pours out again on his drugs. She has begged him to stop but that is what and who he is. And she loves him in spite of it. She really loves him.

And in this way, a whole line of maids from before Betty and after Mandy, scrape the plates resentfully, but for a reason.

Raphaella perches in the pine tree, feels the wind slightly ruffle her feathers. She shifts her tiny clawed feet along the branch a little, tightens her grip. The lake is calm this evening. Barely moving. She wonders where all the fish are. Is there no wind on the water at all? Yes, a ripple, but barely discernible. In a moment, she will fly. Lift her wings and stretch across the water, making a reflection of her belly in the lake. Now. Spread wings. Lift. She's off. Flying across the water. Gliding. Free.

On the other side of the lake sits that bird again. An older, smaller bird. She is more hesitant about flying. Takes longer to leave the security of the branch. But eventually, she does it. Maybe it is that one ripple of wind that gives her the impetus. But she does it. Does not fly as freely, as confidently, as the approaching bird, but flies nevertheless. In the middle of the lake, the larger bird passes the smaller one. Their beady eyes see each other but there is no stopping. Each lands on the branch of the other's tree. One bird is Raphaella. The other is Martha.

Inside the cottage, Raphaella dries herself with a towel and lights her candles. They have burned at different rates, made individual sculptures of themselves. A secular shrine. The flames seem to compete with each other, some leaping higher than the rest for effect. Gymnasts. Acrobats. Show-offs. Flirts.

She slips a white chenille dress on, silver threads running through the fabric. Ties a silver necklace round her forehead. Paints her lips red. Looks in the mirror. Is pleased with what she sees. She is dressing for herself. Tonight, she will wear silver gloves. She puts each one on, flicks back her long dark hair, admires herself for what she is. Pours wine. Wanders into her studio. Looks again at her white, blue, yellow rectangles with snail trails down them. She will paint tonight. When the lake and woods have settled, are quiet again.

*   *   *

A knock at the door. Joe. Red-haired, jeans, old shirt, so different to Oliver and his dark-haired foppishness that the contrast makes her laugh aloud.

"What's the joke?"

Bloke, thinks Raphaella. He is carrying a huge basket of fruit and vegetables. His body is solid, thickset.

"I thought you weren't coming," says Raphaella.

"Sorry. Mum's so difficult. She mopes around while we have to do everything. Poor Dad. I just couldn't wait to get away. I mean, she's always been a bit unusual, let's say, but now, now, she's well and truly flipped."

He kisses Raphaella and puts his basket down. He smells of earth, grass and horse shit. Raphaella loves it. Feels as if he's grown from the soil himself.

She unpacks the basket. Lettuces curve into themselves, pears taper to black stalks, berries squirt their red stains on to Raphaella's hands. Bananas bend. Raphaella sees oranges, apples, remembers her mother's destruction of her square fruit painting. And there is asparagus in the basket, thin and elegant. And a huge bottle of olive oil. And bread. And more besides.

"I'll need more supplies soon," says Raphaella. "I've got a list for you."

She hands Joe a piece of paper and he sees at first glance the familiar items: wine, white candles, wholemeal bread, cheese.

He wonders, as he has done many times before, whether she is agoraphobic. She hardly ever goes anywhere. He does not know she has been a bird tonight.

Chapter One: Home Life

Raphaella Turner was born on 1st May 1961 in an elegant Georgian house, North London, where her parents still live.

17

Her father is a judge, her mother daughter to the famous late milliner, Georgina Hendricks, and a keen amateur painter.

Oliver has exchanged coffee for wine. Feels stronger now than before. Knows this book needs to be written. There is something inevitable about it. Deletes amateur before painter. Anxious. Continues.

An accomplished and capable child, Raphaella showed precocious ability in painting, piano-playing and writing stories. Her father often absent at work, her mother was a major influence on Raphaella and her younger sister, Charlotte, also now a painter. Another major influence was Georgina Hendricks, Raphaella's late grandmother, whose millinery workshop the young girl loved to visit. The business has long since gone but people in the area remember the girl arriving for frequent visits and emerging with yet another hat, which she had been allowed to make. At that time, Vera Bramhall was a young woman who lived opposite the hat shop and she remembers seeing Raphaella:

"She would arrive in some smart car and people would look out of their windows when it drove up. My kids – three of them – would stare out and say, 'Look mummy, there's that princess.' That's what they called her – the princess. She always had lovely clothes. Real nice, they were. Her father was a High Court judge, so it was alright for her, wasn't it? Born with a silver spoon, I used to say. Anyway, she'd be in there for hours and then when she come out, she'd be wearing a hat what she'd made with her gran. Oh, dead smart, it was. Course, we was all green with envy, wasn't we? Back to scrubbing the doorstep, I'd think to meself. It'll be a fine day when someone makes me a hat, that's for sure."

This early experimenting with colour and design, both at home and with her grandmother, gave Raphaella an early interest in and understanding of artistic endeavours.

Raphaella runs her hand over the felt top of a huge red hat. Among brims and rims and mounds of material sits Georgina Hendricks, hatmaker extraordinaire and much-loved grandmother of Raphaella.

"Hello, Granny."

The little girl hugs her grandmother and is warmly greeted. For Raphaella, this workshop and the hat shop at the front are a haven, a heaven of warmth and love and colour.

"Who wants to make a hat today?" asks Granny Hendricks, as if she needs to ask. As elegant as her daughter, Gertrude, Georgina has something warmer and more loveable about her. Her customers dote on her to find or make the right hat for each wedding, christening, horserace, smart occasion. She hands Raphaella, as she always does, a ready made-up hat, newly stitched, and waves her arm around the worktable.

"Choose what you like," she says.

Granny Hendricks does this with Charlotte, too, but on different days: she insists that each girl has time alone with her. Charlotte makes her hats pretty with flowers and netting.

Not Raphaella, though. She chooses sequins, and feathers and bits of taffeta, ribbons, silks, buttons, and stitches them on with Granny's help. And as they work, they talk.

"How's school?"

"Hate it," says Raphaella. "I wish I could be here with you all the time."

Granny laughs. "You can't be – you need to be properly educated – but one day you will make your own colourful creations, I am sure. You're such an imaginative girl."

"But I like being with you."

"You would be very lonely here with me, after a while. I work most of the time and then I'm alone, in the evenings, reading quietly."

"Where's Grandad?"

"You're asking me that again! I've told you. We didn't see eye to eye, darling. We each lead our own lives now. I much prefer to be on my own."

Raphaella looks up at the intriguing lady with her hair twisted into a bun and tidy clothes, a white band where her ring was, surrounded by feathers and buttons. She seems to the young girl an exotic, brightly-plumed bird living her life in paradise.

Raphaella's hat is finished. She puts it on and stares into the glass. It is crazy and bright and bits dangle in all directions. Girl and grandmother shriek with laughter, hug, a joint reflection in a single mirror, Raphaella with her hat on, falling in love, once again, with herself.

From the age of five, Raphaella attended Woodlands Preparatory School near where she lived. There, she was encouraged in her painting by Miss Redding.

"Raphaella Turner," shouts Miss Redding. "I am asking you to copy the flowers in the vase and not to invent what they look like. Look at Henrietta's."

Raphaella stares at Miss Redding from the corner of her eye. She wonders whether Miss Redding and her mother were trained at the same boring art school. She sees Henrietta Marchamp's dull painting. Thin one-dimensional flowers flop limply in a vase. They look as if they are composed of

20

water. Never in a million years will Raphaella paint like that. What would be the point? It is an insult to the flowers, she thinks to herself, smiling. Then she looks at her own paper. Cuboid flowerheads stand erect on rectangular stems. The vase is solid and opaque. Yes, hers is the right way, the only way, she's convinced of it.

Oliver leans his head back and yawns, looks at the screen. It's all too nice, too perfect. Miss Redding. The sister. The father. Oliver knows that there is more to uncover. But how? Where? The Turners are tight and closed. He will have to find his information elsewhere. Maybe Charlotte, the sister? Somewhere.

Chapter
IV

"Betty? Is that you?"

Betty climbs the dark stairs up to their attic bedsit. Nick is waiting on the bed for her. He looks grey today, his deep eyes ringed with black.

"Where ya been?"

"Sorry," says Betty, kissing him. "Old cow wanted extra washing done, din't she?"

"Where's the dosh?" Nick looks up for a moment. "I bin waiting."

" 'ere, love." Betty hands him the money, knocks her shoes off. She settles beside him on the bed. Nick sighs relief and lies beside her, thrusts his hand roughly up her skirt, down her pants.

"Love ya," he says. Kisses her. "Love ya, Betty. I do."

She stops his hand. "Nick," she whispers. "Nick. When you gonna stop with the drugs, love? Sort yourself out?"

His face freezes. "You want me to fuck off, then. Is that it?"

"No," says Betty. "Of course not. I love ya, don't I?"

"That's alright, then," and Nick slips his hand down Betty's pants again. This time she doesn't stop him.

"He works very long hours, I'm afraid." Mrs Turner is speaking to Oliver through a gap in a barely open door. Oliver is not being invited in. "It will be hard to catch him."

"Well, I'd like to talk to him, if I may." Oliver, public-school frozen smile. "Otherwise, I'll just have to guess at things."

Mrs Turner frowns angrily. Is this nasty little journalist blackmailing her? She shuts the door slowly.

"And I need Charlotte's address, please," he says.

Mrs Turner hesitates. She does not want him to think that she is hiding information.

"Wait there."

A few minutes later, Mrs Turner passes Oliver a piece of paper with an address written on it in italics. *Charlotte Mountford. The Rectory.* And the name of a village in Dorset.

"Thank you," he says and is gone. Triumphant.

Raphaella is a tree tonight.

Slender and tall, her thin arms are branches tapering to green. She is still. The lake is quiet. A heron skims the water, sweeping his giant shadow over the landscape. And she spots the other bird again. Raphaella has wondered if the bird is always a bird-woman or whether she is ever an other-shape – a tree or rock, as Raphaella is. But now she is a bird.

Raphaella, rooted to the ground, wishes that the bird would come and sit on her branch. She beckons by waving her arm-branches slowly, appealingly. First, the bird flies past but does not settle. Raphaella rustles her branch again. This time, to Raphaella's delight, the bird circles the tree once and perches on her lowest branch. Her claw-feet cling to the bough and Raphaella feels warm inside, as if there has been some kind of completion, or satisfaction. That bird has chosen to sit on her. And Raphaella feels the slight weight on her with happiness and realises that something important has happened. And she feels tears spill inside her. Someone significant has arrived. Something has happened. A warmth. A presence. And she cannot explain it but she knows that this is the start of something. And it feels so good.

"Raphaella! Come here at once."

Miss Redding's voice, as sharp as glass. Raphaella feels it slice through her head, her fingers, her skin. The little girl looks around at her classmates. The girls are dressed in purple uniforms, edged with gold. They look pleased at Raphaella's troubles.

She walks to the front of the classroom. Her stick-insect teacher is holding up Raphaella's work.

"Look! Did the flowers have square heads?" The girls giggle. "Were the stalks blue? I don't think you're taking art lessons very seriously, young lady."

Yes, thinks Raphaella. I'm taking them very seriously indeed. "You will write out a hundred times: I will paint things as they are."

Yes, thinks Raphaella, that's right: I will paint them as they are, not as they appear.

All through lunch, Raphaella sits alone in the classroom, hearing the muffled laughter of girls in the playground as she writes out with glee and gratitude:

I will paint things as they are.

I will paint things as they are.

I will paint things as they are.

Yes, she thinks. Thank you for helping me, Miss Redding.

I shall always paint things as they are.

In her studio, tonight, Raphaella is painting things as they are. She looks outside to the lake where the water is creased and pleated silk. She takes her fattest brush, spreads white paint lines across her vast blue canvas. Green strokes are trees beside the lake. She looks from canvas to water, water to canvas. A glaze of sun spreads itself across the colours.

I shall always paint things as they are.

Oliver looks round the dark room. The paintings, he thinks, are rather similar to Mrs Turner's – insipid watercolour landscapes, a few of Charlotte's own anonymous paintings, none of Raphaella's.

Charlotte is as cold as her mother; only in her mid-thirties, but looks older. Her hair is tied up in a bun. Her children, Louisa and Harriet, run outside in the vicarage garden. An elderly gardener digs over an empty flowerbed, slowly, his left hand clutching his lower back from time to time.

Charlotte laughs, sneeringly. "An easygoing child? You're joking, surely."

Oliver checks the volume control on his tape machine. "Oh. But your mother –"

"She's loyal, isn't she? First daughter and all that. She's not going to admit that the girl was impossible. A spoilt brat. Child from hell, she was."

"But you don't mind telling me all this?"

"What difference does it make to me? I never see her, anyway." She hooks three fingers through the handle of the teapot. "Earl Grey?"

"Martha?" says Gertrude Turner. She is sitting opposite her husband at their dining table. "Why Martha?"

"She seems the obvious choice," says Julian, looking down at his soup. His young wife is pretty but he is not attracted to her. Never has been. Even the five years of making love to her in the hope that Gertrude may conceive – for her sake, not his – have disappointed him. He has not felt the excitement and lust that he wanted to feel. He has not been hungry for her. His hunger has been for others. Martha is one of them. Betty another.

"I don't know," says Gertrude. "Dr Williams says we have to be patient. That it will happen. But your idea. Your scheme." She has pushed her plate away from her. "How will you handle it?"

"Well, this is what I thought. I'll agree the sum with her. You know how badly her family needs the money. Failing farm and all that. She'll tell them she got pregnant and won't name the father. We'll take the baby as soon as it's born."

"But everyone will know I've not been pregnant. They'll see."

"We'll have to move away. Just for six months or so. Christopher's offered me a place with a legal firm in the States. I think we should take this chance."

Gertrude lifts a fork and twists it in the palm of her hand, over and over. She thinks of a baby, any baby. One which could be hers.

Julian thinks of Martha with her dark hair and elusive eyes. She will be his – again.

From an early age, Raphaella was keen on painting but she was determined to represent life and objects the way she saw them. Her teacher, Miss Redding, now retired, remembers the strong-headed little girl:

"She was wilful, that's true, but I encouraged her to look carefully at what she was painting. I have never had any acknowledgement from her for the help I gave, of course, but I do feel that under my guidance, she began to paint with confidence and certainty. I helped her on her way, I believe."

At the age of eleven, Raphaella left her prep school and went to a private girls' school, St Mary's, in North London.

Oliver sits back and drinks his wine. Looks at the words on the screen. There are times when they swarm in front of him like ugly, meaningless flies. He wonders what he is doing.

Has his life come to this? Agent for a painter who doesn't care; writer of a book about someone who doesn't care; lover of a woman who doesn't care. That callous harshness of Raphaella is, at times, a lure to him; at others a gross disappointment. It makes him feel like a parasite, someone who doesn't live his own life but lives vicariously. One who preys on others. He had meant to be his own man but he feels, on days like these, like the mere shadow of the man he had hoped to be. He has not settled on which gender to love, which way to turn. Maybe this biography is a waste of time. Maybe he is a waste of space. A void. An inconvenience.

And because Raphaella is a fish tonight, she is underwater. Her eyes shine and glaze as currents pass over them, but she can still see. She is breathing, seeing, lifting her fins gently in and out at the side of her turquoise body. She flicks her tail and darts between water-weed and quillwort, green spikes and stalks. So much space here, she thinks, underwater. Underused. We build on earth, we build up to the sky, we fill more and more space above ground. But here, beneath the water, is space and opportunity. Bubbles float from her gaping mouth. Her eyes bulge. I want to build here. Construct something huge and strong and concrete. And no one will know. It will be built as a secret. But out of what? Her fins brush the sand. A few grains fly up. Settle.

Inside her room, where white candles stand tall and thick with wax, Raphaella fills a glass with white wine. Fills her mouth with the taste of cool white. Lights a candle. Tucks her feet under her on the sofa and sleeps. She dreams of fish and birds and moon and stars and her huge brush is painting, painting them all.

27

Chapter
V

"Martha," says Julian, running his large hand slowly down the young girl's thigh. "I know you've been on the pill, but I'd like you to stop taking it."

Martha starts, amazed. "But why? What about your wife?"

Julian smiles. "It's for her that I'm saying this. She wants a baby. I told you that we've been trying. But no luck. So I thought – and I know this is a lot to ask of you – that if you would be willing to carry a baby for her, for us, then –"

"You mean she knows about us."

Julian laughs confidently. "Of course not. As far as she's aware, you clean the cottage and that's it. But I suggested you, as you're young and –" he kisses her forehead, "so gorgeous, darling. What a beautiful baby we'd make."

"But what about us, Julian? Are you still promising that you'll leave her one day and marry me? That's what you said, didn't you?"

"Yes, of course I will. But don't you see, it will be easier once she's got a child. She won't care whether I'm there or not, then. She'll be preoccupied."

Martha edges away from her lover. Sees the lake outside the cottage lift and fall like a heavy sleeper. "So you want me to carry the baby for nine months, and then just give it away?"

"I shall pay you, of course, Martha. Think of your parents and the farm. You'll have no worries about the future. Your family will be well looked after."

"You think money can buy everything, Julian."

"It can't buy another person as lovely as you, Martha. We will make that baby together. Let's start now." His mouth is on her, his tongue on her tongue, his fingers on her breasts. "I love you."

Yes, thinks Raphaella, standing at the side of the lake as a rock, as herself. In that place there will be a building. It could be a temple, a castle or a dome. It could be an amphitheatre, but it will be big and there will be tiny windows and the fish will swim in and out of those tiny openings and I will live and swim there and no one will find me. Her toes are crusty and hard and her back is arched into a giant rock. She can feel ants crawling upon her surface. She is solid, they are small and yet she cannot shake them off. She feels the solidity of who she is and the enormous potential of the wide lake which sits there, waiting.

Oliver is standing at the kitchen table. His bare knees below school shorts are round and dimpled. His mother is reading his school report. Her face is tight, grey, as if she has just received a telegram to say her son has been killed in action or that her house has gone up in flames.

"This is very disappointing," she says. "All this money your father is paying for your education. And these results. And they're still warning you about your handwriting and your spelling and your general attitude. Slovenly, idle."

She turns to the child and, clutching the report in one fist, swipes the child's face with the other. Oliver stumbles slightly but stands, legs together, his face throbbing red and hot below his left eye, as if someone has pressed an iron on it. And he can feel the swelling rise and boil. It may explode in a moment. He may be scarred for life. He watches his mother rip the report up into halves, then quarters, then little ragged squares and throw the scraps in the bin. Some of them

29

fall, like lost mosaic tiles, on to the floor. And Oliver does not know, he does not know which is more painful, the smack, or the watching himself being torn up. The paper with his name on it. And suddenly, he can stand it no longer and, clutching his swollen face, he runs upstairs and cries until his bed is sodden with tears and his whole body convulses with anger and shame and exhaustion. And eventually, hours later, he sleeps. But he does not dream.

"So, how's your book?" asks Raphaella.

Suddenly, Oliver recognises, in her tone, the voice of his mother, sneering and contemptuous.

"My book," he says defensively, "is fine. In spite of no help from you, or perhaps because of no help from you, it is progressing well. Thank you."

Raphaella has made them each a seafood salad. Curly green leaves, fresh fish and shellfish. Lobster. They sit by the open window of the cottage looking out to the lake. It is a wide blue yawn tonight, a stretch, a smile.

"Tell me about it." Mocking. "The book." She lifts a prawn to her mouth, extracts the flesh with her teeth, spits the shell away.

"I thought you weren't interested."

"I'm curious. To know what you've discovered about me that I didn't know before. You are the expert, after all. On me."

Her sarcasm cuts deep. Oliver eats his salad, drinks his wine, tears warm, crusty bread and dips it into olive oil. Looks out to the lake. Remembers the swelling, can feel it under his left eye as if it is suddenly there again. Raw.

"No, really. What have you uncovered?"

"Nothing that you don't know. But things I didn't know. That your father is hard and cold. That your mother and Miss Redding helped you more than you will admit."

Raphaella sneers, laughs aloud, crudely, Oliver thinks.

"Right about my father. My mother and Miss Redding? That bat from hell? Encouragement. What a joke."

"And Charlotte."

"Her? You've been to see her? So, what do you think of my dysfunctional family, then?"

Oliver does not answer for a moment. Closes his knife and fork. Pushes his plate away.

"Why do artists always want to make it appear that they've done it all themselves? They never want to acknowledge any help from teachers or family. 'No, they didn't help. I am totally self-taught.' "

"That's rubbish." Raphaella pours them more wine, herself first. "I don't want to say that. It just happens to be the truth. You see, I told you that you'd learn nothing about me through interviewing others. Can't you see that?"

"I don't agree. I'm learning a lot –"

"About what other people want to say. Or how they perceive it. Me. My work. Not the truth. You will never discover that. It doesn't exist. And that's why I told you that all that matters are the paintings themselves. They stand alone. Not how they got there or what led me to paint them, but what they are. They are the evidence – not what some mediocre old teacher does or doesn't remember about me during so-called art lessons." She looks angry now; her cheeks burn.

"I have always said that you were arrogant. Talented and arrogant. You think your paintings are the whole world. They say it all."

"Yes," says Raphaella, calmer now, "of course they do." She's standing up. "If they didn't, what on earth would be the point in painting them?"

And again they find themselves in bed, though neither is particularly bothered about it. It seems a natural conclusion to the evening, punctuation at the end of a sentence. Nothing more than that. And although it is far from unpleasant – the mouths, breasts, warmth of genitals – both doubt as they perform. Raphaella is thinking of her painting, the white space which she will fill with marks and dots. Oliver's entered her now. His eyes are closed, he is crying. He sleeps with men, with women. He does not know that he also sleeps with birds, with rocks, with trees.

"Good morning, girls, and welcome to St Mary's." The headmistress, Miss Matthews, is short and stout. Raphaella thinks, her body is a cube balanced on little legs. "We hope that you will be very happy here." I won't be, thinks Raphaella. That's obvious. "Now, as I call your name, I want you to proceed to your class. Loretta Armstrong, Denise Ashworth, Rose Atterman…"

"She's pregnant?" says Gertrude, gasping. "Is she?"

"Yes." Julian is pleased with himself. His wife will have what she wants and he has certainly had what he wants. Many times. Before the agreement and after. He thinks now of Martha's smooth skin and her tiny waist. Of the pleasure of entering her, when he was hard inside her.

"When is the baby due?"

"June," says Julian. "I have spoken to Christopher. We will leave for the States in a month's time. Be there six months. It will all work out. I told you to trust me."

Gertrude sits down, clasps a hand to her chest. It has suddenly hit her. She will be a mother. A mother of a baby which her husband has made with – no, she mustn't think of that. The child will be hers. No one will know. She looks at her husband. He, too, looks pleased. There is so much she wants to ask him. Did he enjoy sleeping with the cleaning girl? She and Julian hardly ever – haven't – did he enjoy it?

Did he? She hopes he didn't. She prays he didn't. She wants to ask him. Doesn't. Dreads the answer. The truth. Turns away from her husband. Finds herself holding her arms in a cradle shape, rocking backwards and forwards. Backwards and forwards. Loving the baby who does not exist. Who is not hers. Who never will be.

Chapter
VI

"Martha, love. Come and have your bread before it's cold. It's fresh from the oven."

The girl walks quietly into the kitchen, takes her place at the wooden table with her parents.

"Thanks, Mum."

Her father stirs his soup. Blows at his spoon. Is silent, as usual.

"You been cleaning the cottage, again?"

"Yes."

"Like more soup, love?" Mum, soothing.

"No. Thanks."

"You're quiet today, Martha." Her mother, Helga, stands, ladle in air. Looks concerned. "Anything wrong?"

"Well, yes. There is, actually. Mum, Dad. Please listen."

Her parents are worried. The room feels so still.

"I'm... I don't know how you're going to feel about this. I don't think you're going to be at all pleased."

"Tell us then, love."

"Well, I'm... I'm... expecting a baby."

Helga's eyes instantly fill with tears. Her father is so frozen that he seems suddenly like another piece of furniture in the sparse kitchen.

"Martha. You're seventeen. You've got your whole life ahead of you." Helga is next to Martha now, holds her daughter to her.

"Who's the father?" Her own father, suddenly white, sits upright. "What's his name? Come on. Name him."

"No, Dad. I can't. He's gone."

"Gone?" asks Helga. "Where's he gone to?"

"He's a waster. It was a terrible mistake. I'll go away if you want me to. I don't want to bring shame upon you."

"My darling." Helga holds her tightly, feels her daughter's thick dark hair curl on her own cheek. "We would never want you to go. How could you bring shame on anyone? We love you. You know that. We'll always help you."

"I'll kill that rogue if I ever catch him." Her father's fist is clenched. "What about your life? And your work here on the farm? We need your help. And the cottage cleaning? And what about Mr and Mrs Turner? What are they going to think? A respectable couple like that."

"It won't affect them. I can carry on cleaning. We need the money."

"What will they say?" asks her mother. "They've always paid you, treated you so well."

Raphaella is a shell tonight. Large-lipped, lined with pink, she lies on the sand, imprinting a dent beneath her. The waves crease. The breeze irons them smooth. A pale moon yawns and spreads itself like a glaze over the shell. The light nudges a shadow away. Raphaella is at peace. Feels that the water and sand are there for her purposes and that she is the centre of the world. Near her on the sand lies a smaller, less brightly coloured shell. It is not as beautiful, lacks the lustre of the larger shell, but also stamps its serrated imprint on the sand.

Julian slides his hand over Martha's belly. Yes, he is sure he can feel the slight curve beginning. Slips his hand over her shape and down to her legs, inside her thighs, feels her to be moist. His mouth is on her, his tongue in her.

"Julian," says Martha, stroking his head between her legs. "Don't harm the baby. Careful."

"I won't, sweetheart. Nor would I hurt you." And he's kissing her mouth now. "Darling. We leave for New York tomorrow. How will I bear six months without you? It will be sheer torture for me."

Martha searches his good-looking face, his pale eyes. How she wishes she could love him. Or maybe she does.

"I've got the money for you." Takes wads of notes from his briefcase. "And this."

He passes Martha a box. She removes its lid, unpeels tissue paper to reveal silk. Pure white silk. Lifts it out. It is a nightdress. Martha has never felt such material in her life. Did not know material could be like that. Lifts it to her face. Feels water slipping down her cheek.

"Julian," she says and kisses him.

"Put it on," he says, and she undresses, takes off her simple, country dress and slips the white silk over her head. The nightdress drops like liquid down her body to her ankles.

"Darling," he says. "And I will make sure you have more money. You will always have enough."

"But how can I give this to my parents?" She looks at the wads of money that sit bundled together. She can barely believe it is money. It looks so strange, so much of it. It seems meaningless there. "They already think you and Mrs Turner pay me very well, just to clean the cottage. How can I explain it?"

"You will find a way. And Martha – never stop loving me."

She smiles. I haven't started, she thinks.

Gertrude stands in the centre of Manhattan and arches her neck upwards. Skyscrapers lift their heads and necks like haughty birds. Traffic buzzes around them. Yellow taxis zoom past. The noise is relentless.

"How do you like it?" asks Julian.

Gertrude puts her hand to her ear. "What?"

Julian shouts. "How do you like it? Manhattan?"

She nods. "Can we go and have some lunch?"

Inside a restaurant on Fifth Avenue, they look out at cars and streets and buildings.

Gertrude looks elegant in skirt and jacket, scarf coiled at her neck, immaculate make-up. She looks older than she really is, frumpy. Not a part of the colour and extravagance of this busy scene. Julian cannot stop thinking of Martha and her thighs, the curves of her slim body through the silk nightdress, standing like a long lily, her dark hair frothing on her shoulders. Gertrude could not be like Martha, not in a million years. Why can't she be? And why can't he stop thinking of Martha? Why even here, thousands of miles away, amid the smoke and fumes, can he smell her? Taste her?

Betty mounts the stairs to their attic flat. She is rushing, has been to see her mother on the way home from work.

"Nick?" she calls. "I'm 'ome."

She opens the door. Sees him lying, ashen-faced. Sees the syringes scattered on the floor. Nick is deeply asleep, looks dead almost. For an awful moment, Betty finds herself wishing that he were. That he were gone. Then she could start her life again. Then she wouldn't be a maid. Wouldn't be a slave for Mrs Turner, for Nick. She could be herself. Live her own life.

Betty perches on the edge of the bed and takes her shoes off, rubs her tired feet. Catches sight of herself in the mirror. She looks sixty-two, she thinks, not twenty-two. Her hair is a shambles, her cheeks tired and lifeless.

"Nick," she says, irritably. "Nick, wake up."

Martha finds Helga feeding the chickens. She dips her hand into the bucket, then sprinkles seed lightly as if it were water. The chickens gather at her feet, peck furiously. Martha touches Helga's shoulder.

"Here, Mother. Let me help with that."

"No, Martha. Not in your state." She turns to look at her daughter. The bulge is growing now. "We must look after you... and the baby."

"Mum. I still don't know. I think I want to give it away."

"Oh, you're not still insisting on that, are you? How can you speak like that? That's your child. Did your father and I give you away? Even though it's been a struggle, trying to keep this farm going and to feed us all? No. You're our child."

"But that's different, Mum. I was born from love. You wanted me. I didn't want this child. I don't think I'll feel anything for it."

Her mother puts the bucket down, winds her arm around her daughter's shoulder. "Of course you will. The minute you see it —"

"No, Mum." Martha moves away. "I don't want to keep the child. I've told you. I... I've found someone to have it. A couple who can't have a child. They desperately want it. It will bring them great joy. And... and they will pay me – us – something –"

"Selling a child? Martha, what has happened to you? You've always been such a good girl."

"It's not selling, Mum. They are giving me something and I'm giving them something. That's all. We're helping each other. And just think how useful that money will be for us with the farm." Martha points to the old outbuildings with crumbling brickwork and broken roofs. "Please. Try to understand."

Her mother tips the remaining crumbs from the bucket, wipes her hands on her apron and walks into the house.

Inside her room, Helga lights the sabbath candles, covers her face in front of God, prays to Him, cries to Him, sleeps in front of Him.

Raphaella sits in the playground and looks at the girls who swarm around her like manic insects. She feels contempt for them, nothing but contempt, at the silly way they plait their hair and try to be different in spite of their brown blazers and brown skirts and little white ankle socks. They will all marry within ten years and have babies and be even more boring than they are now. And she? She will paint and change from bird to shell and be different. For ever since she was young, she has known. She is special.

Chapter
VII

"I can't. I can't push any more." Martha is lying in bed, with Helga beside her and a home midwife, Mrs Carter. Martha screams, yells with pain, feels her mother dab her forehead with a flannel. "Help me. Just get this baby out. I'm dying."

"Now, Martha," says Mrs Carter. "It won't help to shout like that. Please keep calm. You must push, but like I showed you. Come on."

"Martha, my love," says Helga. "I know you can do it. Please do what Mrs Carter says."

"That's it," says Mrs Carter, lifting her watch from her uniformed bosom. "Excellent. Push."

Downstairs in the kitchen, Martha's father pushes his plate away from him. He cannot eat. He can hear the screams of his unmarried daughter giving birth to a baby which she refuses to keep, but will sell for money. The last few months, he has not been able to sleep. Has felt tight pains pulling around his heart. It's overwork, his wife says. But he knows it isn't. He's milked cows since he was a boy. It's heartbreak, he tells her. To think that his daughter... his Martha... The pains have come again. He can feel them drawing his heart in, as if by string. He feels he is dying. Pushes his handkerchief against his mouth to stop the cries.

Upstairs, Martha gives a final scream. Opens her legs wide. Thinks of Julian on the other side of the world, probably eating and drinking expensive wine, and she is in pain for him, because of him. Hates his guts. Wants him to know what it feels like.

"Good girl," says Mrs Carter. "The head's out now."

And water and blood and a child are coming from Martha now.

Raphaella is a fish tonight. Swims underwater where the sand makes the lake bed murky. Grains lift from the bottom and rise in flecks. Raphaella's fins open and close. Her mouth gapes. Her eyes bulge. Again, she thinks what she has often thought. There is so much space here, below the water. So much wasted space. She wants to build a sandworld here. It will be a building. A structure. A monument. But how? And with whom? For whom? Another fish swims by, flicks its blue tail and stops to stare at Raphaella. This keeps happening. She keeps seeing another fish, bird, shell, which she knows is a woman, like her. It is with this woman that she will build the sandworld.

"You've done very well," says Mrs Carter, instantly losing her sternness and melting into praise. "A lovely little girl. Perfect, she is."

Martha holds the baby in her arms. Its face is small and red, its hair dark and curly, wet against its forehead. Little eyes open slightly. A tiny mouth rounds to an 'o'. Martha thinks she is more beautiful than she could ever have imagined. That she and Julian could have created this! She holds the baby to her. Does not want to let it go.

She turns to look at her mother who is mumbling. *"Baruch atah adonai..."* All through her childhood, her mother has recited Hebrew prayers to herself, has been caught out lighting candles on the sabbath, plaiting bread. Martha has never been told, "You and I are Jewish," but it is there. A secret. An unstated assumption.

41

Martha's mother looks up. "I am thanking God for the baby," she says.

"You say you want to bottle-feed it?" says Mrs Carter, stern again, looking suspiciously at Martha's mother. "I'll go and prepare a bottle for you. Baby will want a feed."

Through her tears, Helga strokes the baby's forehead. It feels soft and warm. Maybe Martha will change her mind. Maybe…

"How do you feel, Martha?" she asks.

"I love her," says Martha quietly, a lump blocking her throat.

Mrs Carter returns with a warm bottle. Martha feeds it to the baby. She sucks slowly, making tiny noises. The three women look towards the child, say nothing. Pitiful, thinks Mrs Carter, shaking her head. Unmarried mother. What future has that poor baby got?

Halfway through the bottle, the baby falls asleep. The sucking gradually stops and the teat slips from its milky lips. The little eyelids close, the eyelashes tiny half-moons on its cheeks. The body softens.

"Here," says Mrs Carter, arms outstretched, "I'll take her from you, shall I?"

"No, thank you," says Martha. "I'd like to hold her a bit longer."

"Oh, alright then. I'll be off. I'll pop round in the morning, shall I?"

"Er, no… no, thank you," says Martha's mother. "We shall be fine."

"Oh." And Mrs Carter packs up her things and goes downstairs.

As she passes through the kitchen, she sees Martha's father sitting at the table. His plate is pushed away from him and he stares out at nothing.

"You've a lovely little grand-daughter," she says to him as she opens the door. No response. "You may go up now, if you'd care to." Nothing. Mrs Carter shrugs her shoulders and goes outside. Funny people, she thinks. Girl unmarried, uninterested father. What is happening to the world?

"Betty," calls Mrs Turner. "We're home."

Mr Turner tips the cab driver, who is placing their cases in the hall. The driver touches his cap and leaves. Betty comes through from the kitchen.

"Sir. Madam." She sees the cases in the hall, the hatboxes, the many bags that say *Macy's* on them. There are big cardboard boxes, too.

"Betty. Help me carry these upstairs."

Betty does as she is told. Mounting the stairs, she wonders what on earth they could have bought so much of. New York must be a maze of nothing but shops. On the side of one of the boxes, she can see the picture of a perambulator. That seems strange. Then, peeping out of one of the bags, baby bonnets and outfits, fluffy, snow- white.

"Guess what?" says Betty to Nick as they lie together that evening.

Nick nuzzles her ear. "You adore me?"

"Well, yes. But that's not what I 'ad in mind. You know the old cow? I think she's up the spout."

"What? Wiv 'im to 'elp? Don't think so. 'E's not up to it."

"Honest to God. She's only gone and brought baby things back wiv 'er. Bags and cases full. Lucky sod. Lives like royalty."

"Mm."

"Do you think we'll ever 'ave kids? Of our own?"

"Nah," says Nick, unbuttoning Betty's dress, "but I don't mind practising."

"So, you mean," says Betty, the following morning, "that I've got to go to this farm by the lake and collect a baby?"

"That's right," says Gertrude. "It's quite simple, really, Betty. And we know we can trust you. But you're not to say anything to anyone. Do you understand?"

"Yes, madam. I think so."

"And, Betty," Julian presses notes into her hand, recalling the smoothness of Betty's neck, her legs, "this is to thank you for your trouble. And to ensure that you keep quiet about it. It's rather a… a delicate matter, you see."

Betty nods, and goes out to where the driver awaits her.

As they drive along the country lanes, Betty in the back of the cab with her money tucked in her pockets, she thinks, Nick will be pleased tonight. And then she sees the trees and avenues they drive through and thinks, this is freedom. She has hardly ever seen the countryside, having been in London all her life, but here, the fields open themselves as if outstretching their arms to welcome and celebrate her and the sky seems huger, more expansive, somehow. The hills fan out; sheep are woolly rounds in fertile meadows. Buttercups and cow parsley bubble in the fields. Betty has never breathed air like this – and it will change her life.

"Who's coming?" asks Helga, holding the baby. "The maid?"

"That's right."

"Whose maid? Who are these people? Are they well-known?"

"No."

"Just wealthy people who can afford to buy babies."

"That's it, Mum. The rich can have what they want. Didn't you know that?"

A knock at the door. Martha's mother hands the baby to her daughter and goes to answer it. A young girl stands there. Betty clears her throat.

"Good afternoon," she says. "I'm 'ere to collect the baby."

Martha's mother leads the girl upstairs. She passes through the kitchen, notices the old man sitting, hollow-eyed, at the table, goes up to the room where a young, dark-haired girl is sitting, propped up in bed, holding a baby. The girl doesn't look much younger than me, thinks Betty.

"I've been sent to fetch the baby," she says.

"Who's sent you?" asks Martha's mother, eyeing the young girl.

"I'm not to say." Betty feels uncomfortable. Here she is, a poor working girl giving instructions to a farming family. Haughtiness doesn't suit her. "Can I take the baby now?"

Martha looks defiantly at her. "No," she says.

"Martha?" Her mother.

"I'm not giving the baby away! I want to keep her. Tell… tell your master and mistress that the baby's mine. Go back and tell them that." Tears are running down her face.

Betty hesitates, turns and runs out to the waiting cab.

"It's coming, Julian! I can see the cab coming."

Julian thinks, Gertrude is more excited than I have ever seen her before. "Oh my God. The baby's coming."

Julian thinks, she is almost simulating birth. Panting. Gasping. Crying. As if she is giving birth to her own child.

The cab stops. Out gets Betty. No baby.

"Julian." Gertrude sounds uncharacteristically feeble. "There's no baby. She's empty-handed."

"She wouldn't give it," says Betty, panting. "Said she wants to keep it."

Gertrude rushes towards Betty. Grabs her shoulder. Shakes her.

"You bloody fool. You stupid girl. We told you to bring the –"

"Alright," says Julian, removing Gertrude's hands from Betty's shoulders. "What does the girl say?"

"That she loves the baby and it's hers and that she won't give it over, sir. Not for nobody."

"OK. Leave it to me. I'll sort her out."

Julian goes to his desk. Sits down and writes. Hears Gertrude sobbing outside the door.

Dear Martha,

I can imagine how hard this is for you. But you know that we entered into an agreement. That baby must come to my wife before it breaks her heart. I will pay you whatever you want. You know what we said: once this is over, I will be with you. I love you. We will have our own children together. Please God, I beg you. Don't let me down. Do this for me.
Julian

He folds the note, puts it in a sealed envelope. "Take this to her – but under no circumstances must you read it. Do you understand?"

Betty nods, takes the note in her hand. In the cab on the way to the farm, Betty carefully peels open the flap of the envelope, unfolds the paper and reads. Gasps. Then she replaces it in the envelope, licks the flap closed and waits to arrive.

Back at the farm, the driver waits in the car again. Once more, Betty goes through the kitchen, past the hollow-eyed man, up the stairs to the bedroom where mother and daughter sit by the baby, asleep in its crib.

"Good afternoon," says Betty. "I bring this from my master."

Martha reads it and tears well up in her eyes. The letter drops beside her on the bed. Martha nods to her mother who picks up the baby, wraps it in a shawl and hands it to Betty. Betty takes the note – and the baby – away.

All night Martha sweats, develops a fever, tosses and turns. She sees over and over herself nodding to her mother and the baby being taken away. As quickly as that. As painfully as that. A nod and a giving away.

By the following morning, the crib is empty and Martha's father is dead.

Chapter
VIII

Raphaella is a bird tonight. But again there has been the presence of the other bird. Tonight, she decides, she will fly nearer her to see what the response is. She moves closer to the other, smaller bird and feels no hostility. Martha longs to be near, too, so stays close, does not move. And gently, as if in a dance, the one's feathers lift and stroke against the wings of the other. So mother discovers daughter. On the sand beside a still lake.

Oliver stands again at the door of Mr and Mrs Turner. It is being kept at a slit each time he comes.

"Mrs Turner," he says. "I want to write about the birth. I want to write about Raphaella's early years. And her teenage years. Please speak to me."

The door opens slowly. Oliver goes in. Stands in the hall. Mrs Turner's face is hard and cold.

"Why are you so hostile to me?" he asks.

"There are things I want to do with my time. Talking to you or anyone else about the past is not one of them. Why should I waste my precious hours helping you to write a book that I don't even want written?"

"And why don't you want it written? What are you so frightened of?"

"Nothing. But what should I gain from it?"

"She's your daughter. She's a famous painter."

"Why? Because she paints rectangles on big canvases?"

"People like them. They are powerful symbols of –"

Mrs Turner laughs aloud. "Her birth was quite painful enough, without me going over it again and again. I can make you a copy of the birth certificate if you want proof. But I don't want any more of these intrusions."

She opens the door to urge him to go. He will not be invited in for melon juice again.

Outside Oliver pauses on the doorstep. Why is she so reticent? Why is the birth certificate so significant to her? What on earth does she have to hide?

Gertrude sits in the living room, holding the baby. She looks down at her dark hair, just like Julian's. The baby is sleeping now. Her face has settled into peace, her eyelashes tiny and perfect, her fingers hanging limp at her side. Julian comes in, sits beside Gertrude on the sofa.

"Are you pleased?"

"Yes, she's beautiful. But − but I keep thinking. She's not mine, Julian. She's not really mine. It's as if I've stolen her."

"You mustn't think or speak like that, Gertrude. I arranged her for us."

"Yes, that's true."

"What about a name?" Julian looks at the baby, strokes its hand. Remembers Martha. Feels for her. It was not like her to try to be deceitful. How she must love that baby. How she must love him.

"I was thinking. As our surname is already a painter's name, I would like her first name to be a painter's, too. Maybe she will be a great painter. Better than her mother."

"That's a thought. But there aren't many women painters. Famous ones."

"No, but I thought − after Raphael − Raphaella. What do you think?"

49

"Beautiful, Gertrude. I like that. Now I must go to work. Christopher is having the birth certificate altered for me."

"I hope he's trustworthy. No one besides him must know."

"No one does or will. Impossible."

Gertrude does not know how long she sits there, holding the baby. The girl is beautiful. There is no doubt about that, and Gertrude is pleased to have her, but it is not love she feels for her. It is something else. A curious mixture of affection – and deep, deep resentment.

"No," says Betty. "I don't know who the girl is, but one thing's clear. That baby belongs to 'im as well."

"You reckon?"

"Well, listen to this." Betty uncrumples the note from her apron pocket. Reads aloud. " '*You know that we entered into an agreement. One day we will have children of our own.*' How does that sound to you?"

"Well, she obviously agreed to it, din't she? So what's the problem?"

Betty folds the note away. "So you think that's fine. For 'im to sleep with a slut and then pretend that child's 'is own?"

"Yeah, if they're all in agreement."

"You didn't see that girl's face, Nick. She loved that baby. It was torture for her to give it away."

"You're too soft, Betty. 'Ere. Give us a kiss."

"Those are always your solutions, aren't they? Money and drugs and sex. There's nothing else in your eyes."

"What's wrong wiv you, eh? Old cow's been getting at you."

"No, Nick." Betty turns to the young man, sprawled across the unmade bed. "I want to do more wiv my life than cleaning and cooking for someone else and fetching babies for 'em and bringin' 'ome money so that you can get stoned." Tears are racing down her cheeks now. She thinks of the wide fields, the way the country lanes ribboned to the lake. The birds. The grass. "I want to be free."

"Oh, of me? Are you saying, of me?" Nick jumps up and grabs her arm with his tight hand. She feels the deep pinch, his fingers clamped on her flesh, stopping her blood. "Of me, d'you mean? Is that what ya mean?" His teeth are hard against each other, his skin taut, his neck red.

"Get off me! Leave me alone." Betty wriggles free and runs, runs down the attic stairs. Out of the door and on to the busy street. She loses herself in the people and smoke, but in her mind she is already in the fields.

"But why is she so hostile towards me? I can't understand it."

"We've never got on. She hates me."

"But why? Mothers don't usually hate their daughters."

Raphaella pours them more white wine. She has arranged green olives beside black in a bowl, white grapes beside dark ones. Oliver declines it all.

"I was a threat to her. I've always challenged her. Her piano teaching, her art teaching. I've made her seem inadequate, I suppose. You're the biographer, not me."

"Well, I'm beginning to wonder. It's going to be very hard if no one will speak to me. You, your father, your mother, your sister. Anyway, I'm just leaving that part of it at the moment and focussing on the work itself. Lucius has all the slides and catalogues, as you know, and many of the originals. At least he's being helpful. But then maybe he has nothing to hide."

"What do you mean by that?"

"There's something uneasy about all of you. Why don't you ever see your parents any more? If they hate you so much, then why did they give you their beloved holiday cottage? None of it makes sense to me."

Oliver takes his wine and walks in to the studio. A window is open, as if pointing on to the lake. A large canvas rests on a double easel. Vertical lines, purple, white and olive green, reach from the top of the canvas to the bottom. Then one of Raphaella's characteristic lines across, as if the colour is always broken by something else. Why?

Martha's face is pale. She lies against white pillows, weak and unhappy. Helga is beside her.

"Martha, love," she whispers. "I've brought you more soup."

Martha shakes her head.

"Come on, my darling. It's been weeks now. I want to see you up and dressed again – on the farm, feeding the chickens, milking the cows, as you always have done."

"Why should I get up? I have no father; I have given my baby away. What have I to live for?"

"For me, Martha. And for our farm. I cannot manage on my own. The buildings are old and decaying; the cows have not been milked; the chickens not fed. We haven't planted our usual crop of vegetables. We'll have to sell the farm if you don't help me. How many more months are you going to lie there? Martha, listen to me, darling."

Martha looks at Helga's tired face, pleading eyes. She suddenly looks ten years older.

She hadn't noticed that she had neglected her own mother. "Pass me my clothes, Mother," she says.

Chapter
IX

"Alright, Mother," says the young girl. "If you hold it upright, I'll knock in the nails."

And Helga obeys, straining her back to hold the fence. Martha pinches nails between her lips, removes one at a time, hammers hard. The fence gradually straightens.

"This is the kind of job Father would have done, with no complaint or trouble at all."

"Well, we have to manage now." Mother and daughter straighten up. "Let's take a break."

They walk back to the farmhouse, Martha's arm threaded through her mother's. To Martha, it is a walk through a once thriving, now decaying enterprise. For the last ten years, her parents have struggled to keep it going, to make any money at all but, with her father gone, it is a lost battle. And yet, in some ways, Helga seems lighter since her father has died. Relieved, almost. She barely refers to him, wears her wedding ring dutifully but seldom utters his name.

Inside the house, Martha boils a kettle, warms a teapot.

"You know, Martha," says her mother. "I was talking to Mrs Ashley the other day. Her Richard is interested in running a farm."

Martha blushes slightly. Richard has always flirted with her on his visits with his mother. The Ashleys' farm is a few lanes away and Martha and Richard have known each other all their lives, although he's a bit older than her.

"Really? But they've got a farm of their own."

"Yes, but his parents are ready to give it up and it's been an even bigger disaster than ours. Richard wants to move on, they say. She even hinted, well – I don't know what you'll think of this." Martha waits. "He wants to take on ours."

Martha puts her tea down. Wonders. The idea of their farm ending and mother not being there any more. "But what would you do, Mother? What about me?"

"Well, maybe I could live in Briar Cottage if he didn't mind. And you? Would you run the farm with him? And you'd still be cleaning Lemon Cottage. Mrs Ashley knows about the… you know, the baby. She and Richard wouldn't tell anyone else."

Martha blushes again. Her mother's shame is almost tangible, even after this time.

"I don't know about that, Mother. It would seem strange living like lodgers on our own farm. I've lived here all my life. And to run it with Richard in charge? I'm not sure."

"Well, at least, let him come and see us and we can talk. No harm in talking, is there?"

"You need to see Mr Turner. What about?" Mrs Turner is holding Raphaella.

Betty looks longingly at the dark-haired, dark-eyed child. Remembers, as she often does, the day she took that baby from her own mother. Raphaella's face is serious, gorgeous. Will I ever have children? Betty wonders.

"I can't say, madam. It's private, confidential like."

Mrs Turner looks suspicious. "Wait there."

Betty shifts from foot to foot. Holds the note in her hand. Dreams of fields. Farms. The shining lake.

Mr Turner comes into the hall. "Yes, Betty? What is it?" She stares at him. He feels inexplicably afraid. "I think you had better come into my study."

Inside the book-lined room, he shuts the door behind them. He sits; Betty stands.

"Now what is it? I've a meeting to go to."

"I've got this note, sir." Betty smiles, wickedly. Lifts it up so that Mr Turner can see it. He catches glimpses of his writing, his words. He jumps up, tries to snatch the note from her. Betty takes it back.

"I've had copies made," she says.

"You little bitch," he hisses. "I told you to show it to the young girl and no one else."

"And that's what I done. No one else has seen it – yet."

"OK. How much do you want, then?"

"Twenty grand."

"Twenty? You must be kidding, girl."

"Or else Mrs Turner sees it. And the papers might be interested, too. Leading judge an' all… "

Mr Turner goes to the safe, takes huge wads of notes, hands them to Betty. She nearly faints. He has that money ready. Ready to keep. Ready to give.

"But you'll have to leave at once. I don't want to see you again, d'you hear?"

"With pleasure. I'd love to quit my job."

"I'll tell Mrs Turner you're leaving straight away. Get out now. And don't come back."

Betty takes the money and note. How powerful paper can be, she thinks. And how she enjoyed that tiny taste of control over a man, a room, which have bound her in duty all these years. She will never clean that floor again or polish that bastard's shoes or let him enter her with his loathsome body.

Outside, on the pavement, Betty feels like a plotter, a conspirator. Tuesday evenings, Nick goes out. Meets his mates. Gets stoned with them. Spends the money she has earned. Back in their attic flat, she packs a few possessions in plastic bags. Writes Nick a note:

Nick.

I've gone. I don't want to see you again. Leaving you some dosh. Try to get yourself sorted.
Betty.

Never before has she sensed such power. All her life she has served others. No longer. Without looking back, Betty leaves the attic room and goes to explain to her mother before heading for the countryside. The creaseless hills.

Mr Turner takes a while to stop shaking, but eventually he comes out of his study. His wife's standing in the hall. The baby's asleep upstairs.

"What's happened? Where's Betty?"

"She's gone, silly little girl. Says she wants to get on with her life."

"That's as much notice as she gives us, after all we've done for her?"

Mr Turner shrugs his shoulders.

"What are we going to do? I can't possibly manage just with a cook and a nanny. I'll need a new maid."

"You'll get one, then. Frankly, we're better off without her. She wasn't much good. Totally unreliable. I've got to go to my meeting, now. I'm already late."

Julian reaches for his hat and stick and Gertrude sees that his hands are shaking. Why should that silly girl leaving have affected him so much? And why did Betty speak to him, not her? She always deals with domestic matters, doesn't she? Doesn't she?

Gertrude stands by the closed door long after her husband has gone out, wondering whether he was sleeping with the girl. Let her not be pregnant, she prays. Gertrude has often wondered what her husband gets up to with other women. And yet how she has loved it on those rare occasions when his firm fingers have explored her body. And how she wishes he would turn to her more often. Even though she is infertile. Even though she is not beautiful. And young. And how Gertrude wishes she did not think about him and the cleaning girl every time she looks at Raphaella – the baby who she tells others is hers, but who is not really hers at all. Never will be.

"All the slides?" Lucius is in the gallery storehouse with Oliver. "Why?"

"I told you about the biography I'm writing of Raphaella. Well, it's proving hard getting information. She's unco-operative, you know what she's like; her parents are obviously hiding something – tight as bloody clams – and her sister's even worse. I've been interviewing people who knew her gran, she was a milliner, and her old schoolteachers, but it's pretty unexciting stuff really. So I reckon it's going to be more weighted towards her work, now. But not so esoteric that only three people in the country will understand it."

"I see. But not too toned down, either."

"Exactly." Oliver looks at the smart man opposite him. Lucius has always seemed to him the epitome of sophistication – cream suit, cream handkerchief edged with green, green socks, beige shoes. And firmly gay, not a hoverer, like Oliver. From time to time, Oliver and Lucius have slept together, but it has never interfered with their work. They have remained gallery owner and art agent, with a special interest in the work of Raphaella Turner. Uncomplicated.

"Will you help me?"

"Of course. I have all the slides and archive material, as you know. And the catalogues. Some of the paintings will be in New York for a while but the unsold ones – if there are any – will return here for the spring exhibition. No problem, Oliver. Lunch?"

Yes, thinks Oliver. Maybe Raphaella was right. Trust him to get it wrong again. Another failure to add to the list. The long list. The paintings will have to speak for themselves. And yes, lunch seems such a good idea.

"So Richard's coming over this evening?" Martha is folding washing in the kitchen, fingering each item to check if it is dry.

"Yes," says Helga. "Around eight, Mrs Ashley said."

"Fine. I'll go to Lemon Cottage then, just to do a bit of cleaning for the Turners. I think it's time I started now that it's spring. They'll be visiting again, now that the weather's better and they'll want to bring the… the baby. Did I tell you? They have a child now."

"No, you didn't mention it. Are you sure you're up to it?" Her mother looks at Martha. Wonders how her daughter really is. "But take care. I don't want you straining yourself."

"I'm fine, Mum." Martha kisses her mother on the cheek, notices how she looks older since Father died. "We need the money."

That early evening, as Martha cycles to the cottage, she thinks of how many lies she has told her mother. In spite of feeling close to her, it has always seemed so natural to deceive. About the baby. Julian. The cottage. Being a bird. Her mother does not know that this evening, Julian has arranged to meet her there. She has not seen him for a long time. Wondered if, after the baby's birth, he would drop her. But he has been in touch again. Wants to meet. And, Martha wonders, as she leans her bicycle against the slats of the yellow house, will I ever have a relationship with someone where there is no deception?

58

Alone in the house, Helga sits quietly and closes her eyes. Those images again. She never knows when they will come: the uniformed men pushing the children and families into the camp; her mother's cries; the terrifying nights; the sound of the Nazis' boots as they patrol; and then the leaving. Helga sent to England, aged fourteen, with no family and no one. The journey on the train. Children packed in. Going nowhere. Working on the farm. Feeling numb and alone. Marrying a farmer. His despising her Judaism. Was she right to marry him? She asks herself the same question over and over again. But then there has been Martha: her purpose, her joy.

And the comfort that no one knows of: her escape by turning into a bird, flying over the farm while her husband lay asleep. Freedom. And her wings lifting her higher into the clouds and her shiny eyes observing all around her and the wind supporting her. And how no one ever knew.

Helga paces from room to room, closes her eyes. Oh God, she cries. God, in whom I wholeheartedly believe, please help me.

And it is then, as it is often in moments of despair, that Helga's hands turn to claws, her mouth narrows to a beak, her wings and feathers appear, as if by magic. And she preens herself, admiring and loving the soft down which covers her body. And she stands on tiptoes, then lifts herself off the ground and takes flight.

Chapter
X

"Oh, Martha. You're here. Darling."

Julian takes Martha in his arms. Senses a slight resistance from her. A tensing of her body.

"Martha. How I've missed you." He kisses her, full on the mouth, runs his hands over her body. Martha moves away.

"Julian," she says. " I was really surprised to hear from you. I'd thought you'd finish with me now that you have the baby."

Julian laughs in an uncomfortable way.

"How could you think that? You know what I promised you."

"I hadn't heard from you for some time. I thought you'd forgotten me."

"Not at all. It's been very difficult with –"

"Does Mrs Turner love my – our – the baby? What does she call her?"

"Raphaella. After an Italian painter, Raphael. She is pleased with the baby. It keeps her busy."

"Do you know what it was like for me to give away that – our child? Do you know how that felt? Do you know that every night I dream of her still, think I'm holding her, touching her face, and when I wake up and she isn't there, I weep. Did you know that? Do you care?"

Martha finds she is crying, shaking, that her body is throbbing with pain. Julian is holding her now, kissing her hair.

"Yes, my darling. I do know that. I feel for you, but one day we will have our own children. And you will love them just the same. Look. I've brought you presents. Fruit and chocolate and something else." He hands Martha a blue box. "Open it."

She lifts the tiny latch, takes out from its velvet bed, a ring with amethysts and diamonds. Martha gasps.

"Martha, this is my promise of marriage to you. Put it on, darling. I love you." And she slips it on her wedding finger and the stones catch the sun and send shafts of light from her finger to the ceiling and back again.

And they kiss and he holds her and it is like it was before – almost.

"And how many cows do you have now?"

Richard, Martha and Helga are standing at the edge of a meadow.

"About thirty, only," says Helga sadly. "That's all we can manage. What with the milking and all. And the chickens. And the crops. Mainly potatoes and corn and fodder for the cattle. Are your parents giving up their farm?"

"Yes, they want to sell up and move on, retire, but I want a new challenge. They'll pay for me to buy this farm, and I'll pay them back over the years. There's great potential here. Much more so than with our land. I've got big plans for this place. Things I could never do on our limited farm."

"But what about Mother?" asks Martha. "Can she – we – stay on at Briar Cottage?"

"Of course, but you, I thought you would work with me on the farm," says Richard, pushing his ginger hair back with his large hand. "After all, you know it so well."

Martha blushes when he looks at her. Although he is only a few years older than her, he seems so manly somehow. His hands are large, his working clothes rough, his face intelligent. He is ambitious. Maybe it is that which scares her slightly. Or maybe it is because he knows that she is the young girl who had a baby by a waster and that a rich couple took the baby away. His parents probably told him. Everyone knows about it. She's a free girl. Something of the gypsy in her, with her dark hair and wild eyes.

"Yes," says Helga, looking a mixture of relieved and sad, "we'll agree a price and go ahead with it. It's the best thing that could happen. Father would have approved of someone building up his farm."

Richard waits, quietly. Martha looks down to the grainy ground and then up at Richard, whose eyes and face are almost smiling.

Even from the other side of the playground, Raphaella can hear the muttering about her. It's obvious: their hand movements and sniggers and turns in her direction mean that she's the centre of their jokes.

"She's weird," says one, just loudly enough to be audible.

"Those bizarre paintings and no interest in boys. Did you see what she did in gym this morning? Miss Fielding says, stretch your arms behind you as if you were about to fly and she – loony legs – only made her neck arch up and her head was all high and it was really spooky. I thought she was going to take off."

"I know," says another. "She's really demented. And when we were all talking about university and careers with Mrs Archer, nutcase Raphaella said, 'I will paint every day of my life' and everyone else thinks, you are odd."

Even though Raphaella sits on the bench by herself and the girls stand in a large group, nothing affects her superiority. She looks at them as if at dirt and shit: she is not only better than they will ever be, but they are not even in her species. Are *they* birds at night? Can *they* paint?

"There," says Julian, as he ushers bags into Lemon Cottage. "She's cleaned it well for our visit."

Gertrude comes in with the nanny carrying Raphaella. And Lucy, the new maid. Immediately, Gertrude feels differently about this cottage, the lake, about this place which she and Julian bought soon after their marriage and which she has always loved visiting. This, this is the place where Julian entered that girl, where he must have kissed her and fingered her and then entered her hard, with passion, maybe, on several occasions and he must have enjoyed it and the girl must have loved it too and that was in Gertrude's home. Lemon Cottage has instantly lost its appeal.

"Ah, great. Look at the lake, Gertrude. Shining, bright."

Gertrude looks out to the lake, which she has loved for years and to her it is dark and flat and is not shining and bright at all. It has lost its sheen as Julian has lost his and she has lost hers and the baby – Gertrude looks to the carpet of the living room where the baby is playing with the nanny. Does Gertrude love that child? Will she ever? What she wanted was her own baby, yet all she has is someone else's. And, worse still, that someone else has had her husband.

"It's wonderful to be here," says Julian, "after such a long gap. You see, you needn't have worried. It's perfectly safe for the child."

For months, nearly a year since Raphaella was born, Gertrude has made excuses about going to their holiday cottage. It would be too cold for the child, not safe enough for her, nothing to do there with a baby. But in the end, Julian had persuaded her, said the break would do them good, so, over a bank holiday weekend here they are – picnicking as they used to by the side of the lake, Julian canoeing, the windows of the cottage flung open to the sun. And it does not feel the same. No, says Gertrude to herself, I shall not come here again.

"Interesting," says Oliver, as Lucius moves on to the next slide, "how many of her paintings, while retaining that typical block look of hers with her beloved rectangles, have lines or fissures down them, from side to side."

"That's true." Click of the machine. "Yes, here again. This one went to Paris, didn't it, that hotelier, Gerard, d'you remember?" Oliver nods. "Obnoxious, he was, but yes, you're right. In this one, with the lemon and cream shapes – they're almost square this time – there's that grey crack. As if nothing can be complete. Everything has to be broken or interrupted. Interfered with, almost."

"Yes. It's so tempting to play art psychologist. Nothing can ever be perfect. It must be damaged in some way. The one thing that's come out of what people have said to me is that Raphaella always seemed distant, difficult, struggling with life, with herself and these paintings, whilst chosen so often for their almost Mediterranean light and beauty, are unsettling. I think so, anyway."

"Yes, but have you seen the really early ones? I bought them from Anna Polinsky, although I think she was reluctant to release them. Even then. I'll show you."

After a few seconds of fiddling with the slide machine, Lucius projects on to the wall grey and black shapes unlike anything Oliver has seen before. They are gloomy and menacing. Some have lids on the boxes almost like coffins.

"What dates are these?" asks Oliver, feeling like a detective.

"Late 70s, early 80s."

"That's interesting. Just when her gran died."

"Spot the biographer," Lucius teases.

But Oliver has suddenly become animated in a way that surprises Lucius. He always thinks of Oliver as rather bland, a little limp, in a way. He used to fancy him but his inertia annoyed him. But suddenly he is a different man.

"I want prints of all of these, please, Lucius, and what I want to do is to provide a catalogue of all the works at the back of the book. There is no complete catalogue of her work, is there? All those in private collections, too?" Lucius shakes his head. "Well," says Oliver, "there soon will be."

Gertrude sits with the baby by the side of the lake. Lucy has spread a rug out on the sand. Raphaella is over a year old now, and walking. She toddles to the water and comes out again, over and over, dipping her toes in the coolness and then retreating – and again. Water, sand; water, sand; water, sand. Suddenly the child turns round to look at her mother, with hostile eyes, Gertrude thinks. Then Raphaella lifts a fistful of sand and chucks it at her mother's face. Sand particles drift through the air and none reach Gertrude's eyes but she stares angrily at the child. Nanny and maid exchange glances.

"No, Raphaella," hisses Gertrude, waving the sand away with a pointed hand. "Naughty." And suddenly she feels hatred for the baby, overwhelming hatred and wants, desperately, to push her daughter into the lake. She scoops her up, the baby crying now, and runs back to the cottage. I could have, sobs Gertrude, I wanted to kill her.

Yes, thinks Oliver, rushing home, to his study, to the chair, computer on, to write. He has seen the way ahead now. He will make it less biographical, putting in some facts but the focus must be on the paintings themselves. Raphaella was right all along. Lucius, too, has proved that to him. And that's how he'll start his book – *The Work and Life of Raphaella Turner*, not the other way around. That's it.

Prologue

Raphaella Turner has made more impact on the art world than any other woman painter. Mention twentieth century male painters and the names come tripping out: David Hockney, Howard Hodgkin, Lucian Freud, Mark Rothko, Kandinsky and so on. But women? Yes, Paula Rego but who else? The answer is: Raphaella Turner. Even those who do not know her name, know her style. Generations of children have grown up with her images in galleries, restaurants, hotels, homes. She has affected and influenced a whole way of painting with her unmistakable huge rectangles and parallelograms with other symbols upon them, lines running down. She has changed the whole way we see painting; the way we see ourselves. She is as much a symbol of modern feminist thinking as Germaine Greer or Susie Orbach; as much a symbol of this century as contraception or television. She is Raphaella Turner.

Born in 1961, the daughter of a judge, she grew up in an affluent home in North London. Her grandmother was the milliner Georgina Hendricks, who made hats for the royal family and was known for her uninhibited lifestyle and her outlandish ways and creations. Her mother, Gertrude, was a keen amateur painter who encouraged both her daughters – Raphaella has a younger sister, Charlotte – to paint. She says: 'There were always paints in the studio and we would often spend the afternoons, the three of us, painting. It became clear early on that Raphaella had her own distinctive style and we encouraged that, of course.'

Summers were spent at their lakeside residence, Lemon Cottage, now Raphaella's permanent home.

* * *

Today, thinks Raphaella, I will get to know her. She is, after all, a beautiful bird, yet I know that she is a bird-woman. And so when Raphaella sits perched on a pine branch today and the other, smaller bird flies past, Raphaella flies with her. Together they soar, the larger, brighter bird; the older, more wary bird as if she has not long been what she is or is slightly frightened of being caught out. Yes, thinks Raphaella, I like the idea of the younger leading the older. So when the large bird flies, Martha flies too, with her, echoing her movements. When the large bird swirls in a swooping circle, so does Martha. When the large bird shakes her feathers and settles on the sand, so does Martha. And when their beady eyes meet and they blink at each other, Raphaella knows that a bond has been formed. Later, on the white sands, they stretch themselves back into women and look at each other: Raphaella, tall and slim with curly, thick black hair cascading down her naked back. Martha, middle-aged, her hair greying now, her skin slightly wrinkled, but her previous beauty apparent in her eyes, her somewhat wary smile.

I have no women friends, thinks Raphaella, but today I have found one. The only one that matters.

Betty opens the door to her cottage and lets herself in. It is small inside, but she has made it cosy. A rug on the living room floor, an immaculately clean kitchen with everything in its place, red tulips in a white vase. Never before has Betty had her own home, a place which was hers and no one else's. And she owns it. With the money Julian has given her, she has bought and signed for this little cottage and no one will take it away from her. She gazes out of the window and watches the sun enter her home as if by arrangement. And, of course, she can always get more money from Julian if she needs it. She opens the chest with her tiny key and looks at the letter in Julian's elegant writing. She kisses it. That has been her saviour. She needs no God while she has that letter.

"If you hold her and calm her," says Richard, "I'll work at this end." He rubs the cow's back. "It's OK, Buttercup, OK. We're going to help you."

Richard's hand is now inside the cow and his face is serious. Martha is impressed by the way Richard focuses on the job, how he doesn't get diverted. This is a man who will probably deliver his wife's babies one day, she smiles.

"Yes," he says. "Good girl, Buttercup. It's coming."

The cow is shifting restlessly, lifting and shaking its head, the pain obvious in its eyes. Yes, thinks Martha. I gave birth to a daughter once, but I allowed her to be taken away. Her eyes were dark, her lips tiny and round, her skin perfect –

"Excellent, Buttercup. That's it now."

Noises of pain come from the cow's mouth. A slippery shape is sliding out. Yes, thinks Martha, stroking Buttercup's face. It's alright now. And then there's a thud and the calf falls to the hay, wet and shiny. Buttercup licks her baby clean, Richard smiles and Martha finds that she is crying.

Richard comes round and puts his arm around Martha's shoulder.

"You mustn't get so upset," he says, his ginger hair more ruffled than usual. "It's just part of life. You've grown up on a farm. You know it's all birth, life, death, don't you?"

"Yes, yes." Martha finds it hard to stop crying. Why can't she have her daughter back? Will this terrible pain and longing for her ever cease? "You don't understand. It's not just about Buttercup, it's about – I –"

"Martha," says Richard. He is looking at her directly now. They are standing in the farmyard. "I do know about your baby. My mum told me. It makes no difference to me. I still feel the same about you –"

Martha smiles her gratitude, and together they walk towards Richard's farmhouse to clean themselves up – and move on.

"Granny," says Raphaella. "Are you alright?"

They are sitting together in their favourite place, the hat workshop, and Raphaella is making an exotic creation with two peacock feathers and lots of sequins. Granny means to laugh at her granddaughter's wild ideas but coughs instead. Phlegm spills from her mouth on to the table. Raphaella runs to get a cloth to wipe it up. Her gran is coughing still.

"Oh, Gran," she says. "Are you alright?"

Gran tries to mutter comfort through her coughs and eventually the fit subsides. When Raphaella wipes up the mess, she sees that there are specks of blood in the mucus.

"Oh, Gran," she says again and hugs the little woman, who seems to get frailer and smaller each time Raphaella sees her. Please, thinks Raphaella. Don't leave me, Gran. Don't go.

"Now, Raphaella." Mrs Archer is sitting so upright opposite Raphaella that the girl thinks her body a perfect right-angle. "As you know, your A-levels are coming up and you are the only girl in your year at St Mary's who has not decided what she is going to do after school. I have asked you to come here today to urge you to consider your future career. You have now left it too late to go to university this year – I have written to you about this, as you know – but you could apply for next year. Miss Reynolds thinks you should be going to art college as that is your passion, but I want to know what you feel."

What to put on your form, you mean, thinks Raphaella. She watches the tight woman, pen poised above her sheet, green print on white paper, waiting.

Well, thinks Raphaella, is there a box for living in a cottage and being a bird?

"Mrs Archer," she begins. "My parents have given me their holiday cottage to live in. It's by a lake and I love it there."

Mrs Archer waits. Yes?

"And I will paint there and maybe I will travel. That is what I am going to do."

"I see." Frosty. "And who will support you, if you don't mind my asking?"

"I will sell my work."

"I see. We'll put 'artist' then, shall we?" And reluctantly she writes the single word on her little form, as if she were writing 'devil' or 'witch'.

"Yes," says Raphaella. "Artist will be fine."

"How dare you?" hisses her father. Raphaella stands upright, looking straight at him.

"How dare you ask for that?"

"Why shouldn't I have it?" says the girl. "Mother hates going there, she always has and you hardly ever go any more. It would be a home for me – get me away from you – and you know how I love it. I would live and paint there."

"But Betty's in there. She's lived there for years. It's her home."

"Well, she'd have to leave, then. Who comes first – your daughter or a bloody maid?"

"You have demanded so much from us," says Julian. "You have destroyed your mother's life –"

"I have? What about you and your women, Father? The ones she knows about and the ones she doesn't –"

71

"That's nothing to do with you. That's private."

"Yeah? And what about the nights you came to me, Father and touched me up like the dirty little shit that you are? Is that private too?"

"Keep your voice down! Your mother's in the other room."

"No, Father. Maybe it's time for her to find out who you really are."

"Shut up, you little bitch. You're nothing but trouble. Take the cottage, then. Get out of our lives so that we can have some peace at last."

Raphaella turns and strides out of the room, triumphant.

"You know, Gertrude," says Julian, that evening after dinner. They are drinking liqueurs by the open French window. Outside, their garden is bushy, full of lupins, delphiniums, roses, butterflies. "I was thinking about Raphaella and her future."

Gertrude snorts.

"What is she going to do with her life?"

"I don't know and don't care," says Gertrude.

For a moment, a rare moment, Julian feels strong waves of sadness engulf him. That baby – she wanted that baby so much – but it has not worked out at all. There has never been a bond between them as Gertrude has with Charlotte.

"But we have to consider it. She doesn't want to go to university. Says she wants to paint, that's all."

"If you can call those ugly shapes painting." Gertrude knocks back her liqueur in one swallow.

"Well, I wondered about letting her have Lemon Cottage. We so rarely use it these days and it would get her off our hands. I'll give her a small allowance and she can live independently. Eighteen is old enough."

"Yes," says Gertrude. "Let her go. You know I haven't enjoyed going there any more – since – and it will release me from her moodiness and tantrums. I've had enough."

"Good," says Julian, rising to leave the room. "That's settled then."

And he goes up the stairs, smiling, ready to tell his daughter that he – or she – has won again.

As the coffin is lowered, Raphaella feels her body stiffen in a way that surprises her. She is nineteen. Her grandmother has died. She understands all this. She spent much of her childhood in Georgina Hendrick's workshop, stitching tiny beads, attaching shiny plastic cherries on to fancy hats. And yet she feels detached as her grandmother departs. Maybe she is frightened that she will cry. Or maybe she senses that her grandmother is distant now? No longer here to feel affection for? The warmth has gone. The vicar mumbles a prayer. It feels alien to Raphaella. Means nothing. She turns away, avoiding the eyes of her mother. Julian comes over, puts his hand on Raphaella's shoulder. She shakes it off.

Back at Lemon Cottage, now Raphaella's home, she is beginning to clear away the linen tablecloths and heavy curtains which her mother had hung there years before and which Betty had tolerated. Raphaella will paint it all white. But that must wait. Raphaella needs to paint her canvases first. In the studio, which at the moment is a pile of rubble, Raphaella places a canvas on an easel and begins to dab. Black paint. Grey. Much of her painting has been like this recently. Maybe when she redecorates the cottage it will change, but at the moment, it is black and dark. A rectangle of grey emerges, slightly left of centre. There is an uneven white margin at the side of the grey. She layers it on thickly, filling the rectangle, making sure no corner is left unpainted. Then a crack of white light, at the edge of the shape. And it is only then, only then, that Raphaella calls out for her grandma and sits down and weeps.

Still, tomorrow, she will paint the cottage white.

"No, Mother," says Martha. "I shall be fine in here. Honestly." Martha likes the little room in Briar Cottage where she might find peace of mind. She unpacks her belongings, the lock of hair from her baby, her father's gold watch, Julian's letters to her. All of those go in the top drawer of her chest.

Downstairs, her mother is unpacking her possessions. Now that she has her own home, she will put out all her family treasures: the silver candlesticks which she has polished periodically, in secret; her father's *yarmulke,* worn for the last time by him in Germany; his *talit* with silvery tassels; the *mezuzah.* For the first time since she has left Germany, she feels she is at home. Yes, she had thought she had found a home when an English man, a farmer, agreed to marry her, when she had Martha, but how her husband had despised the Jews, was ashamed that people might know what she really was. He had mocked her prayers, taunted her for her dark hair, for what seemed to him strange mutterings. Now, with her husband dead and a home to call her own, Martha's mother will enjoy being Jewish again. She takes a nail and hammers her *mezuzah*, slanting, on the doorpost. Then she kisses it and recites a Hebrew blessing. Thank God, she cries. Thank God.

When Martha comes down later and sees the *mezuzah* on the door, she does not question it. Yes, her mother's Judaism has been something she has known about, something that needs no discussion. Martha thought it would be hard to leave the farmhouse and move into the cottage – a comedown after running the farm – but it does not feel that way. It feels like they have arrived somewhere, mother and daughter. They embrace, Martha stroking her mother's hair.

"Mother," she says. "You have always been there for me, after the baby, when father died... you must truly love me."

Her mother's eyes fill with tears. "Martha, my darling," she says. "More than you could ever possibly imagine."

Betty draws the curtains open wide. Outside is the countryside, which she has grown to love. Fields stretch as if pulled from corner to corner, like shaken out sheets. The sky lies wide and blue and open-legged above her. Butterflies carve loops in the air. Swallows swoop in circles round her cottage. Please, says Betty, to herself, to God. Never let Nick find me.

"So, it's alright, Briar Cottage? You won't be cramped?" Richard is gathering hay and tying it into bundles.

"No." Martha smiles. "We love it. It feels like home already."

"Good," says Richard, " 'cos I was going to say, if you wanted to move into the farmhouse with me, there's gallons of room."

Martha feels her cheeks burn. Richard seems to be growing fond of her.

"No, thank you," she says, bending down to pick up some hay which has managed to escape.

"Well," he grins. "Maybe one day, eh?"

When Martha tells her mother of this conversation later, she smiles. "I can see he is keen on you," she says. "He is a lovely man. Kind." And Martha's mother thinks as she sits sewing, how lovely it would be if Martha could have married someone Jewish, a privilege she hadn't had. But who would she meet on a farm? And who would want to marry her when they heard about the child? None of this seems to bother Richard.

The next evening, Martha and Helga invite Richard to dinner. He brings them vegetables from the farm, sunflowers from the field. Martha puts them in a jar and they smile, huge and sunny-faced, behind them all evening. Martha, Helga and Richard sit cramped around the small kitchen table where Martha serves soup and stew and home-made bread.

"I saw something on the doorpost," he says, ripping his bread and dunking it into his soup, a movement which makes Martha blush, although she does not know why.

Martha's mother looks uneasy. She has learned to be wary.

"It is called a *mezuzah*," says Martha. "My mother and I are Jewish."

It is the first time she has said it and although it is true, it seems odd to articulate it. Her mother has not brought her up with much tradition and they live in isolation and yet Martha knows it is the truth. When she looks to her mother, her eyes are glassy with tears.

"That's interesting," says Richard and asks more questions, about synagogue, the sabbath, the holocaust.

Yes, thinks Martha's mother. Marry him if he asks you. He will treat you well. Not torment you, as my husband did me.

"So, you've begun the catalogue?" Lucius grins, sanctimoniously, Oliver thinks.

"Certainly have. I'm not playing around, Lucius. I want to get this done in time for the retrospective so that this book can be on sale then. I've managed to trace a lot of juvenilia. Also much of her work when she first moved into Lemon Cottage. Her style has changed substantially since then, yet there is something of the present Raphaella Turner in it. Look at these."

Once more, ex-lover and ex-lover fill the projector, turn the lights down, look slowly and carefully at a slide sequence of Raphaella's work.

"These were done just after her trip to Italy," explains Oliver.

"Fascinating," says Lucius. "Look how the colours have changed since those grey and black days. Now we have terracotta, sepia. Yellows, ochre. The images seem warmer."

An hour later, Lucius turns the projector off. His mouth finds Oliver's. For a moment, Oliver feels torn between Raphaella and Lucius, woman and man, painter and dealer. But then, Oliver thinks, Lucius's hand unzipping Oliver's trousers and feeling how hard and stiff he is, he has surely been led to the one by the other.

Chapter
XIII

"These are lovely." Raphaella is picking up vegetables from Joe's basket and admiring each one. Aubergines deep as velvet; courgettes striped down their yellow and green backs; lettuces and cabbages which frill at the edges like salacious underwear.

"Not as lovely as you," says Joe and he immediately feels that was a bit corny for Raphaella. You have to be careful with her, what you do, what you say. She ruffles his ginger-haired mop and laughs. He kisses her, strokes her shoulder, but she pushes him away.

"No, Joe. I want to paint."

Joe stands outside on the drive and stares towards the lake. It is a huge blue plate today with nothing on it. He feels small beside it. Sometimes he senses he is nothing. Nothing beside the lake; nothing compared to a smear of paint on Raphaella's canvases; nothing at home where Martha, middle-aged and wan, tries to run the farm and control him and makes him feel like a child, still. Nothing.

"And that, that is the best you can do?" Oliver's mother is holding up his poem. For English. They had to describe a storm. In the context and solitude of his bedroom, it had seemed alright to him. But then his mother had entered, saliva like cuckoo spit at the edge of her mouth. Looked over his shoulder. Picked up the paper. Sneer. Laugh. Suddenly, the limp sheet looks pathetic to him, as well. She's cruel but she is right. Clears her throat. Reads aloud, sarcastically: "And the rain drums on the street/ Lightning in the sky." She rips it into shreds. The white squares float to the floor. "I don't think so," she says.

She leaves his room, but not before she takes his head and knocks it on the desk. Stars whiz in his eyes. He cries. Outside the door, she is laughing.

Raphaella stands on a hill overlooking Florence. Browns and yellows and whites fill her eyes. For so long she has busied herself with greys and blacks and yet here it is – warmth and dust and heat. She can see the River Arno, a shimmering silver ribbon running through the city. She pushes her straw hat firmly on her head and begins the descent, curving her way through gardens and rockeries. Reaching Florence, she stares at all the statues which rise and thrill her, over-ornate, ludicrous. She laughs aloud at them, at the fountains which overdo it, at the Duomo and the churches and the cobbles and cafes. She is in Italy. Not with her parents, not with the school, but as a painter. And how it all lays itself open and offers itself to her. For her.

That night she sleeps in her *pensione* with the windows flung open to the cool air, and her dreams are full of yellows and ochres, as if the world is being grilled, heated, burned, prepared for her – a giant feast.

Siena thrills her the following day; the horsetrack lying still now and curling its way round. Raphaella buys olives and grapes from a little shop where the server keeps bowing to her and blowing kisses. She will go home and paint this, all of this. Or maybe it has been painted for her already.

Standing in the Tuscan hills one day and seeing rows of trellised grapevines stretching out across the hills like the tightly-plaited hair of an African woman, Raphaella looks up to the sky and feels the blues and yellows drop, slip on to the canvases for her, like a meal already prepared.

Back at Lemon Cottage, it is as if the work has been already done for her. The canvases seem to paint themselves, the colours lead her, instead of the other way around; she is helped and guided by her Italian memories, by a fat brush which seems to know its way. The greys and blacks which kept appearing after her grandmother's death have gone and been replaced by Mediterranean blues and yellows and white. Sheer white. Sand and sea and sky and Italy. Blocks of colour float above each other and then, each time, the crack, the fissure. Nothing for her is complete until the whole is broken.

Richard is lying in the grass with Martha. They are looking up at the sky, which is bright and optimistic above their heads. They work together all day on the farm and often take a lunchtime break together. Martha's mother is resting in the cottage; all seems calm. Richard slips his hand into Martha's. There seems little – or nothing – to be concerned about. The farm is thriving. The sky is clear. He is in love with Martha.

"You know," he says. "I think I am the luckiest man alive."

"Really?" Martha rolls over and leans on his chest.

"Yup. I have everything anyone could want. The farm. A home. Enough money to do what I like." He lifts her chin upwards to tilt her face towards him. Her hair is black and wild, her skin clear and alive. "And I have you. I love you, Martha. Marry me. We'll run the farm together. Have children, and they can run around and feed the chickens and ride on the donkey, and it will be heaven." He kisses her, his tongue on hers, yet he feels her resistance. He wants her; has wanted her since he first saw her. Wild creature. He presses

81

his hand on her shirt against her breast. Her hand stops his. She turns away.

That evening, Martha speaks to Helga about Richard's proposal.

"Yes," says her mother, looking up from her needlework, "you could do worse."

Martha thinks that isn't exactly a great recommendation. A negative rather than a positive response.

"But I don't love him. He is a good man and I like working with him, but love? No."

To Martha's surprise, her mother puts down her sewing and stares her daughter in the eye. "Look," she says. "You're lucky to have a man like that ask you to marry him. He has his own farm and home. He is good. His parents are good. What do you expect?"

Martha finds her cheeks burning. She stands up. "Oh, so you mean 'you are a girl who had a baby unmarried; you live on an isolated farm. Who would want you?'"

"You need to stop dreaming, Martha, and face reality. I came here from Germany and had no one to help me and nowhere to live. Your father said he would marry me. I could not think about such luxuries as love. I had to think about survival."

"Fine. Then I'll marry him. If you think that I can do no better and deserve so little, then I'll marry him."

Martha runs out to the meadow where cow parsley and buttercups froth together into a huge yellow and white milkshake. What is life? she asks herself. What am I? What the hell am I doing here? What small amount do I dare to expect?

Betty sits alone in the green field, which has become one of many places in the countryside where she feels comfortable.

Where she feels alone. From time to time she goes to visit her mother in the town, but apart from that sees few people. Oh, and Julian, of course. When Betty needs money, she goes to Julian to get more. It is so easy. There is a pattern to their meetings. First he resists, then she reminds him of the letter and then, sometimes to get a bit extra, she sleeps with him. Hating it. But he is such a wonderful source of income. Sometimes Betty thinks of Nick and wonders what he is doing with his life. Not much, she imagines. She is pleased that she is free of him and yet, and yet – there is something that she misses. Is it the warmth of his skin, or his kisses, or knowing that he was always there waiting for her? One day when Betty goes to see her mother, she can see that she is agitated. Her mother's always nervous, but today, today there is something else.

"Mum," says Betty. "Mum? What's wrong?"

"I couldn't help it," says her mother. She is shaking. " 'e just barged in. Wouldn't take no for an answer."

The bedroom door slides open. It is Nick.

"Married? When? Who is he?"

Martha laughs nervously, surprised at Julian's tone. "Julian. How many more years did you think I'd wait? I have to get on with my own life now. I want children of my own – not to pass on to other people this time, but to keep and bring up myself."

"But I told you –"

"Yes, you've been telling me that for years. But I don't want to wait any longer. I have a life to live as well. In your eyes, maybe it is a worthless life, but still, it is mine. You think with your money and power and education that you can control everything, but no longer."

"But do you love him?"

Martha averts her eyes. "I think he will be good to me. At least he is willing to marry me and live with me and we can have a family together. We work well together too."

"And so do we work well together. Listen, I'll leave Gertrude. I will."

"So you've said a hundred times. I've had enough, Julian. Anyway, I've decided. You don't need to know all the details. I've just come to tell you that I don't want us to meet again. Do you want me to give back the ring you gave me, and the other gifts?"

Julian shakes his head. Martha looks into his eyes and sees that tears are sliding unceasingly down his cheeks. She has never seen him cry before, did not think he was capable of it. Suddenly, she sees him as pathetic, this famous judge, this great man who controls other people's lives, but cannot shape his own. He is nothing. She feels contempt for him. She enjoys the power for a moment, then feels her heart ache for him. She puts her arms round his neck and kisses him chastely, on the cheek. He looks through the window to where Martha slips away from him. She does not look back. And he cannot look forward.

"Oh," says Julian, closing the door. "It's you again."

Betty smiles wickedly. She enjoys the way he dreads her visits. Her control over him.

"Time for more –"

"I've got another idea." Julian sits in his chair. Leaves her standing. "We don't go to Lemon Cottage any more. My wife doesn't like it. Nor do the girls. So we're going abroad a lot more. France, Switzerland. But we want to keep the cottage. In case – well, we just do."

Betty smiles slightly. He is squirming. Never reveals the truth. The whole truth. Nothing but the truth.

"You can live there, provided you keep it clean. We need a cleaner, housekeeper. Just in case."

Betty nearly cries. She will live in a cottage by a lake. She will be part of nature. Be free.

They are drinking port.

"But why do you want to keep it? Let's just sell it." Gertrude feels her pulse race.

"I don't want to do that. Don't you feel any attachment to it at all?" Julian runs his finger around the rim of his glass. Averts his eyes.

Gertrude tries to catch his eye. Fails. Yes, she thinks. Because you and that girl – that is why. You are more sentimental than anyone imagines. You cannot let it go.

"I must go," he says, jumping up suddenly. "I'm giving a lecture to the Law Society this evening." He puts on his coat. "On truth."

Chapter
XIV

Sun spreads itself calmly through the windows of Lemon Cottage. Betty's cottage. Here, where she is at home, at peace, she spends hours thinking, barely believing that she is free. The lake rises and lifts itself to her each morning. The trees sway for her. The birds entertain her with their singing, putting on a daily show for her amusement. It took nearly a year for her heart to stop thumping. Her dreams were barely dreams: terrible tumbling storms of emotions and memories – her dad leaving them, Mum's many addictions and problems, Nick and his dependency and his relentless demands. Now she contents herself with the fields and the hills and the lake. So she finds rest and serenity for the first time. And it is on one of these mid-summer days when she is staring out of the window that the door to her cottage flies open and Nick bursts in.

"So ya 'ere, then. 'Iding, ya little bitch?"

Betty leaps up. A year of calm vanishes instantly. Her heart is fluttering wildly again, a bird in a cage.

"What do you want? Who told you I was 'ere."

"Ya mum, din't she? Why did you think you could get away from me, you stupid cow?"

Nick is beside her now, his face pale and menacing. His eyes are semi-circled with black. His fists are clenched, his arms a series of pinholes.

"Help me," he says.

"No, Nick." Betty is shaking. "I want to be free. I want to just live alone."

" 'O's givin' ya all this dosh, then? What are ya, a little princess or somefing?"

"No, Nick. I want to be on me own. I need peace. I couldn't find it with you." His face is in hers now.

"Give me money. I need it." His face is desperate, ugly. Could Betty possibly ever have loved him?

"OK. Only if you leave me alone. I don't want to see ya again. I've made my own life now."

She goes out to her purse and takes out the last wad of notes Julian gave her. She hands them to Nick. He grabs them.

"What's 'is name, then?"

"Who?"

"Your fella. What's 'e called?"

"I 'aven't got no one. I live on me own. That's the way I want it."

Yes, thinks Betty. I've got it just the way I want it: a man supporting me but no relationship.

After Nick has left, Betty finds his dirty footprints on her rug, smells his foul breath in the rooms, finds her heart racing again.

After the wedding – small and quiet – a broad-minded rabbi comes to the farm to give Richard and Martha her blessing. She has heard how Helga came to this country and married a farmer who humiliated her for her Judaism; she has heard how Martha is marrying another English farmer but one who feels for and understands her. And here they are on the farm with the sun blazing above them and making mirrors of the trees and, with just Richard, Martha and Helga present, the rabbi makes a blessing.

"Baruch atah adonai…"

Helga's eyes fill with tears. She is Jewish; Martha is Jewish. Nothing will ever take that away. Richard seems

87

sanguine – neither moved nor resistant. Maybe his not caring is the only solution. Unlike her husband who hated and despised what she was. For whom it mattered too much. To Richard it does not seem to matter at all.

Richard and Martha kiss.

That night, in a hotel by the sea, Martha turns to the husband she does not love.

"Please," she says. "I want to start a family right away."

Richard smiles. It doesn't seem to matter to him whether they do or don't. Martha wonders whether indifference such as his is perhaps a better solution than Julian's passionate declarations which lead nowhere. And even though he is not really bothered, they make love that night. Without Julian's skill, but with plenty of gentleness and respect and acres of indifference.

And because they are both birds tonight, Raphaella decides it is time, it is time to approach Martha, smaller bird, worried brow. Large bird comes closer to small; eyes meet, beaks in recognition of each other. Then, for the first time, Raphaella lifts her feathery wing and wraps it round the shoulder of the other. The little bird does not move or try to shuffle away. The opposite, in fact. She comes closer to Raphaella and the birds stand silent on the sand, wing over wing, gazing at the lake, blinking.

Then Raphaella lifts her body and shoots beneath the water. Martha follows. And under the lake they are penguin-like, flippers flapping, wings lifting and forcing the water past, bubbles rising from their beaks. And there, in the centre of the lake, deep beneath the water, Raphaella pauses and looks at the place which she has long considered a base for a building, a structure that she and the other bird will construct.

Now, gradually, Raphaella starts scooping the sandbed with her beak and moulding the grains into a wall of sand, moist and cemented. And to her delight, Martha copies her. And so it is on this day, deep beneath the surface of the lake, that Raphaella starts another of her shapes, a collaboration this time – the sandworld.

"Mum, Mum."

Betty pushes open the door to the flat where her mother has lived, unhappily, for years. The door is always open so that her mother's carers can come in when necessary. Usually, Betty comes in, calls her mum's name, the woman answers and then they chat, Betty arranges the flowers she has brought in a vase, unwraps the bread, tidies up. This has gone on for years. But today she calls, "Mum, Mum," and there is no reply.

Betty goes through to the bedroom and there, with the door ajar, she sees the figure of her mother on the floor, her face and head bruised and beaten, her eyes staring open. Betty screams, runs to her mother, holds her, sobs furiously, sees her open purse lying on the floor, and smells the foul stenching breath of someone evil. Nick.

"It's going well. Thanks." Oliver is on the phone to Lucius, explaining his latest dealings. Lucius smiles. It's like talking to an archaeologist who has uncovered some shard of pottery a million years old, or a detective solving a case rather than a writer on art. And although it amuses him, it also bothers him. Is that what Oliver sees painting as? A collection of canvases that one tries to locate rather like trainspotting or a children's treasure hunt? Collect them all and tick them off? Then you've finished? Although Lucius enjoys a good fuck with Oliver and thinks him, well, pleasant and affable enough, he lacks depth. Is shallow. There have been so many opening nights with Oliver at the gallery and Lucius has heard the comments of people who know, people who are discerning, responsive to art, and he has longed for Oliver to make a comment, which makes him think or see anew, but he has waited in vain. And yet he is devoted to his work and to spreading Raphaella's reputation. And all that is good for Lucius.

"You remember Seligman? Well, the family's moved to the States now. Washington. But he has so many of Raphaella's paintings. I'm going over midweek to see and catalogue them."

Jolly good, Oliver, thinks Lucius, smiling, replacing the handset. Tick them off on your little list.

Betty opens the floral curtains and looks out to the lake. This landscape has never ceased to please her. It is of endless interest and serenity. And it took years for it to return after her mother's murder, Nick's arrest and trial. Now with him behind bars and her mother, hopefully, at some kind of strange peace, Betty has worked hard to regain that contentedness she once had, years earlier. And it has not been easy. Her heart thumped for years; her dreams were vivid, haunting nightmares that ruined night and day; her mind was not at ease. But gradually, over the years, she has made Lemon Cottage her home, filled it with fancy things, pretty floral and lace curtains, ornaments everywhere. Made it hers.

It is mid-summer. The trees are feathery around the lake, birds are high above the cottage. And the door bursts open. Betty sits up. Startled. It reminds her of when Nick discovered her years before. But he's in jail now. Who is this?

A tall attractive woman with black thick hair walks proudly into the cottage. Betty knows who she is. Everyone

90

knows about Raphaella, although she sees few people. Eighteen and arrogant, she only faintly resembles the round-cheeked baby whom Betty had to deliver to Julian. But Betty has seen her growing up over the years. When she has gone to Julian to get topped up, Raphaella has been lurking there in the house, always sullen, always hiding or peering round corners as if a half-person. A shadow. They have hardly spoken to each other before. This is the first time. And in Betty's eyes, it is far from pleasant.

"Father says I can have Lemon Cottage now. As my home."

"But he told me I could. I live here. I love it."

"That's too bad. He told me to give you this."

She hands Betty an envelope. Inside there is money and a note. Another one of his wretched notes.

Betty,

I am giving the cottage to Raphaella now. My daughter must come first. There is money here to help you to get another home. I am assuming my orders are understood.
Judge Turner.

Raphaella glares at Betty. "I'm moving in tomorrow," she says, and is gone.

All night and all day, Betty packs away years of her life into boxes and carrier bags. All the time her eyes fill with tears, blurring her vision, so that she has to keep knocking the tears away. Ornaments into bags, precious belongings of her mother's into boxes.

The following day, Betty calls a taxi and loads her stuff in, looking out at the lake and trees which have helped to calm her thumping heart, where she has spent days and days gazing, thinking, recovering.

An hour after Betty's departure, Raphaella arrives. Flings open the windows. Rips down the ghastly flowery curtains at the windows.

Yes, thinks Raphaella. I shall paint the interior of this cottage white.

Betty flings open the windows of Lemon Cottage and gazes out to the lake. It is calm and serene. Just the way she was in her last home. Just the way she will be in this new home. Betty starts arranging her ornaments – some of which she has collected over the years; others her mother gave her. They are ornate: china birds on porcelain twigs; pottery figurines of shepherds and shepherdesses kissing; a golden bell with swirling patterns etched on its surface. The curtains are floral, the bedcovers patterned. Betty keeps some of the furnishings which Gertrude had left there – why not? They are good quality linens, lined curtains. But takes her own, too. Thinks of Julian.

Fifteen years on, Raphaella rips it all down, the awful tasteless curtains and cheap rugs, and begins to paint it all white. When she needs help she pays someone: her grandmother has left her money; her father is an endless source of funds, but she will make her own one day. Yet there is no one who wants to help her, no friends, no family. She is alone. For the first time now she will have her own studio, not one to share with Gertrude and Charlotte, but her own, where she will paint freely in the way she wants, when she wants to. She will dress more exotically than before. She will live on mainly fruit and vegetables. She will be a bird or shell or rock when she chooses to. This, this is freedom. And yet she finds herself thinking of her father.

*　　　　*　　　　*

And with their beaks, they push the sand into ridges, little walls. Round and round they go, so that the bottom ridge will be an enormous circle, a foundation, which they will build up. This will be the base of their sandworld. The circle is marked. Now, with their beaks, they gather sand and build it up, high. Scraping the grains up, up, till they build and grow higher and higher. The first wall is complete. Now they begin to build so that little windows of light appear all around the first floor. It becomes an amphitheatre of light and sand. A first floor, windows, and then the start of the second. Fish flick their tails and swim in and out of the windows. Raphaella waves them away. This sandworld will be hers and Martha's, no one else's. Tired, the bird-women flap to the surface of the lake and out on to the sand where they rest, the larger, younger bird's wing wrapped round the smaller. And they pant and recover and remember the good work they have done.

Oliver stands in the centre of Washington and stares up at the white buildings around him. The centre is formal and exciting: European, he feels. Here, he will discover more about Raphaella's paintings. He walks through the busy streets to the Turpin Gallery and finds the curator, Jeremy le Veux, who shows him the many paintings of Raphaella Turner's he has in the gallery and gives him lists of clients who are willing to show Oliver the works they have in their private collections. That week he goes from restaurant to hotel to private home seeing the work, which he so admires and sometimes doesn't understand. He makes notes, takes measurements of the paintings, asks questions, looks. He feels his catalogue swell and grow. Yes, Lucius would tease him and say it is a shopping list, a trainspotter's notebook, but Oliver knows, knows that this will be the only definitive catalogue of the work of Raphaella Turner. And it will be he who has compiled it.

"You're an idiot. Did you know that? Three out of ten for Maths; four right for English. Are you retarded or something?"

Oliver shifts from foot to foot in the kitchen in his home, watches his mother's face hiss and boil at him, hate and spit at him. She thumps him hard on the chest. He stumbles, falls. He does not reply. Swallows back his tears. Feels there is no point in crying. But one day. One day he will show her.

Betty looks around the tiny cottage and sighs. Another home. Another move. Her heart has begun to thump again. This is alright, rather cramped and dark, yet she will unpack her belongings, make it her own. But nothing will ever replace Lemon Cottage, where the light flows in through open windows, where the lake is a constant presence and comfort outside, where the cedar trees are large and dependable. She is sick of moving, never knowing where she belongs, where she can settle. One day Nick will be out of jail – soon, perhaps, and he will find her and harass her again. Perhaps she will never be free. Her heart is fluttering. Again.

Nick stands outside the jail where he has lived for fifteen years, if you can call it living. He has been plotting revenge on Betty for most of that time, haunted by it, possessed by the aim to get her for what she did to him. Getting him put in jail – someone who loved and cared for her? He feels more than fifteen years older. Feels like an old man. What will he do with his life? Where will he go? Runs his hand along his unshaven face. Feels rough and dirty. Betty. He will get her. Someone will have seen her, will know where she lives. Someone.

Helga and Richard are standing beside Martha. She holds the baby in her arms. Yes, it is true she had hoped for a girl, but this boy, this boy will bring them pleasure and happiness. Helga's eyes are filled with tears. Yes, maybe you could say this is her second grandchild, after that little girl was taken away. No, she mustn't think of that now. Even though Martha cannot help but remember, remember the daughter she gave away. Sometimes she thinks of Julian, wonders who he seduces now that she has gone. Wonders if he would eventually have left his wife and married her. Maybe. But she has a new life. She did not love Julian. She does not love Richard. But she has her mother and the little boy and Richard is good to her, when he takes his wellies off occasionally and leaves the farm behind. Rare. And this little boy, with his daddy's ginger hair and his tiny fingers, he is Martha's son.

"I think," she says to Richard, "we will call him Joe."

Richard nods. He is easy about that, easy about whether he and his wife get on or not, easy about Helga living in Briar Cottage, easy about everything. So easy, so unconcerned, that Martha sometimes wonders if he is even alive. Barely. Richard kisses the baby, kisses his wife and mother-in-law and goes out to tend the sheep. Martha half-wonders if he will kiss them, too.

Raphaella looks around the cottage and smiles. She is pleased with the work she has done. Each room is white, each piece of muslin, cotton, silk, is white. She has tried to make this home as bare and simple as possible. Some of her early paintings and possessions are still in her parents' attic and maybe she will leave them there but this, this is the way she wants her home to be. Her kitchen is new and modern, the walls and tiles and cupboards white. Raphaella herself will be dressed always in bright blues and mauves and greens and velvet and satin, but her rooms will be white.. A backdrop to her. And her paintings. There, in the studio, full of new canvases and paints and untouched brushes. That will be her passion, to fill her white home with coloured paintings. This will be her life. And, for the first time, Raphaella senses a calm descend upon her, an inner calm which seems to filter through the open windows from the lake and surround and enter her with peace. She closes her eyes. Thank you, she says, without knowing whom to thank. There is no God, her grandmother is dead, her parents have disappointed her. She has no one to be grateful to, yet needs to appreciate what she has. And it is at that moment, that moment of calm, of happiness, that the door flings open and a grubby-looking man, whom Raphaella has never seen before, bursts in and begins to attack everything with an axe. Swings at the walls, the windows. The canvases go flying like missiles around the room. Raphaella stands up, screams, tries to grab the man, but he persists.

"I'll get you," he says. "I'll kill you."

And tears fling out of his eyes as he wields his axe, taking huge swipes at anything there is to swipe at. Then he takes a match from his pocket and sets light to the home. Raphaella's home, where she was going to paint and be happy. And flames catch the curtains and the bed and the new canvases fresh and ready for painting with bright colours. And the whole place is alight and broken and torn, and it is as if the cottage itself is bleeding and crying with spreading flames.

Raphaella runs outside, sobbing and screaming, on to the sand beside the lake and weeps, cries, asks herself why, why, who is he? And for a moment, the man turns, cut and

97

bleeding, to catch her eye. It is not Betty, as he thought it would be. It is a funny looking woman in coloured robes. A weird priest or something. And Raphaella stares through her tears at an evil man, a man whom she does not know. This man who has destroyed her home. And all she knows is that she hates and despises him. What she does not know is that he is Nick.

Chapter
XVI

The man has run away. Vanished. Raphaella stands outside her blazing cottage and watches the flames rise and twist in all directions: through the windows, the roof, dancing their way through the defeated curtains. Her previously white home is now orange and angry and blue. The lake lies passive and aloof. How strange, thinks Raphaella, that a few feet away there is water, so much water, yet it cannot put the fire out, does not even sprinkle a drop upon it. Within minutes a fire engine has come. Then another. Men in uniform leap out and begin to work with hoses. They surround the house. Raphaella stands dazed and in a trance, not believing that this is happening, not understanding what the men shout to each other or the roar of the flames seem to call aloud. Another language. A police car arrives, an ambulance. A uniformed woman comes forward and wraps a blanket over Raphaella's shoulders. She thinks the woman a bit odd, all dressed in bright loose clothes, slightly paint-splattered, but she says nothing. Puts Raphaella in the police car. Asks her where her family live. To Raphaella's own amazement, she finds herself giving her parents' address. Who else is there?

"Very interesting," says Oliver. "Fascinating." Oliver has removed his glasses and is peering up close at a series of miniatures, unlike any Raphaella Turners he has seen before. "They are so compact and tiny, it is quite hard to see exactly what they contain."

The curator nods, has taken rather a liking to Oliver Slatton. This refined, cultured English man. "True. But I see elements here which recur in her later work, don't you think?"

Oliver smiles in agreement, rather fancies this suave French man now living in Washington, whose slight accent makes him even more attractive.

"Such as?"

"Well, the boxes, the fractured edges and lines, but also the beginnings or hints of colour. Out of these broken and black boxes come orange streaks, as if she is discovering colour. And look here." He points without touching. "Here. It's like sunlight almost. What I find amazing about her work, is that it's so intensely emotional. I look at these and there is so much feeling in them that I can barely manage not to cry."

Oliver feels slightly uncomfortable. He has no desire to see this middle-aged sophisticate sob. He moves swiftly on to another painting.

"And in this, the same, isn't it? Black and grey boxes, light streaming out of it. Hope, maybe?"

"Mm."

"And there are ten of these?"

"Mm."

"Where did you purchase them?"

"From Lucius Fox, in England."

Oliver smiles. Lucius. How he misses him. The art curator and Oliver Slatton talk more; the one considers the other sentimental; the reverse simplistic. Both initial attractions wane although relations are cordial. Yes, Oliver may obtain slides. Yes, they will be in touch. They shake hands and Oliver re-enters the anonymous streets.

*　　　　　*　　　　　*

Betty sighs and opens her box of ornaments again. How many more times will she have to pack and unpack? She feels restless, looks around this newest, latest cottage and feels no excitement at it. Yes, she can just make out the lake and yellow blob which is – was – Lemon Cottage. Why did she feel compelled to let the fire brigade know? Why did she care, feel devastated when she saw flames destroy the home which was hers but never hers? Why should she care now? The cottage did not belong to her – ever – and that stuck-up eighteen-year-old could burn to death and it wouldn't affect Betty. So why did she ring and save it? Betty cannot answer these questions, senses that as she grows older she feels more and understands less. Why should it matter where she lives? Why does it matter so much? She thinks of her mother, thinks with horror of Nick, of Raphaella, of the lake and then turns to look at her dark cottage again.

Raphaella is back in the bedroom which used to be hers when she was a child, except that it is different. It has become an empty room, bed, shelves, desk, a spare bare room. Raphaella has not been in here since she left home to live in Lemon Cottage and even now she is beyond realising that it is a morgue. Gertrude has removed all the paintings, put them in the attic, turned it into a tomb. Now, Raphaella sits propped up in bed against pillows, and Lisa, the newest maid, is at the door.

"You haven't touched your soup, Miss Turner. Try some. Come on."

As far as Raphaella is concerned, Lisa is in a room several miles away speaking through a muslin screen. Nothing seems real or connected any more. It is as if Raphaella has died and is watching the world from a new position. Angle.

"Or shall I bring you up some tea?"

Raphaella stares at the girl and begins to cry. Tears rise and fill her eyes first, then spill down her face.

Downstairs, Gertrude is on the phone to Julian.

"How is she?" he asks.

"Distant. Strange. Maybe mad. Who knows? She was hardly normal to begin with."

"I'm making some progress on the fire. It seems it was arson. You weren't right about one of Raphaella's candles simply catching light. More sinister than that. It seems an outsider – a man – was seen leaving the cottage. Running away. Nutter, probably. I'll get him. He'll burn alive by the time I'm finished with him."

Martha flicks her wings and dives underwater. She wonders where her fellow bird is this evening. She encircles the beginnings of the sandworld twice and it looks hollow without her friend. Windows are beginning to appear. Shellfish scuttle in and out of the gaps, the openings. The sandworld seems a hollow shell to her, without that larger, more creative bird. The purpose, the vision, the drive, was hers. Without her, there is nothing. Martha feels tears fill her beady eyes and dissolve into her feathers, into the empty sea. And then senses a presence, a feeling that she is near. She turns. The larger bird is back. And together they begin to build again, although the water tonight is murky and their vision blurred, they begin to build on the second floor above the windows, so that it takes on the air of an Arabian temple, a mystical place with many laced and carved windows. They nudge the sand with their beaks, push it along with their spread wings, build and create without a word or sound between them. Creativity in silence. And gradually, gradually, it grows.

Gertrude stands by the door to Raphaella's room and stares at the pale figure whose black hair lies limply on the pillows. She is sleeping, her breath shallow. She spends most of her days like this, it seems, sleeping, waking and refusing food, then sobbing silently before sleeping again. Gertrude would like to have loved this daughter who was never hers, whom she expected to feel something positive towards but never could. The girl is an irritation, a hindrance, a disappointment, a product of the lovemaking – and even possibly love – between her husband and another woman. For money. And it was not that Gertrude could not feel love or maternal passion, because she felt it with Charlotte. But what a different girl – and, of course, her own. Gertrude turns away and goes downstairs. She has a fleeting idea – to maybe touch Raphaella before she leaves, or perhaps tuck the sheet gently around her, but somehow that desire, that possibility, never comes. It simply never comes.

Midnight. And Julian has come in from work. Gertrude is asleep. They have separate rooms now. It seems better. He looks at his sleeping wife, her mouth unattractively open, her snores slight but unappealing. He closes her door and goes to see Raphaella. She, too, is asleep, but in a different way. Her sleep is more worrying and deep. Approaching death, he feels. Her skin is white, her eyes jammed shut, not flickering at all. He kneels at the side of her bed and strokes her hair. The pillow is moist with tears. He brushes the back of his hand against her cool cheek. "God forgive me," he sobs. "Please."

Martha sits at the side of the buttercup meadow and watches Joe. Two years old, he already loves the farm, which has been his only home. He runs and tumbles over and laughs aloud, clutching his hand across his open mouth. Then runs after the chickens which cluck, alarmed, and flap away. Martha smiles, rubs the curve of her stomach with her hand. Please God, let this be a girl. For even with Joe here and the delight he brings, she cannot forget the daughter she made with Julian. Whom she gave away – sold – for money. Each pregnancy, each birth is not only a possibility that she will have a girl but somehow a chance that she can have that girl back again. She does not question the irrationality of her own thoughts; just accepts and clings on to them as friends to each other.

"Oliver? Lucius. How's it going?"

"Doing good, as they say here. I'm seeing a lot of work. The deals with the rights and transparencies are a bit complex, as you'd expect, but I've seen a lot of work. Didn't even know of some of them before."

"Great."

"D'you know Trents? Big gallery in Washington?"

"Sure. They've been around about ten years, I guess."

"That's right. Well, they've got a few of Raphaella's works which I hadn't previously seen."

"Interested in selling, d'you think?"

"Well, that's for you to pursue, not me. But in terms of letting me catalogue them, they're only too pleased. She has been extraordinarily prolific, hasn't she?"

"Sure. Apart from that gap late Sixties, early Seventies. We've never uncovered that, have we?"

"No. We haven't. But none of that seems to matter now. I've totally shifted. Much less interested in the biography than the works themselves. She's right, of course. They say it all. And more besides."

"Well, we'll have a meal when you get back and you can tell me all about it."

Does he mean more than a meal, wonders Oliver. A meal – and a screw?

"Yes," says the midwife. "Excellent. The head's through now. Come on, Mrs Ashley. Take it easy."

Richard is waiting next door. He can hear the screams of Martha. Then the cries of the child. Both grate on him somewhat. But he is a father again. Fine. Then he can get back to the farm. After all, it's haying time.

Martha gives a final shove, then relaxes her legs. Pants and sighs. Thank God. Thank God.

"Well done, Mrs Ashley. You have a lovely little boy."

Martha sits up in bed holding Adam, her second son. She is breastfeeding him, listening to his tiny sucks and slurps as he works at drinking from her large breast. She is staring through the window at the wide farm and stretched countryside outside. She is also waiting, waiting for her love for Adam to arrive. When the midwife announced that the baby was a boy, Martha felt like chucking him out of the window, but she can see, can see from what her mother and Joe tell her that Adam is healthy and beautiful and she is waiting, waiting for her need of him to come.

Joe runs in, kisses his new baby brother on the head and laughs. Runs out. Richard pops in to see if Martha is alright. He is wearing his farming garments as usual, animal smells upon him and his clothes. A strand of hay has stuck to his cheek. He strokes the baby's ginger hair and kisses Martha on the forehead. After he has gone, Martha waits for her love for Richard to come too.

"Lucius."

"Hi there."

Oliver and Lucius are in a chic wine bar. It is on the fifth floor of a huge London block and overlooks St Paul's and the Thames. It is late. London is alight. Alive. Oliver orders them wine. Each clutches the menu, fancying the food, fancying the wine, fancying each other.

"So, it was a successful trip?"

"Great. Yeah. I'm getting so much information and encouragement too. Everyone who cares about Raphaella's work seems to feel the catalogue is really important and so I'm getting plenty of co-operation. I've got tons of material to show you."

"Good."

"Yeah. The tricky part is still her life story bit. The catalogue and analysis of her work are mere slog. That's all. But the biographical part. That's really hard when no one will speak."

"Tricky. Yes."

"I mean, there are periods of her life when things were obviously happening. Her grandmother's death, problems with her parents, at school, that whole dark time around when those amazing miniatures were painted, but no one will speak to me. I can't guess at what happened. It feels like a conspiracy of silence."

The waiter pours him white wine.

"Thank you." Lucius sips, nods and the waiter fills both their glasses. Brings them a bowl of olives in herbs and garlic. Leaves them. "I suppose the only other option is to produce the detailed catalogue to come out in conjunction with the big retro and leave the biography completely. Let the paintings speak for themselves, as our mutual friend is so keen on saying."

"I think you're right. That's what she wants. It's manageable too."

Oliver swallows. Is he failing again? Copping out? His mother would laugh. Defeat. Failure. Backing out of what he intended to do. Isn't he always?

They chat some more, drink some more, eat the olives. Lucius places his hand lightly on Oliver's on the cool table.

"I've missed you," he says, quietly.

*   *   *

107

Gertrude stands at the end of her daughter's bed. Tries yet again to love the pale girl whose dark hair spills on to the pillow behind her. Fails.

"Raphaella," she says firmly. The girl's eyes open. What should Gertrude say? Sorry that I hate you? Why don't you leave? She opens her mouth. "Lisa will bring you soup if you want."

Raphaella opens her lips. Speech is hard for her, too.

"I don't want soup. I want canvas and oils. I want to paint again."

Gertrude stares at her. Why should her daughter have what she wants? After all that she has put them through? And hasn't it been painting and her arrogance that have caused this, anyway? This breakdown, or whatever the doctor likes to call it?

Half an hour later, Lisa brings up soup on a tray and canvas and paints and a selection of brushes. Raphaella nods her thanks and stares for some hours at the canvas. What can she do that will be worthwhile? Until the evening, the canvas lies untouched, the soup uneaten, the paint unopened. And all night. As if they were never there or Raphaella was never there. Painter and paints do not meet.

In the morning, when the sun blows rays through the open window (Lisa considers fresh air good for Miss Turner) Raphaella picks up the canvas and cuts it into squares. Tiny, irregular squares. Twenty of them. She will paint again but only if it is small. Unthreatening. She opens the tube of white paint. Dips the tip of her brush into it. The painter has returned.

Oliver lies in Lucius's arms. They are in his bed in his beautiful apartment, where some of Raphaella Turner's paintings live. Large abstracts, cubes and squares and lines. One is a tumble of browns and yellows, as if autumn had come hurtling into this light room even in spring. Changing the season. Lucius catches Oliver looking at it.

"One of my favourites. I like it when she's bold. Fearless. Like you."

He strokes Oliver's hair. They laugh.

"Not a bad lover yourself," says Oliver. They laugh.

"Actually, you haven't seen the miniatures, have you? The ones I told you about. Tiny. Blacks lately, and greys overlapping. Fantastically powerful."

"No. You mentioned them on the phone. I wonder what the New York chap wants for them. I'd like to have them back." Rolls over to Oliver. "But not as much as I'd like to have you."

Raphaella feels strange at first, holding the brush. It has been months. She had thought, as she lay in bed, that she would never paint again. There seemed to be no reason to, no motivation. No grandmother to show her work to. A hostile mother. A father she rarely saw. A cold sister. And yet, for no reason that she can understand and from no place which she can fathom, something, some impulse leads her to lift the brush, dip it into paint and touch the canvas. She will deal in blacks and whites and greys. Colour does not draw her. She dabs alternately at the twenty tiny pieces of material laid out before her. A grey smudge, a black blob, pressed down but flattened brush end; white around the edge. She works all day and when Lisa brings her a tray with soup and a warm roll, Raphaella places it on the floor and lets it all go cold. At one stage she even dips her brush into the soup and dabs that on too. Why not? A small stain of orange on a colourless backdrop. The next morning she awakes and sees before her some of her finer work. One day, she will paint big and bright. These twenty stark attempts, however, seem to her to

109

say it all: there is nothing, in this life or beyond, worth living for.

Downstairs, Raphaella can hear her father coming in from work as he has done for years. Quietly. Whispers in the hall. His shoes clicking on the tiled hall floor. Then his steps this evening lead him, not to the drawing room for his usual sherry served by the current short-term maid, but upstairs to Raphaella's room. He opens the door, walks past the twenty miniatures and to his daughter's side.

"They've caught him," he says. "The lunatic who tried to burn the cottage. Nicholas Fletcher. Name mean anything to you?"

Raphaella shakes her head.

"Well, he won't be seeing daylight for a while. Now, what about you? Do you want to return to the cottage, start the whole process now of cleaning and redecorating?"

Raphaella's eyes fill with tears. Yes, she nods. I want to go home.

Betty sits down in her small cottage, puts her mug of tea on the floor and unfolds her local paper. To her horror, here he is. The face and unmistakably haunting eyes of Nick stare out at her. She jumps. Reads: "Nicholas Fletcher jailed for life for arson of Lemon Cottage." She knows he was not trying to burn the cottage. He was trying to kill her. As he had killed her poor mother. Now he's in jail again. She is free. Betty flings down the paper, runs out to the nearby lake and smells the freshness in the trees and the mustiness of the hay and lifts her arms and twirls and dances in the air. I am free from him. Tears hurtle down her face. She looks out gratefully at the loyal lake.

*　　　　　*　　　　　*

Some distance away from her, Raphaella is standing with the decorators.

"Yes, I want the outside painted lemon as it was before but the inside completely white. Again. When the carpenter comes, tell me, because I want to speak to him about the floors. I want them wooden."

The decorator writes it all down, gestures with his hand for Raphaella to go inside. She declines.

"I will come when it is painted," she says. "And get on with it as quickly as you can. I want to live here as soon as humanly possible."

Chapter XVIII

Betty stands outside Lemon Cottage and gazes at the flurry of decorators and builders who are threading in and out in lines. That, she thinks, that was my home until *she* took it from me. And then Raphaella arrives, looks away from Betty and enters *her* home, telling the men what goes where, what to do, what next to do after that.

Betty tries to catch her eye, but Raphaella looks the other way. She'll choose what to look at. They're her eyes, aren't they?

"It'll be good for her to have her own home again." Gertrude is sitting opposite Julian. They are drinking coffee with the French windows open to the garden.

"And good for you to have time away from her." When Julian says this, Gertrude feels a mixture of recognition and sadness. The relationship has been far from easy; hideous at times. Yes, she does want Raphaella to get away from her, but she is sad that she feels that. She has never loved her. Why should she? She was not hers to love.

"You little bitch! How dare you speak to me like that? Charlotte has done her piano practice and so will you."

"I won't." The face of the thirteen-year-old is fiery, red. "I'm old enough to choose now and I choose not to play the piano."

"You will if I say you will."

Gertrude takes Raphaella's bony, slender hands and tries to move them up and down the piano. The hands freeze rigid in protest. Hideous plonks of sound come out. Then, to Raphaella's shock, her mother squeezes her daughter's hands with her own.

My hands, thinks Raphaella. My painting hands. More important than anything else. She looks down to where her mother has grabbed her fingers. Red streaks across her skin.

"I loathe you," she hisses, leaving her mother and the room, spinning.

Martha watches Joe and Adam playing on the hillside. Below, the farm stretches green and baggy before her. Richard is directing his workers in a field. He stops at one point and waves to Martha. She lifts her hand and waves back. Politely. The boys, with their father's soft red hair, are picking clutches of grass and throwing it over each other's heads. They laugh to see the mess they have made, the bits of green scattered on their hair.

Martha finds nowadays that her mind so often drifts away. She thinks more and more of Julian. Why, she does not know. Does not understand. It was surely not love that she felt for him. Something else. Something undefined. And what was it exactly that he felt for her? Lust, clearly, but there was something else. He could have bought sex anywhere. And what of the daughter – her daughter – whom she gave away? That thread, that continuity between Helga and Martha and the baby girl; that has gone.

She gathers up her little red-headed boys, shakes the grass cuttings from their hair and leads them home for tea. She feels as if she is a kindergarten teacher taking some children to a farm in the countryside while their parents are at work. See, these are the sheep. These are the hens. She does not feel these children are hers. Her child – her only child – is elsewhere. She strokes the curve of her belly. Maybe this child will be a girl. Not any girl – but that specific girl whom she gave away. They wander down the hill, and back to the farmhouse. Helga is in the kitchen and the boys rush to her. She has been baking. Sometimes she does so in the main house. At other times she enjoys the solitude of her own company and Briar Cottage. Life, it seems to her, hugging her grandsons, is better than ever before. But she is worried about Martha and worried about her own health. Somehow she doesn't, in spite of her happiness, feel quite well.

"I've got the slides," says Oliver, lifting the phone off its cradle and moving into the sitting room of his apartment. Pours himself wine. Lies on the sofa. "Twenty of them. Absolutely incredible. Tiny. Two inch square, I'd say. But not perfect squares. Mis-shapen. Greys, blacks. Patchy, little shapes. Dark. Sinister. So different from the huge yellows and whites Raphaella paints these days. There's one amazing one: a circle of greys with dabs of thick orange paint. But it hardly looks like paint at all. It's sort of crusty."

"Fantastic," says Lucius. "Bring them over tonight, will you – and why not stay a while, overnight?"

The house is complete. Outside it is lemon-slatted as it always was, but inside it is white. Fresh. White sofas, curtains. Wooden floors. Fat candles in piles around the place. Raphaella is thrilled, happier than ever before. And this evening she will throw a party to warm the house. Because, after years of her isolated childhood, she has decided that she wants to have friends, lovers, people around her. She will paint, yes, but she will also have crowds, colourful creatures, characters who will inspire her and adorn the house. She has searched for people to invite. No one from her family, no one from her childhood or school life. She hasn't many friends. She has had to ask others' advice. Had to borrow others' guest lists. Others' friends. And now they come. Men with golden hair and carrying snakes and women with tails. Threes and fours coming together. And carrying bottles of wine and olive oil and flowers in tissue paper and presents piled on the kitchen table and the people float into her small house. They are harlequin-dressed, weird and wonderful. She shakes hands, kisses, finding herself uncomfortable in the role of hostess. She is not used to it, not good at it. But she tries.

"Have some wine. Grab a seat. Come on in." The chirpy words fall uncomfortably from her so-often closed, unfriendly lips.

When they have arrived, she passes round gold plates with passion fruit and cheeses and melon and wine and olives, and people drink and eat. Not smoke, though, she won't allow it since the fire.

Raphaella is dressed in maroon velvet this evening – long dress as usual, cape.

"Hi," she says, finding herself a seat on one of her own sofas. "I'm Raphaella."

"Hello there. I've come with Abby. I'm M Welsh."

"M? Just M?"

He nods.

"Right. Hi, M. Are you a painter as well?"

"No." Swings a leg over the sofa arm. Raphaella notices his genitals bulge through his trousers. Large and swollen. "I do research. On rainbows. At the university."

By three in the morning, the noise is intense and the rooms are warm. People's cheeks are pink with wine and excitement. The cool lake outside does not penetrate the solid walls of the refurbished cottage. Outside, Betty has been unable to sleep, has walked from her cottage to the lake and stands listening to the fun inside. That woman's life is all privilege, she thinks. I am older than her and what is my life? Loneliness and poverty. Hers is one of luxury and indulgence. Is that fair? She turns angrily to the lake. Is that fair, I ask you?

By five the following morning they have left. All but M. Raphaella has lured him to stay, asking if he will tidy up the house with her. There are bottles to be thrown, plates to be washed, candles now lazy and lopsided with heat, waiting to be blown out and controlled. Reshaped.

M has strolled into the studio and is looking at Raphaella's work.

"Interesting," he says. "These tiny ones, what are they about?"

Raphaella laughs. "They aren't about anything." Mocking. "They just are."

"Right. And what about you?"

M has his arm wound round Raphaella's waist. She likes the smell of him, the solidity of him. She's been a virgin too long. Nearly twenty and never been screwed. There's something shameful about that really. To her mind. He begins to kiss her mouth, her breasts, rip the sleeves from her shoulders. Works down her body. They lie on the sofa. The room smells of sweat and melted wax and wine and over-ripe fruit. He opens his own trousers. Removes his shirt. Raphaella's pants. Licks her. Moves his tongue hard inside her.

"I want to fuck you," he says. Raphaella guides him. He's in her now.

Thank God, says Raphaella to herself. It has happened. Thank you, God.

*   *   *

116

"These are amazing." Lucius is sitting in front of Oliver, who operates the slide projector. Tiny images pop up on the screen. Blacks, greys. Stark and clean-cut. "What a find."

"Well, that's not all. This catalogue is growing. My dilemma is whether to still pursue the biography part or just focus on the works themselves."

"Mm. Not so much life and work of, but just the works."

"Exactly. That would please Raphaella, of course, but are people going to be interested in a mere catalogue?"

"Well, let's have some mulled wine and – mull it over." Lucius smiles at his own pun.

Oliver clicks off the projector and joins Lucius on the sofa. He looks at his lover. Yes, the passion is there, has waned from Raphaella, but he doesn't dare reject her. Not while he's working on her. Not yet, anyway. Lucius's fingers touch his. Oliver succumbs.

"So, you research rainbows?"

"Yeah." M and Raphaella are lying in bed. The sun bounces off the lake outside and spreads yellow fingers across her walls. "But it's not as romantic as people think. You see, in the physics department we're doing work on light and colours. Pigmentation. Optical illusions. It has implications for people's problems with vision."

He waits for her to say, as everyone does, "interesting", but she does not. She is not listening. In her mind, she sees rainbows, rough-edged and hazy, curving over her canvases. They make love again – for the third time – and then, as M sleeps, Raphaella slips into her studio and takes her fattest brush and huge curves appear – violet, yellow, blue, green. They stretch from one edge to the other, as if they had started before the canvas began and finished a long way beyond it. Her arm loops. Arches. Huge. Wide. Yes. Enough of blacks and greys, she thinks. Rainbows. Yes.

Chapter
XIX

The sandworld rises, minute by minute. Floor by floor, storey by storey, the windows continue to build up. A sandcastle, a tower, a palace; it is not one but all of these. And they work unceasingly, scraping the sand up with their beaks, pushing the walls with their wings. And they work in tandem, a pair, passing twigs to each other, helping in what they see as their shared project, their endeavour. And there is a new development now. When they have worked enough and helped their temple to rise and grow, they emerge from the lake and stand dripping, two wet birds, on the sand. Then legs sprout, feathers become arms and two women emerge: Raphaella, mid-thirties, Martha, mid-fifties. Speech took a while to come, but now, words slip effortlessly from their lips.

"You know," says Martha, stroking the girl's wild hair. "That building: it's my proudest achievement."

"We couldn't have built it alone. Only together."

And how pleased these women are that they have found each other.

"When I was young, Raffy, I had a baby girl. I stupidly gave her away. I have regretted it all my life."

"I have done things I regret, of course; so many, too many to mention."

They embrace. They do not know they are mother and daughter, although they suspect it. Are frightened to disprove it. Regardless, they each know that this is the one significant relationship in each of their lives.

*   *   *

Martha is alone in the room. Alone that is, but for the little basket by her bed, the basket which looks slightly shabbier each time a boy – yes, a boy – is born. For that morning, at five o'clock, with Richard and Helga by her side, she gave birth to another boy. And as the midwife passes the child to his mother she can see the indifference, the loathing, almost, that the mother displays.

"What are you going to call him?" asks Helga.

Martha turns away. This child deserves no name. She cannot be bothered to think of one.

"What about Joshua?" asks Helga. "Your grandfather was called Joshua."

Martha shrugs. They can call him the devil for all she cares. She turns her back to the baby and tears dampen her pillow. Where is the daughter she is waiting for? Why has she not come? Why did she go away?

Raphaella is in the studio, her hair tied back loosely, her brush leading her from edge to edge of the giant canvas. She mocks herself for having painted small, for having turned to blacks and greys and no-hope colours, when there were purples and yellows waiting to be used. When the brush becomes too feeble for her, she turns to the knife. Scrapes the paint on, plasters it over the canvas so that a massive rainbow flings itself from one side to another: violet, indigo, blue and green, yellow, orange and red. Standing back, Raphaella admires the colours which have hurled themselves at her.

"M," she calls. He is in the sitting room, reading yet another scientific textbook which does not interest her. "Come and see my rainbow."

It takes him a few moments to arrive, but, when he does, he is still clutching his book, finger jammed in at the page he's on.

"Mm," he says. "It's good. Not, of course, an accurate representation of a rainbow, but an impression."

"Not accurate? How?"

"Well, the proportions. You have romanticised the correct dimensions."

"Yes." Raphaella's cheeks are stinging. "Because I'm an artist, that's why, not some boring scientist in a lab coat staring into a test tube."

"So it's OK for you to insult the work I do, but not for me to comment on yours?"

"Because you haven't understood what it is that art does. That's why."

"No, not like the way you have a deep understanding of science, of course. OK, then. What does art do?"

Raphaella hesitates. Cultural theory has never been her strong point. She does not know how to articulate what it is she does every day of her life. Maybe she should have gone to art college after all.

"I can only say what it is to me," she says, ashamed at the impotence of her own words. He waits. "Painting is my life," she says at last.

"And science is mine," says M.

And with those words, he takes his book and leaves.

And she returns to her studio.

In a valley by a stream, Oliver parks his car and looks out at the most beautiful home he has ever seen. Built mainly of glass and some wood and transparent from one side to the other, it is poised like a giant ice cube, unmelting, in the grass. The roof rises up in a spire. It is a glass chapel – nearly.

120

Inside, a distinguished looking couple are showing him into the main room, a huge glass arena with occasional wooden floors. Walls. On these walls, hang a series of six giant rainbows. Painted by Raphaella.

"Oh, they're amazing." Oliver feels himself stagger back. "It's years since I've seen the orignals."

"We love them," the man says, lifting a glass of water to his lips. "They feel so alive, as if they're moving."

"You can't be down when you see them," says his wife. "They're so uplifting."

Oliver peers up close, then steps back, looks carefully. In them, the paint is not smooth or neat. Each arc of each rainbow is jagged and rough, as if frayed. There is an exuberant but haphazard joy in them. He feels Raphaella's happiness in them; unusual for her. They create emotion in him. He feels, somewhat to his embarrassment, that he is about to cry.

Over a cool drink in the living room, the couple, both retired architects, tell Oliver about where they bought the paintings, how they had to be shipped over, how they always attract comment, how they had never heard the name Raphaella Turner before, but they believe they are now worth a small fortune. No, they'd never part with them. They have promised them to their son for his home, an apartment in London overlooking the Thames, when they die. There have been days, they say, when there have been real rainbows in the sky and that one through the glass has smiled on their painting "as if visiting family." Oliver, in turn, tells them about his catalogue, the huge retrospective, how this is going to be a big development.

"And tell us," says the husband, dwarfed beneath the rainbows, "do you know this Miss Turner? Where does she live? What is she like?"

"We've always been curious about her." The wife.

121

"Oh yes, I know her." Oliver smiles, trying not to give too much away. It is surely her enigma that he wants to unveil in his catalogue – not before. "She is rather reclusive, really, lives alone in a cottage by a lake, sees few people, spends her time painting."

"How old is she now?"

"Late thirties."

"So she must have been in her early twenties when she painted these. What was happening in her life then, we wonder?"

"Well," the wife smiles, "you'd know."

Would I? wonders Oliver to himself. What actually do I know? There is a wall of silence around her. I am amassing information about the paintings, that's all, but her life seems more and more of a puzzle to me. He thanks them for their time and refreshment, cannot resist one last look at the rainbows, and slips away.

I hate this cottage, thinks Betty to herself, as she dusts each ornament in turn. The robin on the bough, the tramp and the flower seller, her mother's figurines, small comfort to her. Ironic that Nick tried to burn the cottage with Betty in it but that she, that girl, escaped. Betty would like to burn her down – her precious little cottage and her arty friends. Why should she prosper and Betty live in a place she does not like? She takes Julian's note from a box and unfolds it. Time for another visit, she thinks.

The new maid ushers her in. The house looks the same as when she worked there. Julian sees her in his study.

"What do you want?" he almost growls.

"What do you think? I don't like the place I'm living in. It's grotty and depressing. I need more cash so that I can move."

122

"Tough," says Julian. Sometimes he wonders where his own courage comes from. "You've had enough cash from me. Show the world your stupid note, if you like. You can't prove it's mine. And besides, who cares now? It's so long ago. Sod off."

Outside, Betty folds her note back into her pocket and smiles. He'll regret this and that girl will. She feels victorious – but she also feels lost. Where should her revenge begin? And what shape should it take?

"To us." Raphaella and M clink their glasses, sip champagne.

They have been a couple for a year, the longest relationship Raphaella has had. The only real relationship. Ever. And yet, and yet, she feels far from thrilled about it all. It is clear to them both that there are tensions. M has been busy writing his book on colour, on pigmentation, on light. On, of course, rainbows. And his absorption in his own work has, she feels, cut her out. True, she does not like to leave the cottage much and M has found that frustrating. They do not do what most couples do: there is no going to a bar for a drink or going shopping or to the films. That is not what Raphaella does. Ordinary things. A bit of travelling, yes. Much painting. Much staying in the cottage. She even has her fruit and vegetables and other produce delivered now by Richard Ashley from the nearby farm. He arrives, once a week, says little, brings lots. Even logs for the fire. Raphaella pays and he slips away. She likes people to bring her things, to give her things.

But what does she give me? M wonders. Many evenings now they stay together in the cottage, but barely speak. Sometimes there is some food or wine, some sex, but they are living out their different dreams under the same roof. M works on his book, Raphaella on her painting. She is still hooked on rainbows but also on colour in general; is exploring greens and blues. The arcs of the rainbows have stretched themselves into lines, squeezed themselves into squares, busied the canvas.

"Well, we've managed a year," she says, draining her glass.

"You say it as if it is an endurance test." M combs back his yellow hair with his thin fingers.

"We each have things we want to do."

"Well," sarcastic tone, "I hope I'm not getting in the way of your paintings. I know they come first."

"Yes," she says, fiddling with the blue beads at her neck, "they do. And I'm going to be very busy now because I'm entering a competition. Did I tell you? My first ever."

M shakes his head, wonders whether the index for his book is detailed enough.

"D'you remember Miles at the party? He told me about it. You have to enter a series of paintings on a theme. The prize is a show of one's work. I'm going to enter my rainbows."

M flinches. *My* rainbows? Did she say *my*? Who spoke to her about them? Who introduced the issue? Where's the credit? Besides which, he hates those new paintings she's been doing. Whopping great clumsy things which romanticise rainbows and pretty them, when they are scientific, real, illusions, documented. Isn't his work setting out to dispel the very myths that her paintings expound?

Raphaella looks up to see him grabbing his coat and heading for the door. Sulky idiot. What does he want – copyright payments on the rainbows? What does he own – the bloody sky now, as well? Arrogance of the man. Should she ask permission to use colour, to breathe the air, to paint, for God's sake? Let him go. She turns and walks back to the studio and to her paintings.

Day after day Betty is in a haze. She had not thought that Julian would refuse her. Ever. She thought she had a safety net, which now seems to have vanished. But what does she do? Does she write to a newspaper: Dear Editor, I know of a man who had a child with a woman who he wasn't married to. Yours sincerely Betty Tattersall? So what? Will they care? So Julian has an important job, something to do with the law courts, she believes, but they won't mind that. It probably happens all the time. She knows, she knows that the bitch girl who lives in her cottage is the daughter of Julian and that poor distraught young girl. But what? So what? Betty sits in the dark in the cottage she hates and feels a lethargy spread over her. She has a story to tell – she even has the note – but will anyone care? Will anyone listen? Nick. Now he'd know what to do.

"Baruch atah adonai..."

It is *shabbat*. As always, Martha has cooked a meal in the farmhouse and her family is there and her mother, Helga. In her increasingly frail voice, she does as she always does, lights the candle, brings her home-made plaited *challot*, blesses the wine, passes it round, blesses the boys. Yes, thinks Martha, there are no girls to bless. My daughter is somewhere far away, unblessed. Richard listens politely, indifferent. He plays with the two older boys after their meal as the women wash up, bounces baby Joshua on his knee, but even in the midst of them all he is removed. It was not always this way, thinks Martha, turning to see him, cheeks rosy by the roaring fire, smiling at his boys. She has removed herself from him and he feels it. Never the most exciting or involved man in the world, he seems further removed these days. When he wants to make love to her she often turns away. When he waves to her from a field or meadow as he gathers hay with his men, she lifts her hand to him but hardly waves it. He accepts all this. Is a dutiful husband, father, son to his elderly parents. As loyal to his animals on the farm as he is to his sons. When Martha looks at him, she thinks: is this all that life is? Is this it? Life reduced? She will not try to have another child for a long time, maybe never again, because the disappointment each time a boy is born is intolerable. All she wants is her daughter back.

"Take care, please. Extreme care." Raphaella's voice is calm, firm.

The two men who are winding brown paper and string round her huge canvases sigh slightly, raise eyebrows at each other. Who the hell does she think she is? Her Royal Highness or someone?

"This is very important. The work in there cannot be replaced."

Carefully, they wrap brown paper, tear long strips of sellotape, label the paintings. Then, more to their relief than Raphaella's, it is time to go. She pays them and they take the paintings out to their van and drive away.

"The tomatoes aren't that good this week but I've brought you extra marrows and courgettes."

"Great." Raphaella likes people to bring her things and do jobs for her. This all leaves her free to do what no one else *can* do – paint in the way only she can.

She pays Richard and smiles. He goes beyond the call of duty, bringing her milk, bread, olive oil, stopping off in town to buy her produce which he does not, cannot, grow on the farm. Even toilet paper, he'll get her. She pays fairly. He can't grumble. But recently he senses a strange attraction to this exotic bird who is dressed in turquoise and green and in long robes and jewellery and who paints weird pictures that look like a child's, or as if they could go any way up and no one would be able to tell the difference. This vague stirring in his loins makes him feel uncomfortable. He is married to Martha. He shouldn't be looking at other women in the way that, as Raphaella bends down to take her money from the drawer, he finds himself staring at her cleavage, trying to see her breasts, trying to glimpse her nipples stiffen beneath her dress. This was not the way he used to be or wants to be. He feels uneasy, disloyal, as if he has done something which is only in his thoughts. He thinks her weird and strange, yet fancies her.

That night, Richard wakes up in a sweat. Maybe Joshua has cried out in his sleep. He goes to check but the baby has not stirred. He thinks instantly of Raphaella. No, he thinks, splashing water on his face in the dark bathroom. This has to stop. As soon as Joe is old enough he can take over the delivery for the goods to that woman.

Dear Nick,

I know we have had a difficult relationship, but I want to make amends with you. I know you did not really intend to hurt me on the night of the fire. Please, if you would agree, I'd like to come and visit you in jail. The past is the past. We have to look to the future. There is something I want to talk to you about.
Yours,
Betty.

When she posts the letter in the box, Betty finds herself kissing the envelope first.

The postman slips the letters through Raphaella's door, looks longingly at the lake as he does every day, and drives away. Raphaella has been waiting to hear from the judges for months. How the time has dragged. She has been used to isolation, to having to rely on her own judgement. Now she will hear what others think.

She opens the letter and sits on the sofa to read it.
Anxiously.

Dear Miss Turner,
    *We are delighted to tell you that you are the first prize
winner of our Painting Series competition. The prize as you
know is...*

Yes, smiles Raphaella. For the first time, and not for the last,
I have triumphed.

Chapter
XXI

Raphaella stands in her studio and looks around her, at the various canvases she has completed and those that she has never finished, that somehow eluded her at the end. She has to fill a whole gallery with just her work. She has never even had a painting in a show before. At all. And this will be just her work. And who is she, anyway? For several moments her canvases look weak to her; the colour drains from them; she is filled with doubt. She has not taken enough risks; has been too tame; lacked courage. Her parents, sister, teachers; none has believed in her or encouraged her. Even M, who professes to love her, seems somehow jealous of her work, possessive. Her granny Georgina, she would have been proud. Who will be pleased for her? Who will share in any triumph that she has? She knows people, names to fill party lists with, but they are not friends, they do not care. There is the postman who brings her mail; Richard who brings her food; but other than that there is no one. Feeling for the first time, utterly alone, Raphaella fingers her canvases which stand leaning against a wall. They are insipid; they are inferior. Her exhibition will be an utter failure; at best a disappointment. Why can't her painting be better than it is?

Lucius is speaking to his young assistant, Oliver Slatton.

"So you're telling me that she has no phone, sees no one, never goes out?"

"It appears not. She is a recluse really. Mid-twenties but living like an old lady in a cottage by a lake. Or so I'm told."

"Bloody painters. Who'd work with them? Right. Well, I need you to go and visit her. She lives in Lemon Cottage, by a lake. You'll have to find it. Start explaining to her about the preliminary details, get her to sign a contract. These painters know nothing about percentages. Explain about framing; opening night and so on. You can manage it. Alright?"

Oliver smiles at Lucius. Who would have thought that a gallery owner of that reputation would take him on, Oliver, a young man, straight out of art college? But sometimes, just sometimes, Oliver wonders if there is an ulterior motive behind Lucius's belief in him. Is it the way he brushes the young man's hand as he leaves, the way he touches his lips with a finger, the way he strokes his waist as he passes? Could it be?

"Wait in there."

The warder has ushered Betty through the huge wooden and steel doors that shield the prison from the outside world or protect the outside word from its lethal mixture of rapists, murderers and thieves. Or in Nick's case, arsonists. Would-be killers. Avengers. Crimes of passion. Betty sits in a waiting-room, if she can call it that. It makes her cottage look like a luxury home. A bare room with two ripped chairs and a screen, used, she imagines, for medicals or searches. There are blood smears on the canvas.

When Nick wrote to her to say that she could visit she felt elated, more thrilled than she could reasonably understand. Why did she feel pleased to see someone who had used her and then tried to set fire to her, killed her mother? Yet somehow those events all seem such a long while ago and she feels, now, as if they had been acts committed by a different person. Not Nick. Not Nick whom she loved. Loves. Still loves.

131

"You can go through now." The warder, is it a man or woman? Betty can't tell, ushers her through to another stark room. There are meeting holes almost like reception points in a bank, but barer, nastier. Iron grids separate visitor from prisoner. She is moved through. She sits by her iron grid, waiting. No one there. Then, minutes later, Nick comes in. He looks bad, black rings beneath his eyes, his hair thin, his skin grey and sallow. Deprived of sunlight. Betty's heart drops forward to meet him.

"Nick," she says, and then finds that words elude her. What can she say? How are you? How does she bloody think he is? What have you been doing? Well, not a lot, actually. Where have you been? Nowhere. Luckily, he saves her. His voice is gritty, low, as if the lack of sunlight has changed the way he speaks, too.

"Betty," he says. "I did terrible things to you and to your mother and to – I am learning to read and write here. They have lessons. I even go to chapel. The priest –"

Words fail him. Betty finds his words choking in her throat. Speech has left them both – his has vanished; hers has stuck. His struggle echoes in her ears. Language has let them down. They sit in silence: Betty crying, Nick staring, white. Betty lifts a finger and pokes it through the wire as if trying to tickle an animal at the zoo. Nick lifts his finger too. They touch. Briefly. Barely at all.

Oliver parks the car and steps outside, holding his briefcase. The lake is bright and alive, squirming in the sunlight. He looks towards Lemon Cottage sitting prettily in the light. He knocks at the wooden door. A young woman answers. She is dressed in maroon – lots of material – drapes, dress, tights, shoes. She barely smiles.

"Oliver Slatton," he says. "I work for Lucius Fox. The London gallery –"

Inside, Raphaella pours them wine. Oliver accepts it, settles on the white sofa. She has not spoken. He clears his throat. Will she detect that he is new at this job, that he has never been in sole charge before? Set out on his own? The slap of his mother on his face; the demeaning comments jump to his head. He tries to drive these memories out. Clears his throat again.

"Well, you must have been thrilled to hear that you had won first prize? Congratulations."

Raphaella smiles. Aloof.

"We had over a thousand entries so it is a great, great compliment to you. Now, the plan is to hold the one-man, one-woman, should I say, show in March in Lucius's London gallery. I don't know if you know it?"

Raphaella shakes her head. Oliver chides himself. Of course, Lucius told him she hardly ventured out.

"Well, it is a big gallery, beautiful, white walls, lots of space, natural light with large windows. Could I see your work? I know the rainbow series is of large paintings but I wanted to make sure of the general size so that we can start working out the area, cost of framing. We take a percentage, of course, of any sales, 30%. That's standard…"

Oliver is aware he is gabbling. He has broken out in sweats in his armpits. Why is he so nervous? Is it because it is his first job alone or is it because of her? She says little, smiles wryly, is attractive. That's it. Her legs are just discernible beneath her drape. The wine is strong. He feels drugged, almost. Maybe she's laced his drink. Maybe she's performing black magic on him? No, that's stupid. But there's something about her. Her lips, her breasts leaning through maroon.

As a child, Oliver felt confused about boys and girls. At twelve, when the other boys were beginning to fancy girls or feel something towards boys he felt an odd lurching between the two. Yes, there was Henrietta with her bouncing bosoms as she leapt for the netball, but there was also Edward, long and lanky and slightly effete. Oliver would feel his affections swinging daily, hourly. Not quite knowing. Not feeling sure. That was normal, he told himself, without knowing if it was or wasn't. But as an adult, this has continued. He has slept with men and women at art college, always feeling that he is searching, trying to discover, decide, not finding any answers. When Lucius brushes his lips with his finger – or now with Raphaella smiling in her seductive, mysterious way, he feels he has found no answers yet. Undecided. Could go either way.

"Art college?" Oliver's mother is standing once again in the kitchen, the place which the teenager associates not with home baking and delicious smells, but reprimands. It is the place of reckoning.

"You know how keen I am on painting. It seems the ideal opportunity –"

"Opportunity? To do what? Become even more of a poofter than you are already? How many boys of your age do you know who hang Indian material from their ceilings and paint their walls pink? Go out and get a bloody job like the rest of us."

This time she does not hit Oliver the way she usually does. He wonders if she is afraid that he will hit her back now that he's older. Stronger.

That's it, then, he thinks, sitting in his room. She's said no. I'll have to get into art another way.

"If it's another son," says Martha, "I will not be able to bear it." She has waited for years, has watched the boys grow up and postponed her next attempt. Her attempt to have a girl.

And yet, something in Martha has spurred her on. A voice inside. Have another try. Surely this time it'll be a girl.

"You mustn't speak like that," says Helga. "You will love the baby, no matter what."

They are sitting on the verandah by the farmhouse. Joe and Adam are throwing seed to the chickens. Joshua sulks slightly, left out. Helga smiles at him, encouragingly. Martha does not respond.

Helga rubs her legs. They are tired. She has had to help more with her grandsons than she could possibly have anticipated. It is too much for her, but how can she watch those innocent, ginger-haired boys, being neglected? Martha carries out her duties, keeps them clean, but there is some terrible hollow gap in her relationship with her sons. Something missing.

Martha rubs her belly. She has wanted another try. Needed to have another try. Let it be a girl, she begs of God, of anyone who will listen. Let it be *that* girl. The one I gave away.

Joshua is running with his brothers, chasing the chickens. When Martha told her that she was pregnant again, Helga's heart had sank. She feels her daughter is on a mad, desperate search, hunting for the girl. Please God, she thinks, if you only ever grant me one thing, let this child be a girl. However, she knows that will not be the end of the problem. Martha will spoil that child, neglect the three boys. That will be bad. But if the child is a girl –Helga knows even that girl will not be the girl she gave away. It is futile. It cannot end well. It will come to grief.

Mother and daughter sit looking out at the hills where, somewhere, Richard toils with his men, praying to the same God, for the same thing. And yet curiously, madly, they feel a hundred miles apart.

Chapter
XXII

Richard places the basket of vegetables on the kitchen table. Carrots, lettuces, tomatoes. Their colours leap out. Raphaella loves it when her produce appears each week, as if the outside world is entering in. She takes the cash from her drawer and pays Richard. As her fingers brush his, he decides, this is the last time I will come here. It is not even clear what it is he feels, but an uneasiness – is it lust? – when he touches, looks at her. No, he should be thinking of Martha, but he is not. He thinks of this strange girl with her weird clothes who smells of paint. Joe is old enough, Richard decides, he will deliver the produce to this girl. And Richard won't ever need to see her again. Then there will be no danger. No temptation.

Back at the farm, Helga beckons to him from a window.

"Quickly, the baby's coming."

Ashamed to discover that he has been thinking of the painter woman all the time – Miss Turner, he calls her, but the name seems too normal to him – Richard runs upstairs to find his wife in labour. Joe and Adam and Joshua are around the house, but uncomfortable about their mother screaming and their gran fussing. Joe hides himself away, finds it all intolerable – his mother, never that stable, even more out of control than usual. A bad day. The head emerges, the midwife wipes Martha's face. This will be my last child, thinks Martha. This is a farce. There is a moment of agony while they wait for her pronouncement, hear the baby's kitten-cries.

"Oh," says the midwife. "A lovely little boy."

Oliver stands outside the London gallery and cups his hands to peer in through the window. There are paintings there of dancers, of birds, of abstract figures. Colours leap as if beckoning towards him. Statues carved in bronze. Gold letters are engraved on the glass: Lucius Fox. It sounds so stylish, so grand. How can Oliver enter into such a hallowed place? It is ten minutes before he is able to clear his throat, put his trembling fingers on the handle and push open the door.

A young girl is at the desk. Looks as nervous as Oliver.

"Good morning," she says, barely audible.

"Hello. I – er, I. Well, I wonder if you have any vacancies?"

"Vacancies?"

"Yes, you know, for working here."

The girl fetches Lucius who stands before Oliver and likes what he sees. The young boy is small-framed and pale with dark hair and eyes. He looks wounded, hunted down. Effete.

"How can I help you?"

"Well," says Oliver, blushing at the man's direct manner. "I want to work in an art gallery. I love paintings, you see. And I'm looking for someone to take me on. I don't need to be paid. I just want to learn."

Lucius smiles. "Well, I am looking for someone to help out now that Antonia is leaving. Come through to my office and we'll have a chat."

As Lucius leads Oliver to his room, he smiles. Why am I going through this ritual? he asks himself. I'll definitely take him on. Without a doubt.

*   *   *

137

"No, I think that is too close." Raphaella waves her hand to the left. Oliver lifts the painting. Moves it where he thinks she means. "Down," she commands. "Lower."

Oliver feels his cheeks burning. One day, lady, he thinks, I will not be the lowest of the low, hanging the paintings of an unknown artist for show. Someone else will be doing that and I shall be in Lucius's position, owning the gallery, running it all. Where is he now? Out for lunch with the director of the Tate, probably, while Oliver takes orders from a twenty-something girl with attitude.

Suddenly, she shrieks: "No, no, no! How can anyone focus on the one rainbow when you have squashed them all together like some kind of, some kind of special offer in the shops? I don't want them that close together. Move them."

Oliver lifts the huge rainbow in his hands and slips it across the wall.

"Here?"

"No, that's still too close. Paintings need space."

Great day, this is, thinks Oliver. And we haven't even started on the bloody labels yet.

Amazingly, by that evening, the gallery is ready. Glasses out in rows upon a white-clothed table; the paintings with space enough between them; the labels carefully placed.

"What do you think?" asks Lucius.

Raphaella looks at the tall distinguished man with deep eyes. Maybe she should thank him? For this chance to exhibit? Yet the words never seem to come naturally to her. She says nothing. He looks impressed, by the paintings, by her, by his choice, of course.

In the ladies' toilet, Raphaella stares at herself in the mirror. She is dressed all in maroon and aubergine: long dress, cape on her shoulders, masses of heavy red and purple beads hanging like overripe grapes around her neck. A maroon hat at an angle.

Other guests have started to arrive now. Women come in tailored dresses and black trouser suits. Raphaella knows she stands out, has been used to that all her life. After all, this is her exhibition. She should be a blushing peacock against a black sky.

In the gallery, people are drinking wine, picking at the nuts. Some are even looking at the paintings, Raphaella notices with a smile. She does not know most of these people. They are on Lucius's list, but she has invited some. Not a friend or member of her family among them, but she had asked M to come. Even though, in a way, she knows that their love is fading – if it was ever there – she asked him to come, thought it might be helpful to have him there. Who else should she invite? The milkman? The postman? The man who brings the vegetables whose name she can never quite remember. Is it Richard? Or Roger? Robert? She looks to the door. No M. He has never been reliable. There has always been that hint of reticence in him, reluctance, as if he is not wholly committed. There is something, maybe someone else, his thoughts somewhere. Elsewhere. His rainbows and their wretched pigments?

But he has led me to these, thinks Raphaella, pleased to notice that people are crowding around her twelve rainbows, as if in homage. As if in worship, their heads tilted upwards towards the huge splashed canvases where they have found happiness, bewilderment, questions, answers and maybe themselves. And one by one, the red dots begin to appear, an attack of measles almost. As Lucius, affable as ever, brings guests over to meet the artist, Raphaella cannot help but notice the rash increase. People are buying – the rainbows, the miniatures, the huge whites and greys: they are buying, are loving, are paying for, choosing her work. She will have to relinquish them, the works which she has spent hours and days on. They are, rightly, hers. Raphaella has a sudden desire to chain up all her work, to protect it, to guard it, stop these intruders and thieves from stealing it. It feels like a robbery going on.

"Samuel is a nice name, I think," says Helga, holding the tiny baby. His face is a smudge of pink and cheeks, and his fists are curled. Yes, thinks Helga. Get ready. Prepare for a fight. You will need to.

Martha does not answer. That child will not have a name. He does not deserve a name. She turns on her side and feels the tears drip from her eyes and flop on to the pillow. Four boys: four miserable boys. Where is her daughter? It is all Julian's fault. How could he do that to her? And her daughter not hers now and that Julian and his nasty cold wife will have indulged and loved her and she will love them back and what has Martha got? Nothing. An indifferent husband and four unwanted sons.

The midwife has her coat on.

"I'll be off, then," she says to Helga. "I assume she's bottle-feeding. I've made some up ready in the kitchen." Her eyes meet Helga's.

"Thank you," the older woman says.

Downstairs, Helga warms a bottle and feeds Samuel, as she will call him. By the fire, he sucks quietly at his bottle, and Helga rocks him to sleep. How will she cope? Her own health is failing and now she will have to look after them all. Not that the older boys need as much attention as this baby. Richard is never there; Martha is absent even when she is present. Don't let me die, Lord, prays Helga. What will happen to these boys? *Baruch atah adonai...*

*   *   *

"Thank you for coming," says Lucius, smoothly, uttering pleasantries which Raphaella would never attempt.

"Wow, darling," he says, turning to her after the last guest has left. "Success or success? Now all we have to do is await the reviews. They were all there, the press – major papers – *Guardian*, *Times*, *Independent*, *Daily Telegraph*. Now let's wait and see."

Raphaella smiles at him. "Thank you," she says, finally managing to utter what she knows a nice girl would have said much earlier on.

"Thank you, darling," he replies. "Wine?"

M did not come, thinks Raphaella. M let her down. He did not even bother to come and see the rainbows, her rainbows, which he introduced her to. That is the end of that relationship.

"Yes," says Raphaella defiantly. "Wine would be ideal."

"You said you wanted the newspapers," says Richard, embarrassed to be back again. He places a pile of them along with the groceries on Raphaella's table.

"Thanks," she says. "Yes."

"You don't normally bother with the papers, do you? Something special happen in the news, then?"

Richard blushes at his own friendliness. Blushes because something about Raphaella makes him tingle. Even though she's weird. People roundabouts say she's a demon, bird-woman, that she changes shapes and allsorts, and she does wear funny clobber, there's no doubt about that, but, still. There's something there that attracts him. Mind you, he's so bloody sex-starved with Martha that he'd probably fancy a tree trunk.

"We've been really busy," he says, taking the money from Raphaella. She looks enquiringly at him. "We have four boys now. Three older and a new baby. They keep us occupied, as well as the farm."

"Ah."

Raphaella, he notices, doesn't take the conversation further. She's not very good at these things. Niceties. Doesn't ask their ages or names or anything.

"Better be getting back to it, then."

Raphaella nods, is pleased that he's going. She bends to pick up the papers. Richard catches a hint of her cleavage, blushes, leaves.

Raphaella sits on her white sofa and looks at the review section. The arts pages. One paper has nothing but the others are complimentary: "New painter enters the art world…" , "Her giant bright canvases explode with colour and energy…", "Where has this genius been hiding herself?"

A few hours later, however, Oliver arrives bearing white roses. "I hope you don't mind me invading like this, but I've got some reviews to show you." She denies that she has seen any papers at all.

"You haven't?" He unfolds clippings from his jacket pocket and spreads them on her table. "Look at that. Genius. Bright canvases exploding. Brilliant. Well done."

She smiles.

"I really love your house here. By the lake. It's gorgeous."

And although Raphaella says very little and although Oliver wonders whether he has made a real blunder just arriving like this (his mother would call him gauche) he ends up staying for hours and talking, looking at her giant canvases in her studio which overlooks the lake, sharing her fresh fruit from some nearby farm, she says, and even sleeping with her. For neither of them is it earth-shattering, but a coming together, some sort of artistic union, agent and artist in bed kissing, touching, something shared.

The next day Raphaella writes to M telling him that she does not want to see him again, and Oliver drives back to London where Lucius is pleased with him and the success of the first show he's organised and says he will give him more responsibility in the future. As a reward.

And so Oliver is high and M is low and Raphaella is high and Martha is low. And the lake is still, apart from the occasional breeze which sucks it up and flings it down again.

And years later, by the side of the lake, Raphaella is once again a bird, her wings fluffy and loose, and beside her appears another bird. The mother and child, who still do not know they are mother and child, look at each other and dive beneath the water to continue building their sandworld together.

Chapter
XXIII

Helga and Martha sit side by side. Mother and daughter on the hillside overlooking the farm. It's their favourite spot, one where they have sat and spoken about so much. In the distance, Richard is ploughing the fields. Joe and Adam are helping him, more and more involved. Adam should still be at school really, but Helga notices how Richard keeps him home, educates him in farming. Martha does not seem to care. Joshua runs around them, flinging hay into the air and letting it fall on his hair. Helga holds baby Samuel in her arms. It seems to her that these boys, pleasant though they are, are feral. There is something untamed about them. They are neglected. In spite of Helga's best efforts, their own parents have ignored them; Richard always busy on the farm, Martha lost in her own thoughts and preoccupations. These boys have brought themselves up, or the farm has brought them up. Nature has reared them. Comfortable with the cows and hens and sheep and at home in the stretching fields, they are uneducated, uncultured. Martha has not given them the best of herself, she has not shared her own knowledge with them. Not that she herself is so refined, but she knows a certain amount. She has kept it to herself. She has neglected herself, neglected her husband and almost totally ignored her children.

The baby cries. Helga looks down at the little boy, cuddles him, stares at her daughter who has not even heard the cry. It strikes Helga that Martha hardly ever holds the baby, never says his name. Helga feels weak. The baby is heavy for her. The doctor has told her to rest, not to get too tired. If Helga has one reason for hanging on to life, it is for Samuel's sake.

"Martha," she says, softly. "I love Samuel, you know that, but the doctor has told me not to get too tired. Here. You hold him for a while. Love him."

Martha stares out at the fields, at nothing. "Today is my daughter's birthday," she says.

Martha is right. Although she is aware of nothing else, it is indeed Raphaella's birthday. Not that it means a lot to her. Raphaella is in her studio, painting, happy as she works. Working on a huge canvas, the best, which she now has stretched and delivered to her, she is spreading yellow upwards and across, loving it as the paint floats and oozes outwards. The windows are flung open to the lake. There has not been much celebration, nor did Raphaella expect or desire it. Her 'mother' sent a card with a cheque in it. Raphaella wonders why she does it, on her birthday. They do not see each other, have no contact, and the woman clearly feels nothing for her. There is no hint of affection in the card. To Raphaella. From Mother. A painting by Turner on the front. What is it for? To ease her own conscience? Oliver Slatton sent white roses. He remembered the whiteness of it all. And other than that, Joe made his first delivery. And what a present that turned out to be.

The van drives up but out steps not Richard, but a younger form of Richard, Joe. Tall, thin, red-haired, easily prone to blushing, Joe enters, bearing a basket. In the kitchen he looks uneasily around him.

"You must be Joe," she says. She likes the look of him, the smell of him. His jeans stink as if he has brought the fields in with him. He is handsome like his father but fresher and younger. His eyes shine with life. She can almost see the cows and hens and wheat reflected in them. "Your dad said

145

that you might be doing some delivering to me, as he's so busy with the farm."

Raphaella observes how Joe looks round the cottage, at the whiteness, the jars, the easels through the open door. He looks at her swathes of beads around her neck, the blue velvet cloak she paints in and he is taken in, excited, as if he has been deprived, his vision limited. All at once, he has been awakened. Stunned, speechless for a moment, Joe runs his fingers through his hair.

"Anyway," he says. "I'll leave the vegetables and stuff there. Better get back. There's a new baby in the family as well as the farm to run."

"Yes," says Raphaella, laughing as she presses the money into his hand. In her studio once more, she raises a hand to wave him off as he gets into his van. Delightful young boy, she thinks. Gorgeous.

Betty thinks Nick is looking better.

"Yeah," he says, staring at her through the grid, wishing he could touch her. "I feel better too. I'm praying a lot and writing, too, Betty. I'm gonna get out of here, ya know. I am."

"Yes," says Betty, warmly. She has begun to love him again, not in the way she used to, reluctant grudging love, but really, from the bottom of her soul. She knows he regrets the killing of her mother, the burning of Lemon Cottage, the drugs, the stealing, the lying. He is a new, a different man. And how she longs for him to come out soon.

"They say they'll shorten my sentence, Betty. For good behaviour, you know, and that. I've changed, Betty. I've given up the – I'm clear. Clean. I'm gonna come out. And be free."

"Good," says Betty. " 'cos I've got plans. For you and me. And there's something I want you to help me with."

146

Sometimes they build as women and sometimes they build as birds. Today, they are feathered, nudging the sand into grooves with their frayed wings, mother and daughter, beneath the water, and their beaks slip sand towards sand. They are decorating the fourteenth storey of the sandworld with their beaks, etching tiny circles and half-moons into the walls. Through the window holes, tiny shrimps and other crustaceans slip and wriggle. The bird-women move the creatures away. They are distractions from their work, their building. Neither makes a sound, but they move in unison, the rhythm of their wings and heartbeats, as if synchronised. Their building has grown and although they have constructed every bit of it, it has felt like a natural growth, like watching a flower, somebody else's creation. It has been both hard work and effortless at the same time.

Back on the sand, they are women again, sitting beside each other. They rarely speak. Theirs is a relationship of silence and of depth.

Now, as Martha strokes Raphaella's cheek, she notices as she has often done how like her she is, the dark wild hair frothing on her shoulders, the wide eyes, the slight gypsy in her face. She has never asked her whether she is Raphaella or not, the name she knows Gertrude gave *her* child, partly because too much speech would destroy their relationship, partly because the girl may blame her. After all, she gave her daughter up – for payment, too. But although she does not know officially if Raphaella is her daughter or not, she feels, believes, she is. She senses that she has found her and is happy with that. There must, Martha believes, be a God after all. He has allowed her to be with her girl again and to be building with her, to be creating with her – this surely is fulfilment.

Martha loves her, kisses her on the cheek, lets her hand fall down her daughter's dark hair, wishes her all the goodness that there is in life. And Raphaella feels loved. For the first time, almost, in her life, she feels the warmth and care that love can offer.

On the other side of the lake in a cold little cottage, Betty huddles by the bars of an electric fire. Her mother is dead. And Betty feels no love for Raphaella at all. Quite the reverse.

Chapter
XXIV

The sandworld is so high now that it stretches from the sand bed past underwater foliage rooted to the base and craggy rocks, till, from the structure's peak, the under-surface of the lake can be seen. The women keep building, though, determined to make it reach the skin of the lake. They sculpt carefully, at times knocking bits of the building as they work, but usually managing to do no damage but to improve. Both enjoy the work. They shoo away the fish who visit them and who want to play hide-and-seek in their windows; they brush away the straggly bits of reed and loose water-starwort that float as debris in their way. The area around the sandworld is cleared daily so that the building has space around it. Both women love what they are building, not only because the sight of its storeys and windows and tiny decorations bring them pleasure, but because they have made it together and both women know that this relationship, this bond, is the deepest, closest each has ever experienced. Will ever experience. And that the sandworld matters.

When Raphaella goes to her studio to paint, she finds that the sandworld and Martha have invaded not only her thoughts and dreams but her canvases too. Gone are the huge bending rainbows, which arched across the expanse. Now, there is detail. The yellow honeycomb shapes, which she begins to paint, have details on them, carvings, shapes, etchings, which would mean nothing to anyone, but please Oliver's eyes when he visits.

"These are terrific," he says, so overcome by the new work that he forgets to hand Raphaella the white orchids he has brought her. "They, they look like ancient carvings, more like cave-paintings and mouldings, like Moorish fretwork, than painting."

Raphaella smiles at his hyperbole.

"You're not just a painter, you're an anthropologist," he says, and Raphaella laughs at his innocence, his burble. He tries so hard. And yet the book he's writing worries her. Not because he attempts to take away mystique but because he is over-enthusiastic. He seems lacking in discrimination, likes anything she does, confusing his attraction to her for her work, maybe. He is not critical enough. Lacks judgement. Now, Martha and her dark eyes invade the canvas too. Never in the shape of a human form – why would she want to paint people? – but in the guise of an invasion, an entrance.

Somehow, her painting has changed – Lucius and Oliver are agreed on that – but neither seems able to say how or in which way. Maturity, they put it down to. The one definite fact is that Raphaella, like everyone else, is adding numbers to her age, so what could be more certain than to attribute her change in style with her maturing?

"How is your book coming on?" she asks, as she and Oliver drink wine and watch the lake's light reflected in their glasses, as if the water is being brought inside. Water rather than wine.

"Oh, you're interested now, are you?"

"No, not interested. Just wondered."

"It won't be a biography. Much more a catalogue and analysis. That's all. The way you wanted. Timed to coincide with the big retro."

Raphaella feels herself squirm at his abbreviation. She likes Oliver but sometimes the words he uses make her feel ill. There is something ugly about them. Something awful.

Oliver sees her wince. His mother used to do that when he read or sang or danced. As if the very sight of him repulsed her. He drains his glass. He will leave. Raphaella can be very unappealing at times. Hurtful, in fact.

But she puts her hand on his arm. "Stay," she says. "I'm cooking artichokes tonight."

The next morning, just after Oliver has driven off after another stay-the-night-and-we'll-make-love-dispassion-nately session, the postman brings a letter from M. Raphaella opens it and reads:

Raphaella,

You're probably wondering why I've taken so many years to write to you. It was hard to decide. Should I be frank and risk upsetting you, or not write at all and spare your feelings – but then I realised – it's impossible to hurt you anyway, so here goes.

At first, I did find you appealing. You make yourself so, with your home and clothes and paintings. Who wouldn't be intrigued? But then I found you increasingly self-centred and cold and hard. Take the rainbows. The ideas came from me but instead of acknowledging that, you called them yours, never thanking me, or giving me credit. I thought long and hard about your opening evening and then I reckoned that if I did go you'd only be cold or hard or turn your back on me to speak to someone more important. I felt you always looked down on me. So it's over. You'll find some other admirer, no doubt, and I have found myself another woman, a scientist. She works on algae, actually, but before you laugh, I'll tell you, she seems to know what love is. She knows how to give and to receive love and that is what I need. Artists are too insensitive for me. Scientists are gentler with other people's dreams. M

Raphaella rips the letter into halves, then quarters and throws them in the bin. Good, she thinks, artists need enemies in order to thrive. It can't all be too cosy. And yet, for an instant, she feels something like hurt, like pain. It gets her in the chest. She finds his words haunting her, just for a few hours. Later, however, painting, algae-like green threads strand themselves across the canvas. Making use of what she has been given. Anyway, she knows what love is. That bird-woman gives and receives it, too.

As Helga passes the farmhouse she hears a baby cry. She pushes open the door. There, in his playpen and dirty with food around his face and trails of wiped snot across his cheeks, is Samuel. Alone. His face is tear-stained.

"Poor darling," she cries, running to him and picking him up. "You're dirty and hungry and cold." She wipes his face and hugs him. He stops whimpering. His little hands and cheeks are icy. She goes to the fridge, finds food, warms it up, sets about feeding him. He must have been alone for hours, the other three boys in the field with their father, picking berries, living like gypsies off the land. There is no heating in the house, no food cooked. What the hell is Martha playing at?

Halfway through Helga's feeding Samuel, Martha enters. Her hair is straggly as if it has been wet and dried but not brushed.

"This has gone too far," says Helga. She is livid with her daughter. To be depressed is one thing but to neglect that child… Helga's heart is fluttering in her chest.

"You brought this child into the world, my girl, and you are neglecting him. This is abuse. I shall report you. Much as I love you from the bottom of my heart, I will report you."

Martha looks away, does not answer.

"My family suffered, Martha. Your family suffered under the regime of people who hated us – Nazis who hated Jews and were willing to see us starve and die – and you are damaging your own child. Your own flesh and blood. I can't stand by and watch it, Martha. I can't." No reply. The baby sobs. Helga picks him up and cuddles him, strokes his fine red hair.

"I know you loved your daughter. I know you hate your son, but he is yours, Martha. Love him. He is here. Your daughter has gone."

"No," says Martha, smiling. "She hasn't. I've found her."

That night, Helga cannot sleep for the pains in her chest. She is worried. Is the baby hungry? Is he cold? Richard is useless, her daughter incapable. It is as if the sight has gone from her eyes. Helga switches on the light in her cottage and fumbles for her painkillers. The doctor said not to take too many, but who cares? She tosses and turns all night but cannot sleep. The pain in her chest eases slightly, but the worries in her mind increase. At six the next morning she runs into the farmhouse and finds Richard by a log fire with the baby beside him.

"I'm worried about Samuel, Richard," she says.

"Martha says she hates him. She never feeds him or picks him up. I have the farm to run. The older boys can be with me but not the baby out there. It's too dangerous with the machinery. How am I supposed to manage?"

"You will have to hire someone to look after him. I wish for his sake he was never born."

"Martha won't have that. Someone in her home."

"I would take him in," says Helga, "but with my ill-health, what if something should happen to me?"

153

Richard does not answer, cups his head in his hands. Helga had not noticed how bad he looks. Worn out and fraught. She feels guilty. He took the farm on in good faith, married her daughter and now this. He has been let down. She has been let down.

Martha has disappointed them both.

"There is no other choice," says Helga. "Samuel will have to come and live with me."

"There," says Helga, placing Samuel down on a rug. "You'll be comfy there for a minute." But as she stretches up to her standing position, Helga feels her heart pull and tighten. "Oh God," she says. "Help me to keep going. For this little chap's sake."

She grabs on to the sofa, sits down. The baby smiles at her. She has a grandson; she has lost a daughter. A photograph of Martha as a young girl on the farm stands on the dresser. The girl's face shines out from the frame, the eyes young and hopeful. The green field stretches vast and optimistic behind her. What has happened? What has life done to her?

Helga is waiting for the doctor to come. He has promised he will arrive soon. She feeds the baby, dresses him, waits for his face to gurgle and shine as it should do. It does not. He gives little smiles but his is a face deprived of the knowledge of love and excitement.

When the doctor arrives, he is horrified to find the ill grandmother with the tiny baby.

"Where is Martha?" he says.

Helga explains how her daughter has changed, is depressed, how Helga is looking after the baby now.

"You are too ill, Helga," he says, caringly. "I have had the results back from the hospital now of the cardiogram. Your heart is weak. You have to have as much rest as possible. I will go and see your daughter."

Outside the farmhouse, the doctor pauses. It used to look so attractive, the house, when Helga lived there. Now the paint is peeling and the curtains are dirty. It is neglected. Inside, he finds Martha slumped in a chair. Shocked at her appearance, he draws a chair beside her.

"Martha," he says. "I was very distressed to hear from your mother that you are not well, that she is looking after the baby. It is too much for her."

"I've found my daughter," whispers Martha. "I'm devoted to her."

The doctor flinches. What has happened to that lovely glowing girl? He writes himself a note to prescribe anti-depressants and to seek further help for her. He strokes her hand and leaves, shutting the farmhouse door quietly behind him.

No, thinks Raphaella. The tip of the sandworld must not appear through the surface of the lake or else people will see and view it. She does not want that. Although generally her work is for show – she wants others to view it – not this time. This is the private structure of the two bird-women. And they continue to build each day, Martha excited by the sense of growth and creativity and the evidence of hard work. Storey after storey of tiny windows and curved walls build up, accumulate. Near the top, Raphaella decides to seal it, before it touches the surface of the lake. She curves the walls inwards so that they form a dome at the top of the building. At the summit, there are no tiny windows, just etchings and scratchings on the exterior walls. And the sandworld is complete. And mother and daughter hug and kiss and stand inside their palace where the walls enclose them and where they feel safe, where the fish know they are no longer welcome and where the strands and bits of plants have been cleared away. The sand floor is soft; the walls stable. It is their home which they have built.

Betty stares at the tiny cottage, which she has tried to make a home. Her mother's ornaments stand neatly on the mantelpiece. The china robin, the plastic flowers in a basket, the figurines. The cottage is as clean and tidy as Betty can make it, but when she looks around her, she remembers the cottage by the lake and how it felt like home to her. A real home. For the first time since leaving home. How she loved it. And how that woman chucked her out. One day, she will reclaim it and she and Nick will live there happily together, and they will have babies and Nick will have a job and it will be idyllic. She closes her eyes and dreams of the lake and when she opens her eyes and sees the darkness around her, she shudders at the contrast.

"It's coming together so well," says Oliver, handing Raphaella the white bouquet. She accepts it, invites him in. "Sorry I didn't let you know I was coming this time. No time to write. And as you refuse to get a phone or e-mail –" he stops, knowing these comments are likely to annoy her. "Anyway, I just wanted to let you know how plans are going."

They sit on the white sofa together. The jars on the shelf catch his eye. They make him feel uncomfortable, always have done. He turns to Raphaella, who is dressed entirely in black. He sometimes wonders why she takes so much care over her appearance. She doesn't see anyone.

"The retro will be huge. All your work I have been able to trace is being flown over from the States, from France, from many private lenders as well as, of course, work for sale. Lucius is naturally keen on that. My catalogue is really coming together and the publishers have said that I can have some money for including small copies of some of your paintings. I'll have those made from the slides. You are going to be there, Raphaella, aren't you? I know sometimes you won't come to openings, but for this. For this –"

She nods. Yes, she will be there. A knock at the door. Joe comes in carrying baskets of fruit and vegetables. Oliver looks round at the red-haired boy, turns away again. Raphaella pays Joe, brushes his hand with hers as she passes the money over. Somehow having Oliver – her casual lover – and Joe, her other lover, her better lover, in the same room excites her. Her worlds, her passions are all conveniently nearby – the lake, underneath which the sandworld stands solid, secretly, her home, the studio with her paintings, the bird-woman. She does not know that at that moment Oliver is thinking of Lucius as she thinks of Joe, even after he has closed the door. And even while Oliver and Raphaella eat grilled fish together and then make love, they each think of their other lover.

Joe enters for the second time since he has started to bring the fruit and vegetables to Raphaella.

"Thank you," she says. "Put them over there, will you?"

The boy blushes, just like his father but more attractively. There is something stale about Richard; something fresh about Joe.

"Won't you stay a little?" she asks. The boy – he looks a few years younger than her, eighteen, nineteen, perhaps – shifts nervously.

"I don't know," he says. "I ought to be getting back to the farm. My dad –"

"There's no hurry, surely." She pats the white sofa. He looks self-consciously at his jeans, wipes them clean, does not want to mark her room. His gran has always taught him that. He sits down. To his amazement, Raphaella sits beside him, slides her hand over to his face, strokes his cheeks, chest, and on to his genitals through his jeans. He reddens, feels himself stiffen, go hard. She unzips his trousers, yanks down his underpants and finds him there, a hard root between his legs. And her mouth is on him, sucking, licking. She kneels at his feet, and takes him in her mouth. He gasps, a virgin, he has dreamt of such things but never before – never could he have imagined. His face bursts into sweat, he cries with agony, ecstasy, he does not know what. He must be in a dream. Someone else's dream. But this is real, this is it. And she clambers on to him, lifts her dresses. And from somewhere, he doesn't know where, he finds the power and the strength to take her and he is in her now, on the sofa and pushing and kissing her mouth which smells of him and he comes and she comes and they lie and kiss together and he kisses her breasts. And within the next hour they make love again. Exhausted and excited and satisfied.

And after that, Joe and Raphaella make love, not each time he brings the produce, but when she wants to. And whereas Oliver is a cultured and refined and decent lover, Joe is an animal, wild and naked and beautiful. Just the sight of him moistens her. And Raphaella needs and enjoys them both, just as she needs and enjoys the bird-woman and their sandworld and the painting. And her life is so, is so complete.

Outside, Joe wonders: is that why his dad sent him there? For experience with a woman? Is that what he did when he made his delivery? But Joe will mention nothing. And maybe when he returns to the farm, his cheeks flushed and his hair tangled with perspiration, his father will know. But nothing will be said.

*　　　　*　　　　*

Three a.m. And Helga's heart is banging too fast and so furiously that she knows, she senses, that her life is running out. The baby sleeps peacefully beside her in her bed. And Helga's heart is pounding so fast she feels she is dying. Death. Yes. It is time it came. But for Samuel, she is ready. Samuel cries out in his sleep. And then it occurs to her. If she must die, he must die too.

"Lord," she says, "forgive me, but I will kill him merely to save him. To take him with me to meet you."

She lights a small lamp and takes twenty tablets, one after another, downing them rhythmically, with water. Then, with two teaspoons, she crushes more tablets within them. Grinding them into a white powder. She slips this into a bottle of milk and stands it in boiling water to warm it. He will soon wake for his night-time feed. She knows she is doing right by Samuel. Saving him from a life of neglect and a lack of love and attention. Samuel stirs. She lifts him, tests the milk's temperature on the back of her hand, and sits quietly with him snuggled up against her in the half-light. The baby gulps and slurps, making tiny contented noises as he drinks.

And that is how grandmother and grandson slip away together, on the same night, the baby in the woman's arms. And they leave a world which has not treated them too well. They leave no notes or mark behind them. Say no goodbyes. And by the morning, they are dead.

Chapter
XXVI

"But you must be aware," says Oliver, before driving away, "that there will be media coverage. The press will seek you out. I've tried hard not to disclose your whereabouts to people but, with the retro" (Raphaella flinches at his abbreviation) "and the catalogue, you must realise there will be attention. That's a good thing but I'm warning you in advance."

Raphaella does not answer. Stares coolly at him.

"And one more thing," he says through the wound-down car window. "Lucius and I want to explore the idea of making prints of your work."

"Prints?" She almost spits the words out.

"Yes. Not sure which method we'd use yet but we could get your work reproduced much more cheaply for people who can't afford originals and we could also make cards. Calendars. Don't you see, the potential is huge? Your work is in demand world-wide."

"I don't want prints made of my work. Originals – and that's all."

Oliver laughs, incredulously. "But you're living in the Dark Ages, Raphaella. All painters have their work reproduced in some way if they can. In books, on posters, made into cards. Mugs even. T-shirts. It'll create more openings, be wonderful for you."

"I've said no." Raphaella's cheeks are on flame. "No one will make copies of my work. There is only one of each painting. That's what art is. Original. My paintings aren't mass products like chairs or lavatories."

"But it would be so good for you."

"Good for you and Lucius, you mean."

And that is why Raphaella takes the decision to start building the second sandworld. With Martha's help she works again, a way away, constructing a mock sandworld, a fake, nearer the cottage. They build it on the side of the far bank, underwater. It is, after all, a sham. Not the first one. No, Oliver, she thinks, planning it in her mind. After the original, there is never a second the same. As I shall prove.

The construction is easier this time. After all, this is their second one now and they know how to build it. Will make it for show. Besides, the spirit and passion are not in this one. They work day and night. Martha is hardly at the farm any more. Second storey... third. They build more quickly now, learning from themselves, self-plagiarising, keeping the first, the original in their heads as a model or plan from which to work.

Martha is absent when her mother and youngest son die. It is Richard who worries. He is not surprised that Martha is not home – she often isn't – but even when the boys and he have returned from the fields for lunch, there is no sign of Helga or Samuel. Knocking on the door of Briar Cottage he gets no reply. He pushes the door open. To his horror, what he sees is the figure of his mother-in-law slumped in a chair, holding the limp baby. He feels their pulses, stands numb and shocked, and calls the doctor. Both are dead.

Hours later, Martha returns. Sometimes Richard has tried to question her. Where has she been? With whom? He cannot help but wonder: maybe she has a lover or a secret life? Really, he does not, cannot care. He has the farm to run and three boys to raise. She has abandoned, neglected, disappointed them all. He is left to cope alone. He cannot

162

worry about her welfare, too. Besides, does she give a damn about them? She is crazy, probably. His parents warned him when he married her: her past reputation was no great commendation but he married her nevertheless and it does not really matter to him. Life carries on regardless. He has the farm to run. The cows need milking no matter what. They do not know there is a crisis. Their udders are full. But today, Richard does feel mildly annoyed. Where was Martha when her mother died? Her own son, for God's sake? But there is no point in even speaking to her. When he tells her, "Martha, your mother, your son are dead," she hardly registers, hardly flickers. It will only be later that she will understand.

Even at the funeral Martha hardly reacts. A large coffin and a tiny one are lowered into the ground. They have found a rabbi to say some prayers. They are in Hebrew but he tries to involve everyone. He notices how Martha's eyes do not fill with tears as one would expect the eyes of a mother and daughter to.

And after Samuel and Helga die, Martha retreats as if gradually disconnecting herself from her family. From the farm. She sits alone on the hillside while her boys grow up without her. While her husband toils. And in her mind she has a vision: one pile of sand gets smaller while the other grows. One diminishes, one expands. And she is digging away with her spade, shifting sand from one pile to the other. And as she digs, she smiles.

Martha is building the second sandworld with her daughter. And it does grow, more rapidly than either could have imagined. The women work in silence at the lake edge, the building almost erecting itself with their wingtips hardly touching it. This is the way those paintings felt after

163

Florence, Raphaella remembers: as if they had painted themselves.

It has been a long day. Both women, birds now, sit on the sand and peck at shrimps. They rip the shells off, then discard them with their beaks, tug away at the eyes that stick defiantly to the bodies, eat the insides. They drink water from the lake, blink at each other, fan their wings out to dry. Above them the sky grows dark, lowers its black blind over the sun and cuts it all out, all but the two bird-women sitting on the sand, looking through the water to where the outline of their sham sandworld can be detected.

And after a rest, they begin their work again. Scraping the sand, mixing it with water to make a pasty cement, adding layer upon layer, cutting out tiny windows, etching decorations on the outer walls with their beaks. And when it is finished, and the sham sandworld stands erect and proud on the bank, to attract and lure, they are pleased with their deception.

There is a certain point on the shore where both birds stand, shaking their feathers dry, scratching their backs with pointed beaks, where they can sense the location of both worlds: the sham, jutting out slightly, and the other which cannot be seen, but they, only they, know where it is.

"I've been waiting for you."

Joe puts the basket of produce on the table. Smiles. He's growing in confidence. Used to wait for Raphaella to make the first move but now he takes her. Enjoys controlling someone who thinks she controls everything. Conquering the unconquerable.

He's pulling at her clothes now, unbuttoning her shirt, yanking the material down, lifting her skirt up, pulling at her knickers. His large rough hands, still smelling of manure and hay, rub her cheeks. Raphaella melts at his touch, his rough touch. She has taught him how to please her. And what an excellent student he's been. On the floor, he fucks her, fucks her hard until she feels her body vanish beneath his weight and then, like a little girl, she sleeps upon his chest.

The room is so crowded that Raphaella could almost be lost among the people. Of course she is known, recognised. People lower their voices as she comes past, move their glass of wine into one hand so that they can point discreetly with the other. All around her, Raphaella can see years of her work and life hung up on the walls: the rainbows, the grey and black miniatures, the Florence paintings which painted themselves, the canvases covered after Georgina died, the recent huge blue and yellow and white squares with her hair and threads as fissures cracking the colour. In a way, it makes her feel proud: she has achieved more than she has realised but, in another, it frightens her. Where does she go next? Is there a next?

People smile nervously as they pass: a couple come and speak, but generally they avoid her, are frightened of her. Formidably dressed in black, with gold threads running like a secret through her scarf, she is to be avoided. She is witch doctor and psychic and criminal. She is best left alone.

And the red dots appear, a plague of sales and promises. Money is not – will not – be a problem to Raphaella. There's always her father – and just as she thinks of him, there they are. Her parents walk nervously in at the door, followed by her sister Charlotte and her dull husband and then three (oh, there's a new one) perfect children. They all walk in hesitantly, unsure of the reception they will receive. They approach Raphaella en masse, as if approaching an enemy. Will they be stabbed with a spear or ostracised? They move forward in a huddle. A cameraman snaps at Gertrude. A flash of light. She smiles awkwardly. They are in front of Raphaella now.

"Hello," says Gertrude. "We saw the preview advertised. Rang up and got tickets. I hope that's all —"

Raphaella smiles coldly at her. She would like to hug them, hug them all, fuss over her nieces and nephew, be warm, but it does not come. It does not. What does come are memories of screaming and being hit and hiding miserable in her room. Her father looks smart and distinguished as ever. They do talk for a while but it is stilted and difficult for them all.

"I'm semi-retired now," says Julian.

"That's good," says Raphaella, twisting her glass in her hands. "So you have more time for —" What should she say? For screwing the maids? For diddling people out of their money? She bites her tongue. "For, for travelling."

"Yes," says Gertrude. Her daughter thinks how she has aged, her hair completely grey now. "We've just been to Thailand."

Luckily, the smallest child, a boy, calls out and they all move on. Later, she sees her parents pointing to a large canvas and her father's chequebook comes out. He speaks to a man at the desk. So her parents are buying her paintings, the ones which they detested nearly as much as they detested her. And yet Raphaella cannot help feeling that she is pleased they have come. Her parents have made the time to come to see her work. No M, no friends, but family. And what else, she asks herself, suddenly feeling light and purposeful, what else counts?

The evening is a great success, no one can doubt that. And besides her paintings, Oliver knows, knows for certain, that his catalogue has been much admired. All that work and he has been noticed. Congratulated politely. One paper even commented on it. "Useful catalogue…" Suck that, Mother. Oliver drives Raphaella home that evening and they make love, not with the agricultural passion that Joe brings to her in his farming loins, but with refinement and respect. The next day, Oliver delivers her the papers to her. Rave reviews… great success. And it is then, then, that the media and press begin to arrive.

Chapter
XXVII

Martha and Raphaella are fish tonight. Their mouths opening and shutting, bubbles rise to the surface of the water. Their gills lift and fold. Each time they see their sandworld it is a reminder, an amazing reminder to them of what they have built. A reason for pride. The walls curve round as if enclosing a magical world where no one else is permitted. But them. Mother and daughter, who have never said, "We are mother and daughter", but know they are. Know there is a bond between them which nothing can break. Inside the sandworld, they rest on the sand. The seabed. Martha brings Raphaella water-snails and shrimps, peels the shells for her with her teeth, feeds only the soft flesh, the best flesh, to her daughter. Lies beside her. Strokes her hair. Strokes her large swollen belly, feeling the child within. The child that will be theirs.

Beside the lake, the paparazzi have positioned their tripods and cameras, reluctantly patient. This, they know, will be a long wait. And they've been sent to watch some weird woman who dresses in strange clothing and splashes paint on canvas like nobody's business. I mean, thinks Matt, stubbing out a cigarette on the sand and gazing out to the lake, when it's a pop star or a celebrity, you can understand it, the interest, the curiosity, but with this weird woman. Who cares? Who bloody cares?

The lake is still. Almost stone still.

"Have you ever been on an assignment more bloody boring than this?" he asks Micky, his colleague. Micky shakes his head, offers Matt a fag. Lighting up, they shake their heads. Must be easier ways to earn a living.

"What do you mean, she's gone?"

Oliver's speaking on his mobile beside the lake, turning his back to the crowd of unattractive men perched by their cameras like fishermen waiting for the catch.

"That's what I mean." Oliver hears the shake in his own voice. The lack of conviction. What would his mother say? Screwed up again? "I took her the papers last week, the morning after the retro and showed her the rave reviews."

"Was she pleased with them?"

"Yes, I think so, but you know Raphaella. Never gets over-excited about anything. Doesn't like the fuss."

"Yes, and then?"

"Well, I've been to the cottage a few times to try to see her and I bumped into that farmer guy who brings her food, and he said she hasn't been in and I even went to the cold-fish mother's house and they had heard nothing. So I've let the police know. And they say she's vanished. Completely disappeared."

"That's weird. Did she seem depressed?"

"No. Not at all. The same as usual." He doesn't tell Lucius that they slept together. Selects his facts carefully. "She wasn't looking forward to the press people arriving, but even then I think she would have coped with it."

"I can't understand it. I mean, I know she's unpredictable in some ways but in others she's always there, hardly leaves her home. You know, we'd often wondered if she was agoraphobic, even, hadn't we? Then she just disappears. And there's no suggestion of anything financial, is there?"

169

"No, on the contrary, we haven't sorted our her commissions yet. She'll have no money worries once this is settled – not that she ever did, I don't think."

"And you know nothing about her love life?"

"No," lies Oliver. "I don't think she was really into love."

"No." Pause. "I'll come down as soon as possible."

As Oliver stands at the side of the lake, thinking, thinking, he sees the top of the sham sandworld. On the far side of the lake. The side where no one goes. It is just visible, enough so that at first or even second glance it might not be noticeable but there, yes, there is it. The cameramen have their lenses pointed at it.

I want to go there, thinks Oliver. I think that is where Raphaella is hiding. Little vixen. But I shall wait for Lucius.

The hair of Martha and Raphaella floats behind them. Dreamlike. And they eat and they drink. And the home which is theirs has become like them. Substantial. A homage to them. To the water. But an exclusion area for fish and crustaceans who try to gatecrash. Squatters. They are wiped away by the otherwise loving hands of two generations of woman. And the next generation, swimming in water inside Raphaella's belly, sleeps.

When Lucius arrives, it is nearly night-time. The lake has lifted itself into dusk and the sky has masked its face so as not to overshadow it.

"Sorry," he says when he sees the agitation on Oliver's face. "Any news?"

"None at all. She's well and truly gone. I don't know. Maybe she's playing a trick on us all or maybe she's in real trouble."

"Where do we begin?"

"There," says Oliver, pointing to the sand dome in the distance. "Come on, we've got to find her."

"Eh, Matt," calls Micky. "Wake up. Look."

Matt stirs and points his camera. There, in the depth of water and night, are two rather effete-looking men swimming out in their suits in the lake towards the sand dome. They squirm through the sand-tunnel which has been conveniently built for them and when they reach the sandworld, are amazed. They stand outside, admiring the massive sand dome, the many tiny windows, the etched sides.

"This is amazing," says Lucius.

"Yes." Oliver stands, wide-mouthed. "It reeks of Raphaella – her style, definitely. I think she has built it for us to stay in, to wait for her. I'm sure she will return."

"I believe you are right."

And so both men settle in the giant sandworld and days later, cameras still pointing at them, their furnishings and paintings begin to arrive. Candles, elegant chairs, tall ceramic vases. And they begin to settle in, to make this home their home.

Not many miles away, Raphaella and Martha focus on each other. They can look in each other's eyes without discomfort, can smile, can cry without any sense of unease. And at night, when the stars are casting their shaky reflections through the water, Martha lies in Raphaella's large arms and sleeps against her daughter's breast, feeling the kicks of her unborn grandchild through her daughter's skin. Nearby, they know, people will be awaiting them, mistaking that world for the real one. No, they, mother and daughter, are the only ones who deserve to live in the real home.

171

"Did you get a good shot, eh?" Micky to Matt.

Matt folds away his zoom lens.

"Yeah. Great. Guv'nor will be pleased. I got those two blokes in their suits, right, swimming towards that funny sand thing. You reckon she's in there, this painter bird?"

"Dunno. Don't much care so long as I'm getting paid decent."

"Nah. I reckon we've got as much chance of seeing 'er as the Loch Ness monster. Oh-oh, look who's here. Posh nob from the Beeb."

In his suit by the lake stands David Hamil with his cameraman, ready, miked up, to give his verdict on the situation so far.

"And I'm standing here beside the lake where, ten days ago, renowned painter Raphaella Turner disappeared. Behind me" (camera swings) "is the home, Lemon Cottage, where she lives and paints. Or used to. For no one knows the whereabouts of this painter. No one can understand why a talented, successful woman like her should have vanished. I have with me Oliver Slatton and Lucius Fox, the organisers behind Turner's recent hugely successful retrospective. Mr Fox, if I could start with you, did you get any sense at all from Ms Turner that she was depressed?"

Lucius brushes his wet hair back with his hand. "Not at all, no. I mean, Raphaella is a reclusive character, she doesn't like a lot of media attention, but she seemed very pleased with the way the exhibition was received."

"Would you endorse that, Mr Slatton? After all, you have worked with Ms Turner for many years. In fact, you must know her well. Were there any signs to you that she was depressed or planning to leave her home?"

"Not at all." Oliver wonders about his cheeks. Do they look too red? Too watery? Are his eyes raw? "She seemed just the same as ever. We are very concerned about her. Just want to know that she is safe and well."

"And finally, Mr Fox, do you have any message to give to Ms Turner, should she be watching?"

"Well, just, Raphaella, we hope you are not in any trouble. Please contact us as soon as possible." Camera close-up on Lucius's concerned – if not a little pink – face.

"This is David Hamil for the BBC outside Lemon Cottage. Fiona, back to you in the studio."

Inside their sandworld – the real sandworld – Raphaella and Martha turn off their television set and laugh and laugh and laugh.

Chapter
XXVIII

"But I don't understand it." Oliver pushes the shrimps away from him. He wishes they'd stop flitting around him. It feels, at times, as if he is caught in a hailstorm of pelting crustaceans. Coming at him from all angles. "We both agree that this is the work of Raphaella – who else? But why did she build it on this side of the lake? Not her side? The tame side? Why keep it a secret? Why then abandon it and lead us here? For this building here is surely a sign, a beckoning. It's as if she wants us to be here. But then, where is she? You don't invite people round and then leave the home yourself, do you?"

"You do, if you're Raphaella." Lucius smiles facetiously. "You know her. Anything to be contrary."

"I don't know if that's true." Oliver leans back against the sand, flicks a shrimp away. "In a funny kind of way I see her as rather predictable. Always at home, in a way, a restricted vision – she never speaks of politics or reads papers or anything else. Just stays at home and paints. Insular. You always know where she is. Or used to, anyway, until all this happened. One knows – knew – how she will react to things. Cynically."

"You always seem to understand her so well. It's as if – as if, at times I think you're closer to her than I've realised."

Oliver averts his eyes, snatches at a piece of floating weed. "Not at all."

"Are you sure?"

Even the water does not hide Oliver's insecurity. Even the cool salt water against his cheeks does not stop him from blushing. From feeling ashamed. As he has always felt. That he could be better. That he has done wrong. He thinks now of Raphaella's slender hips, thighs, of entering her. Pleasant, comforting, but not thrilling enough. Not like Lucius and the smell of his manliness. Maybe her disappearance will force him to choose.

Lucius approaches Oliver and under the water, their hands search for each other, the lake slowing down their movements as if they're living in jelly. Slow motion. Yet the water not only hinders, it helps. The moisture, the smoothness. All an aid to the lovemaking that goes on between these two men as Lucius kisses Oliver and then enters him, hard and rigid and desiring, desperately desiring, underwater. Extracting himself from his lover, the trail of sperm floats into ribbon, twists itself into braid and floats away.

Inside their underwater sandworld, Martha and Raphaella have arranged their belongings as they like. White sofas, wooden tables. Candles burn in glass domes. They do not say it to each other – do not need to say it to each other – but the candles burn for Helga, for Samuel, for their rejected families in which neither has ever felt comfortable. For each other. And the flames rise and lick the sides of the glass in which they are encased and the water passes over the glass as if just visiting. Unable to enter and put out the flames, it leaves, unsatisfied. And a hundred tiny flames leap and twist under glass, under water. And the sandworld has become a temple, a homage and a sanctuary for two women who are mother and daughter and who love each other and spend all day stroking and loving each other in a non-sexual, mother and daughter way.

And the fish which flick their tails as they pass, and the water-weed and milfoil which slip and twist near them, do not know the secret – that mother and daughter have found each other and made their own paradise.

Richard has come in from the farm. He serves up a hastily prepared meal to the boys who sit with him round the table. Richard stares at Joe eating his corn, cob in his hand, butter running down his chin. He is a young man now, good-looking, sturdy. Yet since his mother's disappearance he has been withdrawn. This puzzles Richard. Joe was never that close to his mother, but then he has said that Miss Turner has gone too. No more fruit or veg to deliver there. Could it be that Joe is not pining for his mother at all, but that Miss Turner woman instead? Could it be that? No, surely not. She was just a client. An alluringly attractive one. Admittedly. And Adam and Joshua. They are growing up fast now. Adam throws salt over his corn. Rips a hunk of bread. And how has Richard brought them up? They are wild, somehow, untamed. If Martha had still been there or Helga. A woman's touch. But no, he could never marry anyone else. Martha holds him still. Richard looks at the fireplace. A photo of baby Samuel is in the frame. This house has become more associated with the missing than the living: Helga, Samuel, Martha. Now, with his parents dead, what will happen when his three boys move off the farm to travel and discover the world. What then, eh? What then?

Gertrude passes Julian the paper.

"Another bloody headline," she says, lifting the skin from her salmon in one smooth movement.

Julian pushes his plate away, reads aloud:

"Two weeks and still no sign of the missing painter, Raphaella Turner. Police are treating the disappearance as suspicious. No note has been found and her home, Lemon

Cottage, was left in a normal condition as if she expected to return. "

Gertrude knocks back her wine in one. "I'm getting fed up with reporters coming to the door and I'm sick of being photographed each time I walk to the shops."

"Well, send Donna to do the shopping."

"I could do, but I don't want to become a recluse and never go out, do I? Where do you think that silly girl is?"

"Who, Donna?"

"No, dear, our daughter. Our difficult, impossible, demanding daughter. Troublesome even in her absence."

"I don't know. Maybe she's been killed or she's topped herself or she's playing tricks on us all. Again. As if her blotches on canvas aren't some elaborate trick."

"Well, they're just the work of a charlatan. That's obvious. But none of your explanations makes sense. Her exhibition went well. She wouldn't want to hide away. And who would want to kill her? It's probably an act against us. I told you we shouldn't have gone to the preview. It was a huge mistake."

"I'm going to go and phone the police again. See what developments there have been. Imagine what this is doing to my reputation. I'm meant to judge cases, not create them."

Betty smiles through the mesh grid.

"You're looking better, Nick," she says. "I'm so pleased."

"Well, not much longer now, Betty. And then we can be together. Start afresh."

"Yeah. Eh, guess what? That funny girl, you know, Miss Turner, still missing. They reckon she's done 'erself in. There might be no need for us to – you know, after all."

"Let's see, eh? Let me just get outa here first."

177

"You'll soon be out, Nick. And then we'll be together, you and me, and we'll be rich."

"We'll see, eh?"

Walking out of the jail, Betty sees her mother's face. It is a recurring image: her pleading face, Nick doing her in. No, says Betty to herself, looking for help to the blue sky. I can't think of that now. The only way to go is forward. With Nick.

Gertrude pulls her hat further down her face, bends the slanted brim down. One of her mother's last creations before she died. Might be handy in keeping her hidden. But no. She is only halfway down the red steps that lead from her house to the pavement and the cameramen are there. Lenses staring at her like futuristic monsters. Reporters poking microphones in her face. Crowding in on her. Ghastly men chewing gum with their mouths open. Unshaven.

"Mrs Turner, is there any more news of your daughter?"

"Have you any idea where she may be?"

"What do you want to say to her if she's watching?"

"Are you ready to make a statement?"

Gertrude lifts her hat up slightly, in defeat. Her disguise had, she realises, been feeble.

"Well, no, I don't want to make a statement. Of course I'm worried about my daughter. No, I haven't any news. Please, now, if you'll let me go. I want – I wanted to go shopping."

The men stare at her ruthlessly. Some chance, their faces say.

Tears prick Gertrude's eyes. She runs indoors, Donna opens the door and Gertrude flops on to the sofa and sobs.

Inside their sandworld, Martha and Raphaella watch the news with Gertrude's brief appearance and laugh again.

"But why did she leave us?" Adam leans on his hoe and looks to the fields for the answer. It does not come.

" 'Cos she was a selfish cow." Joe.

"Come on, now," says Richard. "I don't want to hear you speaking about your mother like that." Even to him, though, his words sound weak. Lack conviction. Not only the boys have questions. He has them too. Why did she leave him? Her sons? Without a word. Without a note. And is the disappearance of that painter woman linked to Martha leaving, as the press are beginning to suspect?

As if those questions aren't enough, Richard has to face Detective Inspector Bloor again that evening. They sit at the kitchen table. The boys are out somewhere. Richard doesn't ask too many questions. They are old enough now. They come in at three a.m. usually, drunk, stoned, but as long as they help on the farm (and most days they are up to it) he can't expect anything else. He doesn't want to lose them as well. This house is becoming the home of the missing, not the present.

"So it looks increasingly, Mr Ashley," the Inspector looks and sounds rather pleased with himself, "as if the vanishings of the two women are connected." Seeing Richard's expressionless face, he continues. Needs to convince him. "Well, rather a coincidence, isn't it? Two women who live not a million miles away from each other disappear without trace on the same day, in the same way. Neither leaves a note or seems to have a reason for disappearing. Wouldn't you agree?"

Richard is non-committal, suddenly feels, for no reason he can understand or explain, a surge of love for Martha. Misses her.

"Now, I need to ask you a few questions about your wife. I believe she was known for her, er, somewhat erratic behaviour. Would you say she was depressed?"

"She had never been diagnosed as that, no."

"I see." Drains his cup. "Has she ever disappeared before?"

"No, not like this. I mean, she did her own thing. I didn't keep her tied to the farm. She was – is – a free person."

"Of course." Richard pours him more tea. It is cold. "Did your wife, Mrs Ashley, did she know Miss Turner, the painter?"

"No, they never met to my knowledge."

"But you knew her?"

"Yes, not very well. I delivered fruit and veg to her home for several years."

"And why did you stop delivering, Mr Ashley?"

Richard stares through the window. To the stretching fields. "I felt it was time my oldest son, Joe, took over the deliveries and so he did. Are you, I mean, what are you suggesting?"

"Please. I'm not suggesting anything. Mr Ashley, I'm aware that the next few questions are rather personal ones but I need to ask them. Two women have gone missing and it is my job to find them and to sort this business out. I'm sure you understand that. As you are one of the few people who knew both these women, I need your co-operation, you see." No answer. "Mr Ashley, did you and your wife, er, get on?"

"Fairly well."

"No, that's not good enough." Leans forward. "Did you have much of – er, a marriage?"

180

"I suppose we had drifted apart rather, but we were still husband and wife."

"Physically?"

"Physically?"

"Yes, Mr Ashley. Were you and your wife still having a sexual relationship?"

"Really." Richard feels his cheeks burn. Feels sixteen years old. "This is rather personal, you know." A gap. The detective waits for an answer. "No, not for some time now. She wasn't, you know, keen."

"I see. Did she ever have, to your knowledge, a sexual relationship with a woman?"

"No. I don't think so. Why should she have? She wasn't – isn't – like that."

"I believe that your wife had a child before you married her. A daughter. It is my belief, or suspicion, that your wife and Miss Turner might be mother and daughter. Do you know if this is true?"

"I don't know if this is true. No." The detective smiles, self-satisfied. Ah ha, so that's it.

Outside, he unscrews a bottle of tablets and downs two. Let this be an easy case, he mutters.

"Yeah, and guess what else. You know that funny painter woman, Miss Turner, the spoilt bitch what took my cottage off me and what's disappeared? Well, only it 'ad to be on the same day as that girl who I had to take the baby from. You remember that? She's gone an' all."

Nick's eyes widen.

"So you know 'oo's in for it? Old Judge Turner, in't he? I reckon our work's being done for us, Nick, my boy. Gonna be nuffing left for us to do. Shame really. I was looking forward to showing him up in public, but it's all 'appening on its own."

181

Nick looks down. "Look, Betty, I told ya. I'm clean now. I'm not doing any of that stuff no more. I'm off the drugs. I want to keep my hands clean when I come out. Not get into trouble. I'm in touch with God now. He doesn't want me to do bad fings."

"So you're gonna let them get away with it? The way they treated me and you?"

"No, Betty. I don't want to let ya down but I don't want trouble. God is giving me a chance. I'm outa here soon. I don't want to come back in again."

Suddenly, Betty smiles. Funny, in't it, she thinks. Nick's behind bars and turned all goody-goody and she's on the right side of the law and intending bad. Maybe the bars are keeping her in and him out, not the other way around, after all.

"Oh God," says Gertrude, folding the newspaper back, two giant wings behind its own spine. "Listen to this."

"Do I have to, dear? It's been rather á long –"

"New Line on Lakeside Vanishings. Police are now investigating a possible line, that the two women who have disappeared – Martha Ashley and well-known contemporary painter Raphaella Turner – might be mother and daughter. Police are investigating rumours that Mrs Ashley gave birth to a girl before she married Richard Ashley. Local people are being questioned. Detective Inspector Bloor who is leading the enquiry released the following statement this morning: "The fact that neither woman left a note makes the whole sequence of events highly suspicious. We have reason to believe that neither woman has been murdered or harmed as we suspected at first but that both are safe and that they have run away together, possibly flown abroad. We are appealing to people to come forward if they have any information – "

"That's enough." Julian loosens his tie and wipes his face with a handkerchief. "We're doomed. If this goes much further, what do you think it will do to my reputation and career? It's bad enough now, everyone asking where our daughter is, but because she's weird we can cover that and just say that she's unpredictable, but if they discover that she's not your daughter, we've had it. And the money?" Julian looks to Gertrude appealingly. "What are we going to do?" She shakes her head despairingly. "I can offer this Bloor man money, but it might backfire."

"Money is not always the answer, Julian," she says. "Not this time, anyway. What about Charlotte? What is she going to think? What will happen to us all?"

"Eh, this is interesting." Betty kneels on her tiny living room floor and spreads the newspaper wide. Reads aloud: "New mother and daughter lead... new line of enquiry... please would people come forward... Yes. This is my chance. Maybe Nick is right. Maybe there is a God after all."

Betty goes to the phone and dials the number printed in the paper.

"Hello," she says. Her hand and voice are trembling. "Please can I 'ave a word with Detective Inspector Bloor? Yes, my name is Betty Tattersall and I 'ave some information on the vanishing women case that 'e might be interested in."

Chapter
XXX

"Do come in and take a seat, Miss Tattersall. I'm very grateful to you for coming in to the station." Betty smiles. "I just felt that from what you said on the phone, that it might be easier to meet face to face." He gestures with his hand to a plastic seat. Betty sits down, finds herself feeling strangely nervous. She has planned this moment, desired this moment when she takes revenge, exposes Julian Turner, but now that it has come to it...

Detective Bloor turns on the tape machine. He sees her flinch.

"Now, please, Miss Tattersall. Just relax. Let's take it slowly. From the beginning. You said on the phone that you used to work for Julian Turner. You mean the Judge Turner, don't you? Father of the missing painter, of course?"

"That's right. I was the maid there."

"I see. And when was that?"

"1960 – 61. No maids stay there very long 'cos they treat their staff bad. Don't pay 'em well and that Mrs Turner, she works you to the ground and 'e, well, 'e's intimate with the maids, if you know what I mean."

"I see. Go on."

"Well, they was married many years and putting two and two together, as you do, I reckoned they couldn't have children."

"I see. Do you know that for certain or did you just surmise, I mean, guess?"

"I guessed, but when you work in an 'ouse you get a feeling, if you know what I mean. They used to row something awful."

"Right. Go on."

"Well, it was in the winter of 1961. Mr and Mrs Turner went away to live in New York for about six months. They kept us staff on but reduced our work and pay. We 'ad to carry on as normal, like. When they got back, the first thing I noticed was that she had bought tons of fings – boxes, all with baby fings. I thought, she must be expecting. But no bump or nuffing showing and nuffing was said, like."

"I see. You're doing well, Miss Tattersall. Please continue."

"Well, they'd only been back a few days when 'e –"

"Judge Turner?"

"Yeah. 'e calls me into the room and 'e says that I've got to go on a special trip. And 'e gives me the name of a farm and sends me with the driver. When I get there, I'm to collect a baby."

Detective Inspector Bloor leans forward on his chair.

"That's all you were told? Collect the baby?"

She nods.

"Didn't you ask any questions? Didn't you think that was a bit strange?"

"Yeah, I did think that but, if you asked questions there, you got into trouble and I couldn't afford to lose my job. I had someone else to support besides myself. My mother, you know."

"Go on, Miss Tattersall."

"Well, the driver took me to this farm. Gorgeous countryside, it was. Near a lake. I went into the farmhouse. There was an old guy there, sitting at a kitchen table. He looked upset. Head in his 'ands. Then I was taken upstairs. A young girl was in bed. There were two other women there, as well. I don't know who they were. Older women. The young girl, about my age then, thirty years ago so let's say eighteen, nineteen, was holding a baby. I said that I'd come to fetch the baby and she must 'and it over. She looked very upset, the girl, and said she wouldn't. It was 'ers. I felt sorry for 'er."

"How extraordinary."

"So I went 'ome and told Mr Turner and 'e 'it the roof. 'Go back again,' 'e says, 'and take this note. But don't you read it, mind.' I went back again, but in the car, I, well, I read the note." She blushes. But surely this minor offence will seem nothing compared to what she is describing.

"What did the note say, Miss Tattersall?"

She dips her hand into her bag and brings out the note. Not one of the many copies she's made, this time, but the original. Its creases have almost torn now and it looks old and worn but it is still legible.

The detective lays it gently on the table and reads aloud:

Dear Martha,

I can imagine how hard this is for you. But you know that we entered into an agreement. That baby must come to my wife before it breaks her heart. I will pay you whatever you want. You know what we said. Once this is over, I will be with you. I love you. We will have our own children together. Please God, I beg you. Don't let me down. Do this for me.
Julian

"I showed her the note and she 'anded me the baby. Only I kept the note. I know it was wrong, like, but after all 'e'd done to me, physical like, I felt angry with him. I took the baby back to their house and that was the child they brought up as their own. Raphaella Turner, they called her. Dead posh name, if you ask me, but that's the way they are. Those types. They think they rule the world. Can buy everything with –"

"You're absolutely sure that the baby that you fetched from the farm was Miss Turner?"

"Positive. Gorgeous she was, though I 'ate to admit it. Dark hair, big dark eyes. Pink cheeks. Lovely child. Shame she turned out the way she did, really."

"Anyway, you took the baby home to the couple and they brought her up as their own. Did you ever see the young woman again, the one who had the child for them?"

"No, never."

"Did you know her name?"

"No, but I know that she lived on the farm where the woman has vanished from so I think I can put two and two together."

"We'll get you some photographs to identify her from. Did you stay in the home of the Turners for much longer after this?"

"No."

"Why did you leave? Where did you go to?"

"Well, for a while, Mr Turner, 'e gave me money to keep me quiet about the baby."

Detective Bloor smiles. Evilly, Betty thinks.

"You mean you blackmailed him? With the note as evidence?"

"No. I never. I wouldn't do that. No. 'e just gave me money and said I was to shut up. I 'ad my mother to support, so I took it. But then I decided to leave. I didn't feel good about staying in a place like that. With crooks."

"I see. And did you keep in touch with the baby?"

"No, but I saw 'er growing up like. Seen 'er in the paper. And then years later, Mr Turner, 'e said I could live in Lemon Cottage by the lake."

"Why would he do that so long after?"

187

"I dunno. His wife didn't want to go there no more. I don't know why 'cos she used to love it there. So it was empty. 'E said I could clean it and then live there rent free. But then that girl – the one who was the baby – she came and chucked me out, didn't she? After I'd made it my own home and I loved it there. She just come along and threw me out."

"Dear me."

"Yeah, and so I 'ad to find somewhere else to go. And it weren't nearly as nice as Lemon Cottage."

"Now, in my investigations I discovered there was a fire there. A bad fire. It was gutted. Were you living there then?"

"No, I'd moved out by then. Serves her right that she was there. Wasn't hurt. But right shook up. Went back to her parents' house for a while, I believe."

"Yes, that's right. And a man was put in jail for arson."

"Yeah, so I'm told."

"Well, Miss Tattersall. You've been enormously helpful, I must say. You may go now but I might like to contact you again, if that is alright."

Betty puts her coat and hat on. Nods.

"But just before you go, Miss Tattersall, does the name Nicholas Fletcher mean anything to you?"

Betty pauses a second. "No," she says. "Nothing at all."

Chapter
XXXI

"But wouldn't you have thought she'd turn up? At some stage?" Oliver is lying on one of the black leather sofas he has brought with him into the sham sandworld. It goes rather well here, he thinks, looking round at the pleated lampshades and the clear-cut prints and lithographs secured against the inner walls of the dome. The lake shimmering outside.

"That's what one would expect. Otherwise, why would she lure us here?" Lucius's face suddenly flares red. "But then, Oliver, why are you talking about her all the time? Why can't we just focus on us and forget about her? Does she mean so much to you?"

Oliver also reddens so that, now, two scarlet-faced men are submerged at the bottom of the lake. "No, not at all. Not in personal terms." His lies sting him as he speaks. "But she is our artist. We discovered and nurtured her. I think she owes us something. We wanted the – artistic relationship – to continue, didn't we?"

"Yes, you're right. And I don't mind being here for a while, but I feel sort of manipulated. As if she has brought us here and then doesn't even come to see us. I mean, the gallery is alright. I'm e-mailing Marcus every day and he's doing well there but I don't want to be here for ever, underwater. I'm beginning to feel sort of soggy."

"I know, Lucius. I don't want to be here for ever either. And I feel annoyed with Raphaella as well, but let's wait a bit longer, eh? I'm sure she'll come soon. She must do."

As Oliver speaks, and then leans his head against Lucius's shoulder, he feels the cut of his own deceit. For it is

189

not just anger that he feels against Raphaella – even her name annoys him now – because of their artistic relationship, as he's resorted to calling it, but because of their own affair. They are – were – lovers, after all, weren't they? But it's more than that. She detected his own ambivalence and that's fair enough. They never claimed undying love to each other or commitment or fidelity. But there's something else. His mother's face comes to him often here. Even though she's dead now and he's underwater, for God's sake, she's still there. The pain, the humiliation, the rejection is here again. And somehow it is linked with Raphaella. Women whom he has loved – for it may well be love – have abandoned him, let him down, made him look a fool. Yes, maybe that is it. Lucius is stroking Oliver's cheek now. The cheek that his mother struck. The cheek that Raphaella leaned her dark hair against. He loves Raphaella. And she is gone. Luckily, crying is easy in the lake. The tears that slip down Oliver's cheeks go unnoticed by Lucius who does not see how they merge and dissolve in the vastness of the water.

"Hey, boys." Richard is calling up the stairs. "For God's sake, get down here. Now."

No answer.

Richard sighs and looks out to the fields. At first, he didn't mind the boys drinking and clubbing in the city till all hours – they're young men, he told himself, why not? – but now things have changed. Before, they were always able to combine their late nights with getting up in the morning – perhaps a bit later than he would have liked. But now, now it has gone too far. They can't work. They can't get up. He is being left to manage the farm on his own and the deliveries as well. And it's not as if the farm is doing that well. Richard looks out at the broken fences, the dwindling herd of sheep. Paying staff will be too expensive. With his parents dead there's no one to turn to. He will have to struggle on his own. And in a way he doesn't blame the boys anyway. It is because of what has happened to them. They've lost their mother, grandmother, brother. Although he still finds himself feeling strangely loving towards Martha, he also has begun to hate her. How could she, how could she have done this to him? To her own sons? The only answer now is to muddle on making what money he can – he's advertised Briar Cottage for rent – and hoping the boys will help out where they can. He had hoped that one of them would have carried on with the farm when he got too old but none seems at all interested. And there's something besides that. A kind of desolate loneliness. He's on his own now. Abandoned. Oh well, he sighs. Back to work.

"This is becoming too much." Julian is pacing around the hall of their home. "It's on the news, in the papers – 'New Line of Enquiry: Raphaella Turner love-child of Judge and Young Farm Girl.' I'd like to take one of those bloody detective's lines of enquiry and strangle him with it."

Gertrude has tears running, spilling down her face. "We made a huge mistake, Julian. I never thought anyone would know. Not this many years later, anyway. Why? Why has it happened?"

"I'll tell you why. It's that bloody daughter of ours, isn't it? She's planned this so-called vanishing so that we would get exposed. She's probably sunning herself on a beach in France somewhere while we're all going through hell."

"We shouldn't have done it. We were wrong."

"There's no point saying that now, Gertrude. You wanted a child and that's what we decided to do."

"But the papers are saying, Julian, that Martha may have been your lover anyway. That's not true, is it? Tell me that's not true."

"Of course it isn't! Who are you going to believe – me or some filth in a tabloid paper? That woman's obviously being paid to tell her story to some sleazy journalist. She'll say anything for money."

Gertrude sits down. Doesn't answer. Wishes her husband would stop pacing and storming around and catch her eye.

"Look, we're getting side-tracked by arguing with each other. The point is, what are we going to do about it? We can't stay here with those wretched news reporters snooping around outside our house day and night. I will retire. It's probably time anyway. How can I function with this going on? How can I make legal judgements on other people's lives when my own life is being scrutinised and examined?"

"But where will we go to?" Gertrude still can't catch his eye. "Wherever we go, people will find us. We can't go abroad. Not while all this is being investigated. That will make us look really guilty. We will have to stay nearby. But where?"

"We'll go to Lemon Cottage." Julian looks relieved by his own suggestion. "Can you face it?"

Gertrude nods. "I'll get Donna to help me start packing straight away," she says.

"That's it," says Raphaella to Martha. "I love the way you are letting the paint go on freely. Just relax your elbow slightly."

Martha paints her canvas, with her daughter beside her. She likes the way that the young woman is teaching the older. Maybe that's the way it should be. Sometimes, Martha does think of her sons, the three living and the one dead, and of her mother and occasionally, even, of Richard. But there seems no doubt to her that she is in the right place. With the daughter she holds so dear.

"I've always wanted to paint, you know."

Raphaella smiles, hugs the woman from whom bubbles float, from whom love flows.

Raphaella opens her mouth to call Martha but, instead, Mother comes out. It is no distance, it seems to her, from Martha to Mother and she has travelled it. They are no longer fish or bird or rocks. No need to hide in any shape other than what they are: mother and daughter. And it is on this day that Martha first calls her daughter by her name, but by her own version of her name: Raffy. And although Raphaella has never let anyone else shorten her name, her mother can. Only her mother can.

Betty walks along the country lane which leads from the road to the farm. In the distance, she can see the lake. It flashes at her like a blinking eye. Luring her. Telling her secrets. The lanes are fringed with translucent trees. Avenues of trees. Leaves flashing in the sun. It is a glorious day. A glorious place. She thinks of Nick as she walks along. Poor man. Stuck behind bars, deprived of the sunlight. Soon, she will bring him to the countryside, let him be free and enjoy nature. He deserves it. He has suffered enough.

She walks up the path to the farmhouse door. Puffing, she stops for breath. It has been a long walk. She's getting on now. She is shocked by how dishevelled it all looks. Run down. Broken fences. Splintering window-panes. Nearly forty years ago – for it must be that long – it didn't look that good either. She remembers thinking it needed work then but now, it's even worse. It has declined. She knocks on the door. A red-haired, middle-aged man opens it.

"Yes?"

Betty holds up the advert, cut out from the local paper. "I've come to see the cottage," she says.

Chapter
XXXII

Richard opens the door to Briar Cottage.

"It's only small," he apologises.

Betty's eyes are wide. Outside, yes, it looked a little shabby, ivy overgrown, the chimney collapsed, the wooden door with peeling paint, but inside it is warm and cosy. She could certainly make this a home for herself. For her and Nick. But she won't mention him now. Richard will wonder where he is. Doesn't want to mention prison, does she? That'll make a good impression. She peers through a dust-smeared window. Out to the farm. Dots of sheep in the distant hills.

"How much rent do you want?"

"Fifty a week. Including bills."

Betty smiles. "Yes," she says. "We – I'll take it."

"It seems strange being here again after so many years." Gertrude stands in the doorway to Lemon Cottage. "We'll manage for a while, although it's so small."

"I'm not worried about it being small," says Julian nervously, ushering his wife and suitcases in. "What concerns me is those photographers standing by the lake." He points to where Micky and Matt, having caught snaps of Miss Turner's parents as they drove up, are now smoking and looking out to the lake.

"Did you get 'em?" Matt.

"Yeah." Micky stubs out his fag on the sand. "Bit bloody boring, in't it, here? Standing around for hours, waiting to

194

catch a glimpse of someone. Where do you reckon this bird is, then?"

Matt shrugs his shoulders. Passes another fag to Micky.

"I reckon she's buzzed off somewhere and is having a good laugh while everyone else gets themselves into a tizz about it. Must be nice to be famous."

"D'you reckon? Maybe not for her. Maybe she's gone and topped herself? Couldn't take it?"

"Nah. She's organised this all to suit herself. And nobody else. Mark my words."

Inside Lemon Cottage, Gertrude is looking around her daughter's things. Having not visited the cottage since her daughter had moved in there – rather, having never been invited – it is intriguing to her to see how Raphaella has arranged her home, her life. White sofas, white walls. On the mantelpiece, there is a series of glass jars each with different contents in it: buttons, shells. Strange, really. There is nothing living or pretty. Everything is sparse as if reduced. Eliminated. Gertrude is not surprised that there are no photographs of anyone there. Nothing sentimental. Nothing, it seems to Gertrude, representing the past. As if it has been blotted out. The memories cleaned with disinfectant or bleach. In the studio, a half-completed painting stands on a double easel. Gertrude fingers the large canvases, stacked in piles against the wall. Gertrude looks through them, one at a time. They are enigmas to her, repetitive, undeveloped, crude. Paint is smeared on thickly in large meaningless shapes. Nothing there, it seems to her, is beautiful. Almost deliberately ugly. Not one dab of paint compares with the beauty of the lake outside which, in the spring sunlight, is wriggling with energy. Alive.

In the living room, Julian is tugging at a locked drawer. He hopes to find some clues here. There is some fruit in a bowl but no other food left behind. In the studio, one painting, incomplete. Had his daughter planned to go? Yes, in a way, it feels like someone going on holiday, using up their last supplies, leaving everything tidy. But she may have been taken. Snatched. Why the painting unfinished? Does that mean she plans to return? He tugs again at the unlocked drawer. There is no note left behind. But then, who would she write to? She doesn't know anyone. No one's expecting her. He tugs again. The drawer yanks open and art books tumble out.

"Gertrude," calls Julian. "Look what I've found here."

She comes through and kneels beside him. They pile the books up together: Kandinsky, Rego, Hodgkin, Klee, Heron, Rothko.

"They're her art books," says Gertrude. "Influences on her."

"Then why lock them up? Why not put them on a shelf like other people? It is as if she wants to keep them a secret. Why?"

"If you're asking why that, then why everything else? Why is she the way she is? Why did we ever agree to the deceit in the first place? Why?"

That evening, they get into bed, their daughter's bed. The bed, Gertrude knows, that Julian and Martha made love in. Just once? Or hundreds of times? Gertrude cannot sleep. Lies on her back with her eyes wide open, hoping that her husband might lift his hand and reach out to touch her. He does not.

Betty opens the box, yet again, and takes out the ornaments her mother gave her. China robin on bough. Beggarman with balloons. Arranges them on the mantelpiece. She will paint this cottage. Make it pretty. Later, she hangs her floral curtains up. They are a bit long for these narrow windows. She sits all afternoon, stitching up the hems, pins placed carefully in her mouth, needle and thread dipping in and out of the fabric as she thinks of Nick. How he will love this place: the green hills, the sheep, the fresh sweet air. It will be a haven to him after his bare cell and the barbed wire coils around the tops of the prison walls. Caging him in. For what he has done. And what he has done recurs to her when she is asleep and when she is awake. What he did. To her mother. To the cottage. Intending to burn her. No, she mustn't think of that now. He has made mistakes. Everyone has. That is behind them now. Then why, why, as she sews the final stitch and tears the cotton with her teeth, does her mother's face haunt her still?

"And everywhere you look, it's green," says Betty through the iron mesh. "Green and fresh and the air is, well, it's lovely. And the lake is not very far away." She stops in her tracks. Of course she mustn't dwell on the lake because that will lead him to think about the cottage. The one he burned. "And the farmer," she continues, "Mr Ashley, he's ever so nice and I'm sure there'll be work for you on the farm 'cos it's really run down and his boys don't do much to help. Just lounge around, and they're grown men, not youngsters. You'd like to work on the farm, wouldn't you? Nick?"

"Let me just get outa 'ere first, Betty, alright?"

Betty's face falls. Whenever she tries to talk to him of his future – their future – he seems to refuse to look forward. She tries so hard not to look back, but he seems stuck in the present in the same way that he's stuck in jail. What should she say to him? The future doesn't seem to exist for him, to excite him: the past is so full of demons and errors; the present is empty. There seems to be nothing out there – or in there – for him.

Leaving the jail today, the giant steel doors closed behind her, Betty feels bleak. Maybe Nick is right. There is nothing for them to look forward to. Money is running out and she can hardly go to Julian and ask for more now that she has exposed him. What are she and Nick going to do together? How are they going to live? Can she ever really forgive him? Even their plans for revenge have fizzled out. With Raphaella and Martha gone and Julian exposed, what else is there to do? Back in her cottage, Betty feels slightly better. At least she feels safe. There is a knock at the door. Richard is there.

"Oh hello, Mr Ashley." Betty smooths her skirt out.

"I just wondered if there's anything you need," he says.

"It's strange, isn't it?" says Lucius, knocking a pike away with his fist, "that here, where there is no hint of Raphaella – none of her paintings, no dealings with her, no sign of her – that I am so much more aware of her than ever before."

They are in the lake again, where they spend so much of their time, at the foot of the sandworld.

Oliver sighs. Not that topic again. Lucius seems to be obsessed with Raphaella, talks of her all the time, asking questions more than providing answers. Oliver almost admitted the other evening that he and Raphaella had been lovers. Not that there was any love – but there was sex. And that is what he cannot tell Lucius and yet Lucius is angling to find out. And Lucius is right: here, where Raphaella is absent, she's more present than ever.

"Do you think so?" says Oliver. "I never think of her at all."

"Raffy," says Martha. "What I love about being here in the water in the sandworld with you, is that we are close. And we are open. And that we love each other." And she closes her eyes and curls up against her daughter's chest and sleeps,

198

the bubbles escaping, slipping through her nostrils as she dreams.

Raphaella feels her mother's breath upon her, feels the kicks of her unborn child, the child whose father may be a cultured and slightly bland lover or a wild, animalistic farmer's son. Raphaella remembers Oliver's dark-haired foppishness; Joe's red-haired loose, ragged mischief, his gorgeous body, the sheer smell of him. How long ago that seems now. No sex, no painting, no changing shape into birds, trees or rocks. None of that seems important now that she has found Martha, Mother, home.

Chapter XXXIII

Julian and Gertrude jump when they hear the knock at the cottage door.

"Don't answer," says Julian. "It will be one of those filthy media people wanting their little pictures."

But the knock comes again, harder, more determined and a voice: "Open up. I know you're in there. Detective Inspector Bloor."

"Oh God, Julian, we'd better open the door."

And he does. And there stands, clipboard in gloved hand, the serious raincoated body of Detective Inspector Bloor. His other hand displays an identity card with his grave face photographed on it.

"You'd better come in," says Julian, smiling awkwardly. "I'm Julian Turner."

"I know," says the detective, opening the back flaps of his raincoat as if they were wings, before sitting on a white sofa and looking disdainfully around. Prefer repro, antique desks myself, he thinks, drawing a pen from his coat pocket.

"Tea?" says Gertrude, trying to sound cheerful and failing utterly.

"Milk, no sugar, thank you," says the detective and sits in silence until the tray arrives and the three of them then sit drinking tea in the home of the absentee.

"You are aware, of course, of the controversy surrounding your daughter's disappearance. It seems that Miss Turner has gone somewhere, we don't know where, with her natural mother."

"Who has told you this?" Julian tries to keep his temper. Whispers to himself. "As if I don't know."

"I am not at liberty to reveal that at present," says the detective. Sips his tea. Wishes it were stronger. Never mind. "Are you denying this?"

Julian looks down. He knows enough about the law to take a risk.

"Of course I am. You have no proof whatsoever that my wife and I are not the natural parents of Raphaella." But the detective has caught the glance shot by Gertrude to her husband. He makes a note of it. "If you are more willing to listen to the prattle and gossip of maids than to a respected man like me, then there's not much point in me saying anything. Gertrude, fetch the birth certificate, please." Gertrude returns a few minutes later. The detective looks at it, seems reassured.

"I am aware of your position as a judge."

"Well then, listen to what I have to say and not to some gossipmonger."

"Fair enough. How do you explain your daughter's disappearance and that of Martha Ashley?"

"I cannot. That's your job, surely."

"Did you know Martha Ashley?"

"Yes, we did." Gertrude jumps in before her husband has the chance to lie again. "She used to clean the cottage for us years ago when she was young. However, after her marriage and her own family, we have had no contact with her at all. We didn't know that our daughter had any contact with this woman either. For all we know, she hasn't."

"Rather a coincidence, though, I'm sure you'll agree, Mrs Turner, that they both vanished on the same day, don't you think?" Neither Turner answers. It seems a question for him to deal with rather than them. He's being paid to solve this enigma.

"Did you see much of your daughter?"

"She liked to live her own life," Gertrude explains rationally, "but, of course, we supported her work and were at her last exhibition. The preview night, naturally."

"She seems, by all accounts, to have been rather a loner. Do you know if she had friends?"

"Very few. She never mixed well, even when she was at school."

"And what about the view expressed in some quarters, that she and Mrs Ashley were, er, in a relationship? A delicate matter to bring up, I realise."

"Well," Julian leans forward, "we felt that her sexuality was her own affair. It is obvious what has happened here, Inspector. But we don't want her to be humiliated. We understand that our daughter was being hounded for many years because of her leanings. There was even an arson attempt on the cottage many years ago when it was first disclosed. We live in an intolerant world, Inspector. Recently, there were those who were stalking and taunting her about her sexuality. I suspect that she and her lover, Martha, couldn't stand it any longer and have run away."

"But it's strange that she shouldn't have said anything to you, her parents. She'd know you would be worried, surely?"

"Maybe it got too much for her?"

"Mm. Why then have you moved into her home?"

Julian places his hand on his wife's, the first physical contact for months.

"To await our daughter's return," he says.

Outside the cottage, Micky and Matt flash their cameras at the detective leaving the house and at the two heads peering out of the door of the cottage. Then Bloor stands below the window of the cottage and listens to the argument at the window above him:

"Why did you make up all that rubbish about her sexuality? He'll easily disprove that."

"What else do you suggest? What we did was not illegal, but it will ruin our lives. Do you want that? He hasn't got a leg to stand on. Who is he going to believe – some silly maid from nearly forty years ago or us? Don't worry. Trust me."

"Maybe that's the problem, Julian. Maybe I don't trust you. How many lies have you told me, let alone the police?"

The detective hears a door slam, turns his tape recorder off and walks away.

"That's good, Mother," says Raphaella. "I like the way you've made the stripes wave and curve into each other a little rather than being straight lines alone."

Martha smiles, hugs her daughter. In fact, Raphaella has been surprised at her mother's limitations, her lack of talent, her inability to learn. This does not diminish her love for her but it has been a surprise. Where has her own talent for painting come from then? Not from any specific teacher, not from her natural mother, her supposed mother, Gertrude, whose taste was old-fashioned and unbending, and certainly not from her father who never seems to look long enough to observe. What is she? Where has she emerged from? And where will she end up?

Later that night, when Martha and Raphaella are lying on the floor of the lake and gazing at the refractions of the stars in the water, Martha strokes her daughter's swollen belly. They have spoken about so much, yet there is one area they have not discussed: fathers. Who is Raphaella's real father and why did Martha sleep with him? Who is the father of Raffy's baby?

And so it is tonight, when the stars are liquid above their watery feet, that fathers are discussed.

"So who was my father then, Mother?"

Martha sighs. Reaches out her hand to catch the reflection of a star. The light twists, slips through her fingers.

"Julian. Your real father. We were in love. He said he would marry me. But then – well, he stayed with Gertrude and I married Richard. And that was that."

Raphaella strokes her mother's cheeks. "I loved you instantly, Raffy. Wanted to keep you. But my parents were ashamed as I was unmarried. And Julian abandoned me."

"Bastard," hisses Raphaella. "Men."

"Yes," smiles Martha, stroking her daughter's stomach. "Men. And who is your man? The father of your child? My grandchild?"

Raphaella flinches. Should she tell Martha that the child will be her grandchild in two ways: the baby of both her daughter and her son. If it is Joe's.

"A man called Oliver," says Raphaella. "He is my art agent and we – well, we have been involved in a way for years."

"Do you love him?"

"No. I love you, though." And so, beneath the water, the deceit continues as mother and daughter lick each other's tears away.

"Do come in," says Betty, nervously. "After all, it is your cottage."

"Not at all," says Richard, accepting the invitation anyway. "As long as you're living here I want you to regard this as your home."

Betty smiles her gratitude.

Over tea and biscuits, Betty and Richard talk quietly. Each thinks that life has given the other a hard deal.

"And so you manage alone, now, with the farm and the boys?"

"Well." Richard looks down, feels shy with Betty and yet strangely comforted by a woman's voice. Eyes. "The boys are adults now. Do their own thing. If they give me a bit of help with the farm, that's fine. And sometimes I have to pay for a bit of help as well."

"I have a friend who may be coming to visit here soon. If that's alright? He would like to help you."

"That would be great. But I get by. Just plug away really."

"And the house and the cooking?"

Richard smiles. "Well, I'm not the greatest cook around, but I make sure the boys get fed. And the house. Well, it's a bit neglected really."

"It must be lonely for you, Mr Ashley. With your wife gone, I mean."

Richard stands up. "I really ought to be going. Thank you for the tea. And let's stop this Mr Ashley nonsense. Please call me Richard."

Chapter XXXIV

Betty wakes with a start, pulls open the curtains to reveal a blue spring day. She has been dreaming. Delightful dream: she and Richard running the farm together, and the house all prettily done up with new checked curtains tied back at the windows, and fresh paint on the house and chickens in the yard, and the boys all gone, and bread baking in the oven and cakes cooling on the window-sill, and a hen clucking in the yard. Yes, today, before she visits Nick, she will bake cake and bread for Richard and take them as a gift.

The delight on his face – though hidden slightly by shyness and surprise – is worth it.

"What's all this?" he laughs. It is a while since someone has pampered, focused on him.

"I've baked them for you," says Betty. "A woman's touch. Are you going to invite me in, then?"

Once in the kitchen, Betty clears the crumbs from the table and lays out her cakes, buns and rock cakes as if spread for a Women's Institute sale.

"Well, I'm, er, I'm amazed. I'll put the kettle on."

"What about your boys? Would they like some cakes?"

"Oh, they're not up yet. They were, er, out late last night. Joe's a bit down these days. He's taken his mother's vanishing rather badly."

"Of course," says Betty, looking round at the neglected farmhouse and comparing it to the idyll in her dream. "It's hard to be deserted. I should know."

*   *   *

Betty smiles at Nick through the iron mesh, smiling at him, smiling at the contrast between the farm cottage and the jail.

"Not long to go now, Nick, eh? You're nearly done."

He does not reply. Avoids her eyes.

"What's up, Nick? You want to be free, don't you? You know we're gonna be together. On the farm. In the little cottage."

"Yeah, I know. But I'm not sure if I'm ready. To leave, ya know. 'Ere. I feel, sort of, safe 'ere. I'm busy. I'm working in the carpentry place and I'm serving God. Maybe I'm better 'ere."

Betty leans back. Her mind is whirling with Lemon Cottage and the Turners' home and Briar Cottage and Richard's farmhouse and the jail. What should she do? Where should she live? And Nick? And why can she not get Richard's gentle face out of her mind?

"This is too much." Julian is pacing up and down the cottage, the newspaper spread out wide in front of him. His voice is sarcastic. Angry. " 'Farm Girl Paid to Have Baby with Judge.' What is the world coming to? A series of sleazy headlines for everyone to ogle at?"

"You can't blame the world, Julian. We did wrong and now we're being punished for it."

"Oh dear, Gertrude, you're not going to turn to God now, are you? Give us all a break."

"It's nothing to do with God, Julian. It's just plain common sense and logic. We were deceitful. Now we've been caught out. What do you think Charlotte will think of us? When we can face her and tell her where we are?"

"She'll have to cope, won't she? as we're having to cope. My reputation has gone. What are we going to do?"

"We'll have to leave. Go."

"Where to? That sneaky little detective has told us we're not allowed to go abroad while the enquiry is pending. We can't keep running. Where else can we go? Each time we leave the cottage we are flashed and snapped at by those vipers."

Gertrude is standing by the window now, looking out to the lake. "I don't know," she says slowly, looking to the water for answers. "But we need to leave. Today."

"But you're always coming back to her." Oliver rakes his wet hair with his fingers. "You're obsessed with her. I try to change the subject, swim, play, but you keep on talking about her. Why?"

"Because," hisses Lucius, "don't you see? She's behind this all. She is the reason we are here. She is the manipulator who has engineered this, so that instead of running my gallery and now losing God knows how much every day, I am sitting here underwater, waiting, waiting for her. And I'm fed up with it. There's nothing to do here. Once I've answered all my e-mails and faxes, I'm redundant. The water's beginning to get to me, I suppose. Too much of it. And I feel wet and soaked all the time. I want to go home. I want to dry out. I want to run my gallery again."

"OK, then. You go. I'll stay here and wait, and you go home. How about that?"

"Oh no," says Lucius. "If you're waiting for her, I'll wait too."

"So you're the only person I can be honest with, Raffy."

Raphaella smiles, strokes her mother's arms. "Of course," she says. "We'll stay here together, look after each other, care, comfort, entertain."

It occurs to her that they speak to each other not only the language of love, but the language of lovers. The words she ought to have used with M. With Joe. With Oliver. She has reserved them, saved them, for her mother. As if her mother is her lover, her beloved. They stroke each other's cheeks. Then Raphaella gives her mother another informal lesson in painting and Martha gives her daughter an informal lesson in loving.

"I can't believe it. I just can't."

Her husband, Mark, comes up to her, puts his hand on her shoulder. Turns to their daughters. "Harriet. Louise. Go upstairs and play now, please. And quietly. Charles is having his nap."

"What's wrong with Mummy?" Harriet.

"Why's she crying?" Louise.

Mark calls the nanny and she takes the girls quietly upstairs.

Mark and Charlotte sit side by side on the settee, looking out to their perfect garden.

"I suppose looking back, Mother always treated me as the favourite. Well, Raphaella was such a monster that I never questioned it. Only Granny preferred her to me. But to think that father had a child with that woman – she used to clean the cottage for God's sake – and then pretended she was their own. I mean, it stinks."

Mark, never one for long speeches, lets his wife speak. Sob.

"Maybe I was conceived with a maid as well. Who knows? And to keep that deceit for so long. I want to speak to my parents and yet when I phone the house, they're not there. Gone away, the staff tell me. Well, that's great, isn't it? I need them to confess to me and they've absconded. For a holiday, no doubt. Well, I want to speak to them. Or rather listen. While they, once and for all, tell me the truth."

"I'm sure there's an explanation." Mark – cool, serene.

"Really? You heard the detective on the news. You've seen the headlines. I've had to find out the whole sleazy truth along with the rest of the population. It's so humiliating. I want to find them, Mark. Where on earth do you think they can be?"

Chapter
XXXV

"There. Can't you see it?"

Gertrude is standing beside Julian and pointing. She loves to be this close to him, to feel, smell his breath upon her shoulder as he looks but does not see. She smiles. "You've never been very visual, have you? You never notice things. There. Look, jutting out on the far side of the lake. A sort of dome."

"Ah. I see now. I wonder what it is?"

"I don't know, but it looks to me like one of Raphaella's crazy contraptions, don't you think so? I can just make out decorations or scratchings on the surface of the sand. I think we should take refuge there, Julian. Just me and you. What do you say?"

She slips her hand through his arm, pulls herself close to him. Oh God. In spite of it all – the infidelities, the coldness, the mess they've got themselves into – there's something about the sheer presence of him which she loves. His body is rigid and cold against hers. Unbending. Tears fill her eyes. She has no mother. No daughter. Her other daughter probably despises her now. But she has Julian and she loves him. But to love someone who does not love you back, to crave someone who does not crave you, is agony.

"I love you," she whispers. "I love you, Julian."

He places his hand on her shoulder. That's all. That's all, but it's something. It's a beginning.

"I'll start packing our belongings," she says, her shoulder where his touch was, still glowing, warm.

"These are delicious, Betty." Richard is sitting in the kitchen of his farmhouse, drinking tea and eating Betty's cakes. He feels warmed from the inside, from the tea, from the food, from Betty's company. It is good to feel this again after the months, years of loneliness with Martha, with his wife.

"I'm pleased you like them. You know," she looks round her, "you could make this house really attractive. Homely. I could help you to make new curtains and paint the walls."

"Why should you? It's not your job."

"I know. But it would give me pleasure. I've got plenty of free time."

"Are you retired, Betty? You've mentioned work a few times."

"Yeah. I worked for, for a wealthy couple as their maid for years. And many other families besides. Then I, I came into bit of money. Not a lot, but enough for me to live carefully and rent."

Richard nods, asks no further questions, does not wish to intrude. He likes this woman: his own age, down-to-earth, her once pretty face worn somehow. There is a warmth there which fills and delights him.

She smiles back at him. The poor man. Neglected and abandoned, and what harm has he done? Always the same, she thinks. Those who are innocent are punished, whereas the likes of the Turners get away with everything. So unfair.

Gertrude and Julian attempt, but fail, to slip unnoticed through the front door of Lemon Cottage. Micky and Matt, nearly dead and stale from weeks of inactivity and waiting, leap to their feet and start flashing, snapping.

"Look at 'em," says Matt, laughing evilly. "How the mighty have fallen."

And Micky laughs as he photographs the Turners, scuttling crab-like across the sand, their heads down, shame stamped on their bodies.

At the edge of the shore, they put down their suitcases and take their shoes off.

"Let's start swimming." Gertrude leads, leaps into the lake and her hair and skirt flow backwards behind her. She feels like a stone caryatid released into water and she feels free. Julian is stiffer, more like an ironing board underwater but he follows his wife. Together they swim, ignoring the tiny fish which flick past them and the few bits of algae that get caught in their hair.

Then they see a tunnel, made of sand, like a huge yellow drainpipe. Again, Gertrude leads them through, enjoying the power and leadership. Theirs has been a marriage in which Julian has led and she has followed, but underwater this changes. He seems content to follow as if the water has drained his powers or tranquillised him. Every few moments, Gertrude turns her head and looks back: there's Julian, the water bending him gradually, his face softening in the lake.

Through the tunnel they swim, until they reach the huge sand structure with its curvaceous walls and massive dome and etched walls: the sham sandworld.

"This is amazing," says Gertrude and Julian nods his agreement. "It's a lakeside palace, or temple. It's unbelievable."

Gertrude rubs her fingers along the outer wall, feels the carvings and etchings there, senses her daughter's stamp there.

As Gertrude and Julian enter the structure, they see two men on a black leather sofa: Oliver and Lucius. They jump.

"Oh," says Oliver. "We weren't expecting company."

"No." Lucius is at his shoulder. "We thought we'd be alone here."

213

"We're Raphaella's parents. I'm Julian Turner –" he holds his hand out and the men shake it in turns, " – and this is my wife, Gertrude." She smiles.

"I see." Lucius's body relaxes a little. "Well, you'd better sit down." So on one black leather sofa sit Lucius and Oliver (rather close to each other, Gertrude notices) and on the other sofa (not very close together, Oliver notices) sit Julian and Gertrude.

"Of course, we're very worried about our daughter. We don't know where she is."

"So are we," says Oliver. "We don't know where she is, either, and so we're staying here in the hope that she'll return."

"I see," says Gertrude. "But don't I recognise you? Weren't you the man who was writing the book?"

"Yes." Oliver shifts, a little nervous at being spotted. Is there no privacy these days? Not even in a lake? "But I abandoned it in the end. Your daughter managed to persuade me that what counts is not the life story but the paintings themselves. I, I do apologise for having troubled you."

"Not at all." Gertrude smiles so coldly, Lucius worries that she might turn the water into ice. "So you – you never wrote it then?"

"No, just a catalogue to go with the exhibition. That's all."

"He's very modest." Lucius. "It was an extensive piece of work, a huge amount of research and the first comprehensive catalogue of your daughter's work ever."

The Turners nod.

"Well…" Oliver looks down. A man in his early forties and this is all he's achieved: a slim catalogue of the work of a painter who seems to have vanished off the face of the earth. His mother's sneering face is there, even now.

"Yes, we saw it at the opening night. We were there, of course." Julian fiddles with his socks. "We were – are – very close to Raphaella. Wouldn't have missed it for the world."

"So where do you think she's gone to... as you were so close?" Oliver.

"We just don't know. She was worried about her sexuality being disclosed, of course. This was her main concern. We'd spoken about it often."

"Her sexuality?" Oliver and Lucius speak simultaneously.

"Yes." Julian is nudged by Gertrude, leaves his socks alone. He will have to just accept that they are waterlogged and that his shoes are squelchy and that his hair is matted. "She was – is – gay, of course. Did you not know that?"

"No." The boys speak in chorus again, each slightly annoyed at the other's quick response.

"Not that we minded," Gertrude is quick to point out. "We're very liberal, very tolerant, but you know what some people are like. Well, Raphaella was worried that now that fame had found her, or now that she'd found fame, whichever, she was concerned that people would discriminate against her or turn against her work."

"Gay? Raphaella?" Oliver rakes his hair. "I don't think so."

"Don't you?" Lucius. "Why not?"

"Well, I, er I – I – er, don't know but she, she had a partner for a while. M, she called him."

"M?" Gertrude flinches at the name. Was it human? M? What kind of a name is that? Her daughter had a partner? Called M?

"Yes. Yes, she did. He inspired that series of rainbows, you know?"

"Yes, we know. He was important to her, this N?"

"M."

"M. That's right. By the way, we bought two paintings and haven't settled up." Julian takes his cheque book out of his jacket pocket. "Would you like a cheque now? Or do you take a credit card?"

"We'll settle up later," says Lucius. He is too happy to think about money now. He's laughing at himself, smiling inwardly. All this time he's been worried that Oliver was sleeping with Raphaella and the woman's gay. Of course. It all makes sense now.

Gay? Oliver can't believe it. He and Raphaella were lovers. Or were they? Yes, she was detached always. Kind of cold and distant. Maybe she didn't fancy him – guys. But then why did she sleep with him? And M? Why? What has she been playing at? Using him? But for what?

"Here we are," says Lucius, popping a bottle of champagne. "This will be well cooled now. It's been chilling in the lake overnight. Let's celebrate – that we've found each other and can wait together."

"Really?" Julian is astounded at the generosity of stranger to stranger.

"Why not?" Lucius smiles. "There's plenty of room here for us all. We can wait together."

"Oh, thank you," say the Turners as they clink their glasses and watch the bubbles of the champagne rise.

"Yes," says Oliver. Humiliated again, he thinks. "Cheers," he says, glumly.

216

Chapter
XXXVI

"Now, do try some of my fish and then I'll show you to your rooms."

"Thank you," says Julian, suddenly cheerful. "Excellent service. Better than The Savoy!"

"Delicious," says Gertrude. "Do you use lemon in the sauce?"

"Yes, adds a bit of tang, I think. But I'm fast running out of those supplies, of course. As I was saying, Oliver and I are most happy for you to stay here with us in this structure, building, call it what you will."

"Are you sure?" Gertrude's chewing, finding the fish a bit tough. Feels like she is gumming a rubber football. Maybe it needed marinating longer. "We don't want to intrude."

"Not at all." Lucius has become more charming than before. Oliver growls at him slightly. Why the sudden mood change, then? Raphaella – gay? "There's plenty of room." He smiles at Oliver. "We sleep here so if you two wanted to bed down or sand bed down here," he waves his arm, points a finger, "that would be fine. En-suite bath facilities, as you can see. Constant water supply. Sea-view. Shall I show you to your room, madam? Sir?"

"This is so good of you, Betty."

Richard and Betty sit once again at the kitchen table, but the room has changed. The pretty curtains which Betty has made and hung have brightened the room. She has put flowers in a vase, plants in a window box so that they seem to smile, yellow and bright, through the glass.

"You've made such a difference to the house. To me." Richard has made himself shy by his own words, a perennial problem for him. He wants to be warm, has always had the desire to be close to people but it never seems to happen. His relationships always seems to take place through screens of glass. His late parents, Martha, his sons: none of these has been warm and intimate. Is it his fault? he asks himself almost daily. Does he shut himself out? Does he not try hard enough? Does he too easily accept defeat? It's easier with Betty. Why? Maybe because she is less educated than him, he does not know, but she is easy to be with. His eyes can meet hers. They can laugh together, though neither has that much to laugh about. They can be together, chatting, laughing, reminiscing without any uneasiness.

"I'm pleased you've come to Briar Cottage," and Richard manages not to blush or to avert his eyes.

"Me too."

"I'm meant to be helping you by finding you a home and yet it's really you who has helped me."

"How?" Betty smiles and even though her crow's feet screw up and the lines on her neck need ironing out, she looks pretty in this spring light.

"Because my life's, well, pretty crap at the moment. Parents gone, farm failing, wife vanished, one dead son and three who can barely get out of bed and be vertical and yet here I am, laughing. And that's because of you. And we don't even really know each other, do we?"

"In what way?"

"Well, where did you come from? Where have you lived? Have you a family? Who is this man you've mentioned who might come and live with you and help me on the farm?"

218

"Oh, he's just someone who I've known for years. He's had a really hard time and I thought I might be able to help him."

"All these men who you help, Betty."

"Well, not really, but I think he'd like the farm."

"Sure. Where is he now?"

" 'e's – 'e's working elsewhere. But what about you, Richard? What can I do to help you? Would you like me to speak to the boys for you?"

"No, that's for me to do."

"Have you tried talking to them?"

Richard looks up. His eyes seem brighter somehow, as if he's only just been made aware of something. "No, I haven't. You're right, Betty. We must start talking. Soon. I'm so grateful to you. You help me through."

Betty smiles: what would you think, she wonders, if I told you that I took your wife's daughter away? It was me who started all of this. Me.

"Look at the markings on these walls, Julian. Whatever we think of the way Raphaella has behaved, to think that she has made these, carved and etched these." She runs her fingers in the grooves, feels the curves, the marks. "What an incredible achievement."

Julian looks but then turns away. Gertrude laughs.

"Now come on," she says. "You never look properly. It's always a quick glimpse with you and then you turn your head. Why don't you come up close to the walls? Look carefully?"

And to her surprise, he does. Peers up close, lifts his glasses up so that nothing comes between him and the decorations.

"You're right," he says. "It is pretty extraordinary."

"And look at this, Julian, as well." He turns from the wall to look at his wife. She has slipped her dress off and is standing naked in the water. Her hair waves behind her. Her pubic hair lifts and fluffs. Her skin is pink and fresh. Her face is more beautiful than he has noticed for a while. Her body is not perfect: it is the flesh and outline of a middle-aged woman, her belly sagging slightly, her legs puckered at the thighs, but it is his wife whom he loves. And he had forgotten that.

"How about more blue here?" Raphaella points to where her mother has tentatively dabbed paint. Her movements are restricted, cautious, her paintings lacking a kind of energy, it seems to Raphaella. "I'd be inclined to leave it there. Don't overwork it."

"Thank you, Raffy." Martha stands back from her painting and admires it. She feels a deep contentment which she had, for years, only dreamed of. She is here, underwater, with her daughter and she's painting, which she wanted to do for years. What more could she hope for? Yes, sometimes she thinks of Richard and her boys but there is something lacking in her feelings towards them. They are men. Maybe she is not good with men. Maybe she was meant to be mother of a daughter and that is all. They probably do not miss her. And what of Helga and baby Samuel? Yes, Martha feels guilt for them, but they are safe now. Tucked away. And all that she needs to focus on is her painting and Raffy. All is well.

This evening, Martha lights candles. She does not say it but they are lit for her mother and her boys, all four of them and for Richard. She lights them as *yartzeit* for the dead, for her family is dead to her. Over. There is affection in her feelings for them but they are feelings for those who no longer live.

The hundred candle flames bend and falter in the water but are never extinguished. They reflect and multiply themselves in her daughter's eyes – shining and alive with light and warmth. And the water laps gently round the candles to emphasise but never to extinguish them.

Chapter
XXXVII

"Joe? Joe? Are you awake?" Richard is sitting on the edge of his son's bed. He realises, being there, that he has not been in this room for years, let alone sat beside his child as if he were a baby. For Joe is in his thirties, for God's sake. He strokes the red hair of the man who is his son, his child, the child he has forgotten to pay attention to.

"Joe? It's, it's Dad." The word leaps uncomfortably from his throat, slips through his lips as if it is alien territory. He has not been a good father, he feels, has been too busy with his farm, his own sadness, to notice the suffering of his sons.

The man stirs a little. Richard draws the curtain, then partly closes it as the sun clearly hurts his son's eyes. How debauched Joe looks; puffy in his cheeks, black circles under his eyes, his skin unhealthy and marked. Too much drinking, drugs perhaps, late nights, bad diet. He has allowed himself to decay, to deteriorate. He has not deemed his own welfare and health to be important.

"Why are you sitting here? What's up?" Joe reaches for a cup of water – God knows how many days that has been there for – and drinks. Even then, his lips look paper dry.

"I'm worried about you, Joe. I want to talk to you."

Joe pulls the covers over his shoulders. Defensive. "I'm alright."

"I don't think so. I want to say, Joe, that if you feel the time has come for you and your brothers to move on, to get jobs elsewhere, I'd understand that."

"Why? Do you want shot of us?"

Richard smiles warmly. "Not at all. But you are a grown man now. I don't want you to feel bound to me. Like you've got to stay here. I'd miss you – but I'd be OK. You mustn't stay on the farm because of guilt or duty."

"What else am I meant to do? What qualifications have I got? Friends?" He sits up now.

Richard suddenly feels, as he often does these days, a shot of anger against Martha. She has seriously let these boys down. He couldn't do it all: he had the farm to run, an income to earn. She failed them, obsessed by her own quest for her daughter, her self-centredness. She allowed one son to die and the other three to squander their talents. She took her own mother for granted. Missing her, longing for her: that's faded now. But the fury grows daily.

"Besides," says Joe, "I want to wait for Mum to return."

Tugged back from his own thoughts, Richard flinches.

"You miss her, don't you?"

Joe nods. Of course, he really misses Raphaella, her eccentricity, her touch, the smell of her. Making love to her with the lake listening outside keeping their secret. Should he tell his father? Should he tell him that the woman he is pining for – really pining for – is not Martha but Raphaella, the daughter who so obsessed his mother that she let them all down? He doesn't, steers the conversation sideways.

"Do you think that what everyone's saying is true? That Miss Turner is Mum's daughter from before she married you and that they've gone away together?"

"Well, there are other theories floating around as well. But that one seems most likely. I knew your mother had had a child before I married her. But I didn't know the effect it would have on her. On all of us."

"I wish she'd come back." Joe's eyes fill with tears. His father places his hand on his. "We need to do more to find her. We're just waiting."

The men embrace, each pitying the other. Themselves.

Gertrude turns to Julian, rests her head on his chest. They are bedded on the sand, with the water shiny through the windows and the shrimps and fish eyeing them, suspiciously. Gertrude hisses the crustaceans away, so that they don't disturb Julian. He's sleeping now, so peacefully. He has slept so well since they've been living in the water. She is so pleased, for him, for her.

Last night they made love, the first time for years. Yes, there was an awkwardness about it, like returning to a house you have not inhabited for ages and yes, she thought of all the others whom he'd entered too. But still: they are husband and wife and here they are, together, still. For they have been getting on so well the last few weeks. They spend some time with Lucius and Oliver – what lovely men – but they spend much time together. The other day, Julian gathered shells for Gertrude and arranged them for her. They swim, they talk, they eat. Their furniture has arrived now. They joke about how one room of the house is the boys' black leather and modern prints and the Turners' part, watercolours and antiques. They needed to be here. How strange life is: that their daughter's disappearance has led them to a lakeside to live with two gay chaps and to heal their marriage. She strokes Julian's chest. She is pleased to see him smile in his sleep. She does not know that he's still dreaming of Martha.

Raphaella's stomach is so big now that Martha senses the baby will come soon. Raphaella likes to feel the baby kick and turn. She feels she herself has changed. She will be a mother. She does not paint any more. She spends her days idly, happily, with her mother, awaiting the chance to be a mother herself. Sometimes she misses Joe, his thick loins and messy hair, but she knows it is simply animal lust, not anything beyond that. One could hardly have a good discussion about art with the man. And Oliver: feeble and bland in bed. She could hardly miss him. She does not change shape any more either, not a rock or fish or bird. She has found her own mother and her own motherhood and everything is calmer now. More serious. And yet something has been lost. Raphaella does not know what it is but something has gone missing. Maybe it is desire. Energy.

"But we don't feel you're doing enough."

Richard is taken back by the force of his own words. He is standing in the police station talking to the detective.

"We are, we have been, Mr Ashley," Bloor stutters. "But we don't really feel there is more we can do. It seems clear to us now that your wife has chosen – she is an adult, after all – to go and live with her daughter. You yourself confessed to me that that was her mission or quest. We launched a big campaign to try to find them. There was huge media coverage, as you know. I don't see what else we can do."

"So the case is closed, as far as you're concerned?"

"Not at all. We are still investigating, and until we find your wife and her daughter, we keep looking, but I don't see there is much more we can do. I don't know if you've heard, Mr Ashley, but it now seems that Miss Turner's parents and her art agent and gallery owner have gone too. They all seem to be in on it."

"The whole bloody world's vanishing. Do you think they're all involved in some, I don't know, fraud together or swindling?"

"It's certainly crossed my mind, but there is no evidence of that. Nothing untoward. Mr Turner retired from his legal work but there is nothing suspicious about that. He was of retirement age and all his accounts were justified and settled."

"You're asking questions all the time, Inspector. But no answers. No bloody answers at all."

Richard leaves the station and walks down the road. He sees Betty, lifts his hand to wave. She comes over.

"What ya doing here?" she asks, surprised to see Richard not on his farm. He seems out of place in this busy street, in his non-agricultural clothes. No wellies. No checked shirt. No muck on his trousers. No cows or sheep behind his shoulder.

"Oh, I've been to see the detective supposedly looking for my wife. But he's useless. Not doing a thing. I'm going to have to do more myself."

"But you've got the farm to run, Richard. You ain't a detective."

"No, I know, but I took your advice, Betty and spoke to Joe. Or rather, listened to Joe. He's more miserable about his mother going than I realised. I'm not doing enough to help him. Or the other boys. I must be more active now. We must find Martha and be a family again. The boys – we all – need her."

"I understand, Richard. I must go now. I'm, I've got an appointment." She hopes he does not know the prison is near, would not imagine that she was going there. "By the way, you know that friend I told you about? Is it alright if he moves into Briar Cottage? Soon? I can give you more rent or he, Nick is his name, he could help you on the farm."

"Yeah, that's fine, Betty. If I had more help, I could spend more time looking for Martha. I must get back. Sheep need shearing. I asked Adam and Josh to make a start but you know how unreliable they are. See you later."

"Yeah. See you, Richard. I've baked some more cakes. I'll bring them round later."

And they part, Richard to the farm, Betty to the jail: each with thoughts of their own, each aching for the other.

Chapter
XXXVIII

Oliver has seen a change in Lucius since they moved near the water. He seems lighter, happier, more sure of himself. But this morning, when the sunlight is twirling and pirouetting through the lake and all seems well, Lucius looks unhappy. He is clutching a piece of paper.

"What's the matter?" Oliver puts a hand on Lucius's shoulder.

"I've had a fax through. From Marcus. He says things are really bad in the gallery. At first, Raphaella's disappearance made people more drawn to the gallery because of our connection, but now they've sold all her work, you aren't bringing in any new painters and I'm not running it. Money is being lost daily. I don't want it to close, Oliver, not after all those years of slog and grind. I mean, I love living here and of course we're waiting for Raphaella, but we may want to return to the gallery again. When Raphaella comes, then we'll go back."

"What can we do? If she's not painting any more – or getting her paintings to us – how can we sell them? Because it's her work people really want."

"We can't get the originals. Obviously. All we can do is my initial idea: make prints of her work. They'll sell like crazy."

Oliver collapses on to the bed. "But you know she's against that. That's the main reason she ran away, apart from the media coverage. She doesn't want her work made into prints."

"You're very loyal to her, Oliver. How loyal has she been to us? At one stage, I know it's ridiculous now, I thought that you and she were lovers. I know that's not true now, but I still cannot understand your devotion to her. She didn't bother to tell you where she was going, did she? Wasn't that thoughtful – is she ever – to let you know? Yet here you are, trying to protect and defend her ideology."

"But, Lucius, that's the one thing she would hate: prints, copies, fakes."

He turns away from Lucius and looks about him – at the sham in which they live.

Richard laughs, sticks his hoe in the ground and walks towards Betty. "You've been so good for me," he says. "With all that's going on at the moment, who'd have believed that I could still laugh?"

Betty smiles. Says nothing. Richard thinks again how pretty she is. Yes, she is middle-aged. Yes, he can see the lines on her neck, but she is attractive still. He walks towards her.

"It's not that I forget about my troubles when I'm with you but they don't stop me feeling happy. You came along just at the right time."

He winds his large arms around her and she rests her head on his chest. For a moment they stand still, silent, feeling absorbed in the green fields around them, absorbed in each other. They breathe together, Richard's mouth on Betty's hair, the sun warming their necks. He wants to kiss her, has the thought that he has often, the impulse to move his head down and latch his lips on hers. But there is Martha. Not that she has felt faithful enough to him to stay with her husband, her sons, but she is his wife. She may still be there. She may still come back.

Betty takes a deep breath. "You know that friend, Nick, I told you about. Well, 'e's arriving today."

She feels his body stiffen slightly. All along she has deliberately called Nick her friend, not her lover. Not told the whole story. How can she hurt Richard? He has given her a home at low cost, made her feel happy. If she wanted, she knows she could stay there and live with him, run the farm, be happy. In some ways, Betty wishes that Nick wasn't coming to spoil their peace, but she has her duty. Somehow Nick always seems to destroy her chances. Every time.

Richard hesitates. Picks up his hoe. Goes back to his work again.

"You'll be fine. I'll be with ya." Betty looks at Nick. His face is wan, worn. "What's the matter, Nick?"

"I – I'm not ready, Betty. I told ya. I asked them if I could stay. It's peaceful here, in the chapel. But they said no. It's easier here."

Betty feels her heart stretch towards him. "But look, Nick, it's peaceful on the farm. I've got this cottage and you and me, we're gonna live in it and there's this real nice farmer, called Richard. He wants you to help him on the farm – when you're ready, that is."

"I – I'm not sure, Betty. I'm better inside. On my own, in my cell."

"No, you're not. Now come on, Nick. I know this is hard for ya, but I've got this taxi waiting and it's gonna take us home. You and me. Like it used to be." Her mind flashes back to the days when she worked for the Turners, then mounted the stairs to the attic room where she'd find Nick, stoned to high heaven and aggressive. "It's gonna be fine. You'll see."

Betty nods to the prison warder and he unlocks the great steel doors that close the jail in. A burst of sunlight leaps through the doors and nearly blinds them. It warms Betty, startles Nick. He falters. Betty helps him to the taxi and off they go.

The city soon translates its grey streets and shops into green fields, as if swapping currency. Two garages for one field. Spring seems the ideal time to release Nick, thinks Betty. Who could not be welcomed and reassured by the sight of lambs huddling up to their mothers, daffodils and forsythia flaming along the verge? She points out flowers as they go, spots a bird, tells Nick it is a chaffinch. It is as if everything has come out to greet him and she is noticing it on his behalf as they pass.

Nick remains silent. The pity in her rises to meet him. She holds his hand the whole way. Is this the same man who used to knock her around, swear at her, who killed her mother, tried to burn her house down? Life has ground him to nothing, shaken him, turned him inside out, then put a match to what was left. If there is nothing more to Betty's life, it will be this: to make Nick better than he was before – a decent, fulfilled, contented man – loving and loved.

Richard has made vegetable soup. Adam and Joshua are in their rooms, still. He feels somehow they have slipped away from him. They are shadows. But with Joe, there is still a chance. Still some hope. Some desire to find his mother. Maybe they can work together. At least, since Betty's suggestion, they have been talking.

"Great soup, Dad." Joe tears a hunk of bread and dips the corner in his bowl. "Leeks? Carrots?"

"Yeah, and onions from the far field."

"You're a good cook, you know."

"Well, only very limited, homely recipes, but if that's OK for you – great."

"You've coped well since Mum went. But that doesn't mean we should give up trying to look for her – and for Miss Turner."

"No, I agree with you. But I've given up on Inspector Bloor. He doesn't seem to be very effective. He says that your mum's an adult and that if she did find her daughter and wanted to go and live with her, that was her right. That's not a criminal offence."

"But I don't think Mum would do that, do you? I know she's had her problems, but still. And let's say he's wrong and that's something's happened to her? Is he happy to leave it like that? No, we're gonna have to do it ourselves."

Richard wants to say, how on earth are we going to do that? Where do we start? But doesn't. That's too defeatist for Joe. He wants action, answers. Richard cannot let him down.

"More soup, Joe?" he says.

Chapter
XXXIX

"Not at all," says Gertrude, handing a plate of salmon and trout to Oliver. "You've entertained us so many times. And for you, Lucius?" He nods and takes a piece.

"Amazing," says Julian, laughing. "Even underwater the woman can present a feast."

They all laugh as Gertrude hands round her platter.

She smiles at Julian. Life can be so surprising. Who would have thought that after a lifetime of living in North London, with that huge house and the staff and all the problems they've had, that they'd be happiest sitting in a lake eating shellfish with two gay men? And yet, these past few weeks have been great. Lucius and Oliver have given them their space, time, and sometimes they eat together, sometimes apart. And she and Julian have been making love, with contentment and respect if not passion, every night. She and Julian, united. And he seems happier since they came here. He's lost weight, started smiling, looking at her with love when she'd given up every hope of that happening. Thank you, lake, she mutters. That was the answer, after all.

Although Raphaella is happy with her mother, she thinks a lot about the future. Will they stay here for ever? What about when the baby is born? And her shape-changing and painting: will they return?

Martha seems happier than her daughter. She is at peace. She is painting. Up until now her life has been a sham, a role-play-mother to boys who don't connect with her; wife to a man who is good but uninspiring; living on a remote farm, pining for her daughter. This is not pretend now; this is real and it is genuine. If guilt about Richard ever enters her head, she lights another candle for him and embraces her daughter.

"I think that's an excellent idea. What's more, I'll give it financial backing, if you think it's a risk."

"You will?" Lucius smiles his thanks to Julian.

"I don't know about this," says Oliver, yanking a piece of squid from between his teeth. "Raphaella expressly said that she did not want her work made into prints."

"Why ever not?" Gertrude looks indignant.

"It's complicated. She believed – believes – that paintings should exist in the original only and nothing else. Not be reproduced. Duplicated. That art is a one-off."

"Typical Raphaella." Gertrude rolls her eyes. "Why be easy if you can be difficult?"

"No, I don't think that's fair. They are her paintings after all. Surely she has some say as to how they are treated?"

"Not if she buggers off," says Julian. "Did she leave any paperwork? Documentation?"

Lucius shakes his head. "Right then. Let's get on with it. Fax your office today and let's get going. I like the idea of doing business underwater. Therapeutic."

Lucius looks from Julian to Oliver: smile to frown.

Richard looks out of the kitchen window towards Briar Cottage. Betty has put out two chairs and she and her friend are sitting in the sunshine. Richard is washing up, carries on cleaning plates, but looking as he does so. Slowing down his motions. Betty has not been to see Richard for days. How he has missed her gestures of friendship, her smile, her laugh. Who is this mysterious friend of hers? She has said so little about him. He looks ill. Maybe he is dying. Betty is so kind, she would help anyone. Somehow Richard can't imagine him working on the farm. Not with hunched shoulders and a weak frame like that. Pulling up a cabbage would probably kill him.

"Feel the sun on your face," says Betty. "Close your eyes and feel it."

Nick obeys. Betty smiles faintly. The last few days have not been easy, not because Nick has been his old self, aggressive and hostile, but the opposite, in fact: pale, passive, barely awake, hardly alive. She feels she is controlling a puppet, not helping a man to readjust to life outside prison. He has changed since he left jail, as if he felt safe in there, threatened out here. It frightens her. Will he ever recover? Will she be able to help him?

From where she sits, Betty can see Richard at his kitchen window of the farmhouse. She would like to see him but does not feel she can leave Nick. Does not trust him. What would he do? Sometimes he mutters about God, about Jesus. One evening, he said he didn't want to live. She must not, cannot, let him down. She lifts her hand to wave to Richard. He waves back. Just once. She turns to look at Nick.

"I don't know. What's the bloody point of us being here? Can't understand it," says Matt.

"Me neither." Micky lights up a fag, hands one to Matt. "Just to get an occasional shot of movement underwater. Who cares about that? I don't reckon that loony painter's coming back, do you?"

"Nah, not now. Either someone's topped 'er or she's decided she ain't returning. What 'ave we gotta wait 'ere for then?"

"In case she comes, the boss says. I've told him what I think, but he says stay put. Damn boring it is, too."

"So there's four of 'em now, isn't there? The parents of the loony and those two arty poofters."

"That's it? Whoever next, I wonder. A stripper and a kangaroo?"

"At least."

"So far as you're concerned, it's closed?" Richard is surprised by the anger in his own voice. Maybe Joe's persistence and pleading for his father to take action is having some effect on him.

"No, Mr Ashley." Detective Inspector Bloor tries to keep his voice steady. This two-woman vanishing trick has given him strife. He doesn't like failure. Untidy in his books. Enquiry still continuing. "No case is closed until it is solved. But in the sense that we are no longer looking for anyone else connected with the disappearance of your wife and Miss Turner, you are correct. I don't think there is much more I can do. I'm sorry."

"What did he say, Dad?" Joe looks up from the table.

"Nothing helpful. I think we're going to have to go and look for your mother ourselves. Do you think Adam and Josh will come, too?"

"Yeah. I reckon. All this waiting's got to them. I'll have a word."

Richard waits, steps outside the farmhouse, can hear his sons talking in low voices upstairs. He feels there is nothing here to remain for: Betty is keeping her distance. A few times recently he has waved to her, tried to catch her eye from far away, but each time she turns away and looks at Nick. As if Richard needed more rejections. And as for that waif-like figure helping on the farm. What a joke. A boiled turnip would probably be more help. Why is he waiting? What does he expect to happen?

235

Richard opens the door and surveys his farm. He smiles sardonically to himself. At his hopes so many years ago when he thought that this farm would be his passport to success. It's been a passport to hell instead. Perhaps people had been right to be wary of Martha, already a mother. He hadn't seen the dangers. Had seen the farm as having potential. Yes, it had potential. Potential disaster. Losing money rapidly, losing his wife, his parents, his mother-in-law, his baby son, real contact with two of his remaining sons.

Richard turns. At the base of the stairs, his three sons are standing in a line. The rucksacks on their backs are packed.

Chapter
XL

"Hey, watch out. Spoke too soon."

As if in a dance, Matt and Micky stub out their cigarettes on the sand and get ready to aim their cameras. Walking towards them are a middle-aged man and three younger men.

"What's this?" Matt. "The red-haired army?"

For the matching hair colour of the four men makes them undeniably related – father and sons.

"We're looking for the two women who've disappeared." Richard answers their questions before they've asked them. Sometimes he's surprised by his own forcefulness these days. He speaks his mind and strength seems to prevail. As the men walk towards Lemon Cottage, Matt and Micky snap away, pleased to have something to send their newspaper editor rather than endless pictures of a static lake with a sand-dome sticking out of it.

"Yeah. Four blokes, one older than the rest." Matt's on the phone to the paper. Micky can see from his face that the editor's pleased. "Yeah. We'll get them sent right over. Thanks, guv."

Satisfied, the men light up again and position themselves on the sand.

Inside Lemon Cottage, the four men quietly gaze around. White walls, sofas, jars filled with white objects. Studio with neatly stacked paintings – some half-finished – against the wall. It is ages since Richard was here: he remembers the mysterious, yet strangely alluring girl to whom he was attracted. Little did he know then that she was Martha's daughter. Clearly, he smiles to himself, I'm drawn to those dark-haired difficult women – mysterious, problematic. Joe looks around, a lump swelling in his throat. How he and Raphaella made love with passion and fire on those sofas, that floor. How he misses the skin of her, the smell of her, being next to her, being inside her. He says nothing; thinks plenty. Adam and Josh walk around as if spellbound. Don't comment or wonder, just look. Where is their creativity? Richard wonders. Their curiosity? What has happened to these boys who were bright and colourful once? What has their mother – life – done to them?

Martha is happier than ever before. She has no intention of leaving what she has now found: her daughter, her water, her voice. She paints, sure that what she has discovered is more than she had before. Raphaella, increasingly restless, looks enviously at her mother. This contentment, she feels, is non-productive, non-creative. It is static: taking her nowhere. She does not paint any longer, change shape any longer, unless one could call her swelling belly the changing of her shape.

"What is it, Raffy?" Her mother plaits Raphaella's hair with water-weed and strokes her large stomach. "The baby will come soon. Do not fret."

But Raphaella knows now that her satisfaction in fooling others has been short-lived. The novelty has gone. She has to move forward. The baby, yes. And then what next? She feels that rather than the water releasing something within her as it seems to have done for Martha, it has diluted her. She has been dissolved in it, become nebulous – been lost.

And then, one evening, as mother and daughter sit on their white sofas, listening to the news and listening to the familiar report – six weeks now and still no sign of the missing mother and daughter, farmer's wife and painter – there's something else. Just as Raphaella is about to turn off, there come the words that knock her: the failing London gallery which discovered Raphaella Turner is now making mass prints of her work. For sale... Phone this number.

Her work. For prints? How could they? Oliver and Lucius? They knew how she felt about it. That was part of the reason she disappeared. Her paintings should only exist in the original, can only be seen in their first form. They knew that. Know that. Tears fill Raphaella's eyes and slip away into the water. Martha embraces her. You do not understand, thinks Raphaella. You do not have the intellect to understand.

And yet there is something about her mother's touch that warms Raffy; the stroke on her arm that she wants, she needs. She has a mother, Martha, nurturer.

"To our new business deal!" Julian raises his glass and the others clink his and echo: "Business deal! Congratulations!"

"Who would have thought that even here, in the lake in the middle of nowhere, for God's sake, I'd be making money?"

"Well, a good businessman is good wherever he is."

Oliver has never seen Lucius this happy. He has started disliking him, feeling that his happiness stems from other people's misery. Lucius's belief that Raphaella is gay and therefore Oliver faithful; his deal with Julian which he knows Oliver and Raphaella will dislike. Maybe there is malice in him. Maybe he is actually rather loathsome. And yet Gertrude, whom Oliver disliked intensely when he had that mad idea to write his biography of her daughter, he rather likes now. In a way, she is the mother he never had: warm, maternal, caring. Being here in the water has changed everything: perceptions, feelings, hopes.

And while Lucius and Julian congratulate each other and themselves, Gertrude senses Oliver's discomfort.

"What's the matter?" she says, sharing a seat with him.

"I feel uneasy about this print business. Raphaella won't like it."

"But she's not here, is she? She doesn't care what we're all going through." Then, sensing that her words have brought him no comfort: "I care about her, too. She's my daughter. I've always encouraged her painting. How do you think I feel? But I want to support Julian. And I feel that your loyalty is to Lucius. We must help our loved ones, mustn't we? Come on, let's cheer up, hey? I've a few shrimps left over. I saved them just for you."

And she takes him by the hand and feeds him shrimps from the shell and he wants to put his head on her chest, close his eyes and call her Mother.

"It doesn't feel as if she intended to go."

Richard is sitting in the living room of the woman he used to deliver fruit and veg to and they are discussing her vanishing. Who would have thought it? Well, only Joe and Richard are talking. Adam and Josh say very little, apart from asking for food or wondering what time it is.

"It's the way so many of her paintings are half-finished." Joe pauses, looks to his dad.

"I don't know." Richard. "Everything's very tidy. Stacked away."

"But she always was orderly, wasn't she? We're all assuming she has left through her own free will but maybe she was taken. Against her will. Maybe Mum was too. By some strange religious sect or something."

Richard hears the passion in his son's voice. Again he wonders: could it be that Joe is missing Miss Turner more than his mother? Was there something in that relationship? He says nothing, puts his hand on his son's shoulder.

Adam and Josh are by the window, staring out as they seem to always, but this time Richard notices Adam nudging his brother.

"What is it, Adam? Joe?"

Richard and Joe rush to the window. There, in the fading sunlight, is a dome jutting out on the far side of the lake. It appears to be made of sand. It seems to beckon them. Somehow, within that dome, the answers lie. The resolution. Richard winds his arms around his three sturdy sons and smiles.

Chapter
XLI

"No," says Matt, lighting up. "You won't be the first. So far there's been two men going in together, if you get my drift," he winks, "and then this posh pair, weren't they, Micky?"

"Yeah, that's right. You see there's this passageway there," pointing, "and that leads through, I assume, to that dome."

"I see." Richard has taken out beer to the men. It is his way of saying thank you for leaving them alone, not hounding them. Yes, they took some pictures when they first arrived but since then, nothing. Drinking beer, and then Adam and Josh share their fag supply with them, the six men sit on the sand and chat, gazing out to the lake as they speak.

"Have you been in there?" Richard asks. Both men shake their heads.

"The day the boss asks me to do that, I'll quit the job." Micky nods his agreement. "Nah. All we're meant to do is stay 'ere and watch the comings and goings in the cottage and in the lake. That's all. And send the piccies back when we've taken 'em. Isn't that right, Micky?"

Micky nods. "You're not going in the water with ya camera. It'll ruin it."

"And yet," Matt helps himself to more beer, "they go in fully clothed, you know, and their furniture and stuff goes with them."

"No!" Joe.

"Yeah. Honest. It's like they move in there. There's a removal company what specialises in underwater work."

"Do you know who they are, the people already in there?" Richard.

"Nah, but the boss, he reckons they're all connected with the loony painter woman." Joe flinches. "That they're all waiting for her."

"I reckon," says Micky, "that they're all part of one of them strange cults, you know, like religious nutters and they've made a temple there. A shrine, if you know what I mean."

"Still wanna go?" asks Matt, and they all laugh, and so they pass the night eating and smoking by the side of the lake where they eventually fall asleep beneath the stars. And next morning, when the sun comes up, the four men say goodbye and begin their journey.

Betty works in her little kitchen garden, cutting herbs, weeding. The last week has been tough. Yes, she can see signs of improvement with Nick but it has been slow, will continue to be so. He is gaining physical strength, with all her good home cooking and plenty of sleep and fresh air. She is hoping that soon she will be able to get him working with Richard on the farm. That will help them both: Richard could do with some support, and it will make Nick feel better about himself. Besides, she thinks they will get on well.

But it is not quite time for that, yet. Nick is on the way to recovery but he's not there yet. Prison life has knocked the insides out of him. What worries Betty more, she thinks, pulling the brown bits off her parsley, is his mental state. He's not the way he used to be. She's pleased the aggression has gone but there is something else in its place and it's disturbing. He mutters in his sleep about God and Jesus and talks of being saved. Yet he is depressed, without hope. His new-found faith, if it really is that, is not a comfort to him but a source of anguish. What is more, he does not seem to respond to things the way Betty had hoped he would: the trees, the baby lambs, woolly and white as if newly washed in the fields, the buttercups, seem to draw no reaction from him. It is as if something within him has died. Betty tries to be brave and cheerful but she wonders if she has the power to resurrect him.

And there's something else on her mind: she did not know how much she liked – maybe loved – Richard until now. Even while she's with Nick, being nurse and carer, she finds herself gazing towards the farmhouse to look for Richard. My duty lies with Nick, she thinks, walking into Briar Cottage and looking for him. He is slumped in an armchair sleeping, as he does much of the time.

Maybe she will just go and see Richard. It seems rude to neglect him. Maybe he is hurt? She covers Nick with a blanket and tiptoes out to the farmhouse. Richard is not there. She walks down to the fields, to the orchard, but he is nowhere to be seen. No machinery is moving. Neither he nor his lads are anywhere. Betty shivers. The sun has suddenly gone in.

Richard, Joe, Adam and Josh are swim-walking through the tunnel which leads to the sand-dome. When they arrive, what they see is a massive sand structure. It is full of tiny windows, cut out of the walls as if with a pastry cutter. The walls are etched and decorated. It is incredible: a palace, a temple, a magical castle.

They turn the corner, enter the dome, and they see two men sitting on one black sofa, and an older couple on the other. They are drinking wine and cracking water-snails open with their teeth.

"Oh look," laughs Lucius, "the party's getting bigger."

"Hi," says Richard, wondering if that's the right thing to say when you gatecrash someone else's party under a lake. "Didn't mean to barge in on you –"

"Not at all," says Lucius, so cheerful these days that it makes Oliver cringe. "Do come and join us. D'you know everybody?"

As introductions are made and wine poured for Richard and his sons, each realises the connection between the others and Raphaella. Yes, thinks Richard. You are the man who slept with my wife to get your wife a child. Yes, thinks Gertrude. You are the man who is married to the woman who is my daughter's mother. Yes, thinks Joe. You are the man who I thought was also sleeping with Miss Turner. You were often there when I showed up. But now I see you are gay so maybe I was wrong. And in this way, the evening continues, drinking, understanding, seeing more clearly if not completely.

"But of course you must stay," says Lucius, flamboyantly. "There's plenty of room for us all. Gertrude and Julian are over there, and we are here, but there is that whole wing there. We will all wait for Raphaella and Martha together."

"You've got to be joking." Detective Inspector Bloor sinks into his chair in the police station. "What? Has the whole bloody world gone missing?"

"I don't know." Betty sits too, uninvited but feeling as flabbergasted as the Inspector. Bloor opens a screwtop jar, takes two tablets and washes them down with a glass of water. He offers the jar to Betty. She takes two as well and swallows them whole. What is this, she thinks? A police investigation or a self-help group for those who are near collapse?

"Are you sure?"

245

"Yes. I've been going to the farmhouse every day, knocking on the door, and looking in the fields. They've gone, all of them, Richard Ashley and his three sons."

"Maybe they're on holiday or having a little break somewhere?"

"Never. Richard wouldn't leave his animals and all his farming, like. There's something suspicious 'ere, Inspector."

"Something? The whole thing's bleeding suspicious. First, the painter and farmer's wife, then the art agent and gallery owner, followed by the parents of the artist, now the farmer and his three sons. What on earth is going on?"

"I don't know. You're the detective, in't you?"

"Am I? I'm beginning to wonder what the hell I am. This case is quite beyond me. I need a break. I've been doing this job too long."

"What have these people got in common? Are they working together?"

"Could be. I've heard that the gallery is doing very well indeed. Huge increase in their profits. Maybe they're all in business together?"

"Not Richard. Never."

"Or part of some sect?"

"No. That doesn't make sense either."

"Or she, Miss Turner's luring them somewhere and that's where they never return from."

Betty nods; a possibility.

"But somehow the gallery is still operating. How?" The inspector seems to have recovered. His anxiety has transformed itself into curiosity and enthusiasm for this case. "I'll solve it," he says, jumping up. "Do excuse me."

Betty smiles. That's the inspector revived. Now it's back to Nick.

246

Chapter
XLII

Morning. And when Richard and the boys awake in their part of the sandworld, the sun is dripping spiral honey through the water. Richard wakes first, looks around him at the carved walls, the water gently lapping against the building. He wonders what he is doing there, where Martha is, what he has led his boys into. For the previous evening, although Lucius was friendly and invited them to stay, there was tension in the air. Martha never spoke to Richard about her baby born when she was unmarried (she never spoke to him at all, really) but since her disappearance he has fitted together the pieces. Learned more about her in her absence than when she was there. Though, in truth, she was never really there. She was always absent, a million miles away, even when they lay beside each other, back to back in bed. So it's clear to Richard, after only one evening, that Julian, that pompous, arrogant man actually slept with Martha and yet the wife seems to adore him still. And that gay pair, they've been involved with the financial dealings of Miss Turner. And yet it seems more and more likely that she is the daughter of Martha, after all. Why didn't Martha tell him that? He could have ended up having an affair with the daughter of his wife. And he wouldn't have known. She wouldn't have told him. Anger mounts in Richard: he has tried his best, yet he has been kept in the dark. Secrets have not been disclosed to him. He feels, suddenly, as if he has been treated like a fool. The dumb farmer. Not worth confiding in.

Joe wakes and says nothing, just smiles kindly at his father. Maybe he senses his confusion. His anger. He, too, feels bemused and dazed by what has happened, by the cobweb of relationships around him. The way that his life seems to be linked with people whom he does not know. Did that stuck-up bloke last night have a child with his mother? And that dark-haired gay chap – wasn't he often at Raphaella's house when he arrived with the delivery? And if Raphaella is really his mother's child, has he been sleeping with his half-sister?

Joe and Richard sit together and gaze around the sandworld. To their surprise they see, through the tiny windows, Adam and Josh in the water beyond. Usually sleeping late in the morning, the boys are up and dancing, swimming in the water. Richard and Joe can barely believe it but there they are, two grown men laughing and splashing each other as if, as if, they have suddenly been transformed.

"To think that she married that farmer," says Julian. He and Gertrude are lying awake and watching the light filter through the windows. Gertrude has her head on her husband's chest.

"He's rather simple, isn't he?"

"Well, she grew up on a farm and was a cleaning girl. She wasn't going to marry a genius now, was she?"

Gertrude knows that when they talk of Martha, the girl she has not seen for many years, she insults her, but to no avail. What is the point in constantly being rude about a woman whom your husband clearly loves? And yet she cannot help herself. Even lying beside her husband now she wants to criticise the girl for maybe, just maybe, it will turn him against her. For to love someone who really loves someone else is painful.

That's not quite the thought that Oliver has, lying beside Lucius and watching the light fragment the water into angular sections. But that man who arrived last night. Oliver instantly recognised him as the man who ostensibly came to deliver fruit and veg, for God's sake, but was clearly Raphaella's lover. He could see it in her eyes, the yearning, the excitement when he arrived, compared to the polite coolness of her glances towards Oliver. No one can disguise that. It's real. Just as Lucius looks at him with love that Oliver cannot reciprocate.

"I feel rather sorry for that husband of Martha's, don't you?" Lucius stretches himself awake, puts his arm on Oliver's.

"Why's that?"

"Well, his wife has left him, he's got these three no-hopers for sons and what's he supposed to do? I think we should let them stay here if they want to."

Great, thinks Oliver. All I need is that lover of Raphaella's living around here. But, of course, he says nothing. How can hc?

Later, Oliver and Gertrude talk.

"I don't really want those four men here, either," says Gertrude.

"Why's that?" Oliver. Gertrude hesitates. "Come on," smiles Oliver. "I'm not going to write a book about Raphaella. I won't reveal any secrets."

She relaxes. "Martha and Julian slept together so that I could have a child. We were unable to."

"I see. Did you agree to that?"

"Yes, but I still feel uncomfortable about it. Of course there was no IVF then."

"But you had Charlotte later?"

249

"I know. It's strange. I couldn't fall pregnant for years and then two years after Raphaella came to live with us as my daughter, I did conceive."

"That was a long time ago, Gertrude."

"I know, but having Richard here when he's married to Martha and with his sons: it is all a reminder, brings it back again. Why don't you want them here?"

How can Oliver tell her about how he loves Raphaella, more now that she's gone than when she was here? He cannot, will not.

"It's just an intrusion, I suppose. I was getting used to the four of us being here together, waiting for Raphaella and now they're here. But Lucius says we should be kind."

"Well, if Lucius says that, so will Julian. Since their new deal, they're like this." She twists one finger around another, looks across to where Julian and Lucius are scanning the latest fax, nodding their heads in agreement.

By the evening of that day, the Ashleys' furniture has arrived. Neatly divided into three sections, the sandworld has one area of elegant settees and watercolours, another of black sofas and modern prints and now a third: farmhouse cottage curtains (which Betty made) to keep the light out of the tiny windows and floral settees, homely prints. And so the three factions remain, not in total harmony and ease, waiting for Raphaella.

"Now," says Inspector Bloor, chewing his tablets, "let's go through this once more."

Matt and Micky have lit up fags, stand listening to the police chap rambling on.

"You say that first, two men went in together."

"Yeah," says Micky. "Very together, if you get my drift."

"I see," says Bloor, not at all sure that he does.

"And then the Turners, the parents supposedly of –"

"The loony painter woman, we call her," Matt interjects.

"Raphaella Turner, yes. And now you tell me that four red-haired men have gone in?"

"Yes, they have." Micky.

"OK, now this ties in with what Miss Tattersall told me. That Martha's husband, the farmer and his three sons have all left the farm. And tell me, gentlemen, when these folk go through the water, do they return?"

"Nah. Never."

"So we have no way of knowing whether they are alive or not?"

"Well," offers Micky, " they do get their stuff sent in but it's true, you never see them again."

"I see." The inspector chews some more tablets, feels his head. It's burning again. The strain of this job. Why couldn't he have chosen something easier to do as a profession like naked wrestling or flying to the moon? The boss is really going to believe him back at the station when he tells him that these people are all going into the lake and never reappearing. There'll be great jeers about the Loch Ness monster and allsorts. No, there has to be another answer. What is drawing them into the lake? What is keeping them there? Are any of them still alive? Somehow, thinks Bloor, thanking the men and allowing them to take snaps of him before getting in the car, I will solve this.

251

Chapter
XLIII

"Look." Betty is standing with Nick outside the abandoned farmhouse. "The animals are dying. They're hungry, like. The plants need watering. I don't know where Richard is or why he has left this farm which he loves but we must, we must 'elp him. Can you 'elp me to do that, Nick?"

Nick stands by Betty's side and looks out, does not see what she sees. Says nothing.

"Come on," she says, pulling him by the arm.

All morning he trails behind her, a shadow, while she takes the grain and feeds the hens, sweeps the stench-filled sty out, uses the massive hoses and just about manages to water some of the fields. Nick does little: just about holds the hose, broom, bucket if she hands it to him but his grasp is weak, his speech almost non-existent and his help minimal. Some of the animals have died but even this seems not to move him: he occasionally mutters about Jesus or God but his prayers do not transform themselves into actions. By the end of the morning, Betty is exhausted and sits down on a hay bale and sobs. Why has Richard left her? Why has he done this? She hopes, waits, for Nick's comforting hand, his arm on her shoulder. It does not come.

"I think we ought to get more of the rainbow series done as prints." Lucius and Julian are having one of their business meetings. These have become frequent now, and usually take place in the morning. They sit on Lucius's black sofa, poring over spreadsheets and faxes and recent e-mails, congratulating themselves and each other on the amazing

252

success they've had. Raphaella Turner's paintings were in demand anyway, but since her disappearance, the chance of owning one of her prints has taken the public by storm. And is it the mystique, perhaps, which excites them: the painter, gallery owner and business partner are all absent? Doing deals with those who have gone? Certainly the media storm has never stopped thundering, helped along by Matt and Micky's photos and many news items, featuring the faces of the main stars and the miserable face of Inspector Bloor, enduring another grilling.

And in the mornings, when Julian and Lucius discuss money, Gertrude and Oliver sit and are mother and son: talking, laughing, eating together. But now this rhythm has changed. Since Richard and sons arrived last week, nothing is the same.

"It feels different," Gertrude complains to Oliver one morning. They are sitting in Gertrude's part of the sandworld, where elegance and antique furniture meet. "I wish those men would leave. I feel they are critical of us. It makes me feel uneasy."

"I know what you mean, but Lucius won't listen. He says they want Martha to return as much as we want Raphaella to and they are entitled to stay."

"He's very kind, Lucius, isn't he?"

"Yes, he always was but not quite like this. This philanthropy is new, I'd say. It's as if he's changed."

"I understand. I can see the same alteration in Julian. Do you think it's because of this business deal of theirs?"

"I don't know. It may sound odd but I think it's because of the water."

Not very far away, Richard is having the same thought. He is watching Adam and Josh swimming, laughing, enjoying themselves in a laddy but pleasant way, each grabbing the other's foot, imitating the fish which flick past. Since they have arrived here, Richard feels as if something has been released in them. There is a happiness, a new joy from within. And there is no drink here, no opportunity for drugs and late nights and bad company.

Joe notices it too. He comments to his dad as they sit in their farmhouse part of the sandworld.

"You know, Dad, I've never seen Josh and Adam so happy."

"I see what you mean." He laughs at his sons' antics, grabbing each other by the waist and swimming off. "I wish I felt as comfortable here. As welcome."

"In what way?"

"Well, that Lucius chap is OK in that he's made us fairly welcome, and Julian obviously agrees with him on everything, but Oliver's looking at us strangely and as for Gertrude – I don't think she really wants us here. And I just can't believe that Julian and your mother would have had a child together. Why on earth would Martha have agreed to that? He's much older than her."

"You should have told us about her child, Dad. We knew nothing about her until all this came out."

"I know, but your mother never spoke about it. Her. She kept her quiet. I mean, I knew when we got married but she never wanted to discuss it and I felt it was OK to let it pass."

Your usual way, thinks Joe. Keep it low, don't make a fuss. The problem is that I've been sleeping with my mother's daughter, my half-sister. How do you think that makes me feel?

"I know, sir." Bloor is standing (he has not been invited to sit) reporting to his big chief about his progress, or lack of it, on the Turner case. "It must sound ridiculous to you, but this is the honest truth. They all go into the lake and never come back again."

"All of them? So, let me see, the painter and a farmer's wife; the painter's parents (so-called); an art agent and a gallery owner; and now a farmer and his three sons. How does the song go? E-i-e-i-o. Or shall we sing the farmer wants a wife? Eh? They've all just gone into the lake and vanished?"

"That's right. It must sound preposterous –"

"It does –"

"But that's the way it is. There are two cameramen on the shore. They can vouch for it too."

"Handy way of getting rid of a case, isn't it, Bloor? Just say they've gone into a lake and vanished. What about the other cases you're working on at the moment? Hole in the ground? Gap in the sky?"

"Honestly, sir."

"I'll honestly sir you, my friend. What was that request you made about early retirement and a good pension? Not until this case is sewn up tight and sewn up good."

"But sir, the stress, the worry. I'm getting these pains in my chest –"

"Are you? What a shame." Voice rising. "Well, you'll get a bloody bigger pain in your face unless you SOLVE THIS BLOODY CASE. Now go!"

Outside his room, Bloor takes two tablets and pants. Please God, he mutters. Let those people return.

That evening, in an attempt to be friendly, Lucius and Julian invite Richard and sons round to their elegant part of the sandworld. There is a definite unease in the air: polite conversation and awkward stares. Richard at Julian: were you really the father of my wife's child? Joe at Oliver: were you just Raphaella's agent or lover as well?

And the staring and the interrogating eyes make the atmosphere tense. So that in spite of Lucius passing the trout and salmon platter round and more wine being brought in by Julian than anyone can manage, there is a discomfort which does not fade all evening.

And then the candles burn.

Raphaella has had enough of the water. It has been too long, this feeling of sogginess, sensing the water in her hair, her eyes. Making companions of the fish. And it's not just that. It is good to have Martha here. Martha. Mother. To feel that there is a connection with someone else and to be stroked and touched but Martha is different to the woman she thought she knew. Martha is motherly, strokes Raffy's stomach and talks through her daughter's skin to the baby, but there will not be intellectual excitement with Martha. Issues, discussions begin with Martha but they do not really develop. And it's the same with her painting. Raphaella will encourage her, try to take her beyond the obvious, the easy, but it may never go anywhere. But does it matter? Her painting will fulfil one part of her; her mother another.

Yet, what has happened to Raphaella? Without the painting, without her shapes, without her cottage and the jars and the lake and the studio, there is nothing. She has reduced her life so far that there is nothing left. And as for this baby and this massive stomach which she has to hold in front of her. When will the baby come? Will she want it anyway? Will the love come?

It is not that she feels much for any of those people from whom she has run (although she misses Joe's loins) but what is she without them? Without those to fight against and resent, what is she? She feels that she has become the water itself, worse than the water. At least that has form, has movement, has shape. And no one is imitating it as they are copying her paintings. And from now on, that will be how she exists, will be perceived: through cheap prints of her work which do no justice to her colour, her strokes; through a baby, and reflected through the water with no form or figure at all. Watered down.

And what of those people whom she resents and misses, despises and maybe even loves? Were they tricked and lured to the sham sandworld the way that she had hoped and plotted?

And it is that night, after Martha has again interpreted Raphaella's mood as fear about the birth, and has fallen asleep on her daughter's white sofa, that Raphaella, heavily pregnant, swims away. It is odd to swim when pregnant: the usual buoyancy and support of the water is challenged by this downward pull. And yet it carries her: and as Raphaella swims away from the original she sees the reflections, the undersides of irises and water-lilies which make the water seem an ally rather than a weight.

It is a long way to the other place, the other world which she and her mother built with the aim of deceiving. Several times on the journey, Raphaella stops to rest, leaning on rocks or letting her heavy weight settle on the sand bed for repose, for respite.

And then she spots it: the sham, the fake, the deceiver. And it is more beautiful than she remembers it but clearly not the original, the one that she and Martha inhabit. There is something about its angle, its shape, its decorations that remind her of its inauthenticity. It was the afterthought, the shadow, the imitation. And yet, there is something lovely about it. It does not make the same claims as the first, is bashful, modest even, in its expectations.

Swimming up to its windows, Raphaella hears noise and laughter. It is dark now in the water, bright inside the building, and there she sees many people gathered together eating and drinking. She knows most of them: her (alleged) parents, Joe with his father, Martha's husband and their other sons and Oliver and Lucius. And are they gathered there because of her? Maybe they care for her more than she had realised? Maybe it is a surprise party and all they are waiting for is her?

She could so easily call through the windows, enter in, be welcomed. But would she be well-received? And would they be loving her as the artist or the daughter, lover or friend? She thrills at the sight of Joe, feels repulsed by the Turners, angry at Lucius and Oliver who have done what she requested they should not.

And what would she do if she did go in? Be warm to some and attack others?

She hesitates by the window. Tries to listen in. Once, she thinks she hears her name. Someone laughs. A phone rings. There is music. If they are waiting for her, she could surprise them all.

And it's there, pausing, wondering, that Raphaella feels the first pangs in her stomach – a pulling, a contraction. The baby – her baby – is coming. She will return to Martha. It is a sign.

But before she leaves, she takes her hundred candles and places them in jars outside the sandworld. And she lights them, one by one, so that the water curves around the glass and the flickering flames, but docs not quench the fire. Then, after looking one more time at the circle of candles, the sandworld, the people and the light within, she swims away.

It is Oliver who spots the candles first. They are deep in conversation, not wholly easy, not totally without tension as each looks questioningly at the other. Julian and Richard have landed up together and Richard, with the courage which seems to be his companion more and more these days, asks Julian why? Why did he have a child with Martha? Julian answers placatingly, in his judge's voice. Because we discussed it. My wife could not fall pregnant. Yes, yes Richard knows that. But why did Martha do it? Was she tricked? No. Were they lovers? No. Was there money involved? No. Why then? Why? And as Richard gets more frustrated and confused and wonders why he is there with a man who may be a rapist or trickster, Oliver leaps up and points:

"Look out there. Look at those candles. They are a sign. A sign from Raphaella."

"He's right." Lucius. "That is a real Raphaella sign."

"You think she's near here?" Julian.

"Yes." Oliver. "And she wants us to wait for her."

The journey back is harder than the outward swim for Raphaella. Her stomach contracts as she goes, pulling, tightening, as if a belt is being fastened around her middle which she cannot release. Several times she has to stop and rest, rub her stomach, wondering what the pain would be like if she were not in water. At one point, she wonders if she can carry on. Maybe she should have gone into the sham sandworld with the certainty that the father would be there. And what a lot of help would have been on hand. But she couldn't be sure of her reception. Maybe they would have been ready to kill – not greet – her.

She feels drawn back, though, even with this question mark. Drawn back more than pulled forward to Martha, to her real world.

It is late when she returns. The candles have shrunk from sight and leaving behind the light, she reaches darkness. Darkness and Martha. The older woman lies asleep on the sand bed, her arm over her face.

Raphaella collapses with exhaustion, the contractions close now. Martha embraces her, unaware that she had gone, and feels instantly the movement in her daughter's stomach as if it is her own. She rubs her daughter's back, supports her on the sandbed, helps her as best she can, remembering Helga and how she had helped her. Raphaella cries out, cries out again. Martha cries with her, holds her, loves her.

It is the early hours of the morning when Raphaella's child is born.

Chapter
XLV

Martha rubs Raffy's back, her stomach, her feet. Anything she can do to make the delivery easier, she does, all the while reliving her own giving birth to Raffy nearly forty years earlier. How she instantly loved the tiny child. How she had to hand her over as if she had been a ticket to a bus conductor. Well, Raffy will not have to hand her child over, thinks Martha. This baby will be with its mother. Grandmother. She thinks back to Helga. She lost her granddaughter too.

Raphaella cries out, spreads her legs on the sand bed. Pushes. Cries.

Raphaella is pushing now. Although the water eases the contractions, she can still feel them tightening and releasing her. A mild torture. Whose child will this be, she wonders? And will she know? Given the choice between the red-haired bestiality of Joe and the dark-haired refinement of Oliver, she hopes it will be Oliver. Joe is a beast, a field-dweller; Oliver is refined, an aesthete. What a father to have, gentle and responsive.

"You're doing so well," urges Martha. "Push a bit more, Raffy. My girl."

Raphaella's mildly annoyed by her mother's platitudes. They're too obvious, too easy. It seems to her that Martha always takes the easy option with language, with painting. It's not original enough, not hard enough. She takes the short cut. And so as Raphaella becomes a mother, she distances herself from her own mother, separating from her. The time of plaiting hair is over.

Raphaella's baby girl has soft dark hair. It is fine and wet. Martha strokes her head, not knowing that this could be the child of her son and daughter. Martha instantly loves her as she did not love her sons but loved, and still loves, her only daughter. Her affection has been reserved for the female progeny. She cries and strokes the head of the child, suckling now at her mother's swollen breast.

Raphaella looks down at the child and sees a shape: intriguingly tiny fingers and toes, a soft moist head, curled up body, a flower not yet opened. And she sees Oliver in the baby, a dark-haired beauty.

Martha feels love oozing from her. Raphaella does not feel love. Just tiredness and curiosity but also mild resentment. These breasts had previously been her own. Now a little limpet is draining milk from them. Increasingly, it seems to Raphaella, her life is not her own. Her painting, home, freedom, and now milk have been stolen. Usurped. She has been dissolved in the water like a soluble tablet and, whereas the water appears to have defined Martha, it may have drowned Raphaella. And yet, this is something, someone who she wants. Tiny eyelashes curl upon the baby's cheek. Her mouth is a little o. She is my shape, thinks Raffy, the shape of Oliver and me. The shape we made has made this shape.

I will call her Sophie, thinks Martha.

And I will call her Sky, thinks Raffy.

"Oh-oh, look who's here? More visitors than bloody Buckingham Palace. Start snapping." Matt lifts his camera and Micky obeys instructions.

"Whoever now?"

They flash and snap, watching the two incongruous figures as they make their way across the sand towards Lemon Cottage: a woman walks in front and behind her, round-shouldered, a thin man. Yes, thinks Betty, snap your cameras. Once a criminal, always a criminal. Poor Nick. What hope has the poor man got?

It is a relief when they open the door to the cottage and escape the glare of the men. As the door shuts, Matt and Micky cover their lenses and light up their fags, ready to speculate on who the latest arrivals might be.

Neither Betty nor Nick speaks as they enter the cottage: both are choked up with vivid memories of the place and the circumstances they were once in. Betty recalls the freedom and happiness she felt all those years earlier when she found this haven. How she had unpacked her mother's ornaments and settled in, finding peace by the quiet lake and the tapering trees. And then the awful day when that ghastly Miss Turner came and turfed her out. Just like that. On to the sand. With barely time to pack her belongings away.

For Nick, it is an even less happy recalling: when in his rage, he set fire to this cottage, tracking it down, believing that Betty, who had, after all, abandoned him, was living there. And then the triumph as he ran from the cottage, turning back only once to see the flames, defiant and tall. And then the police, knocking on the door and arresting him, and then court and jail and that awful sense of declining independence as they took his liberty, and life, away.

No wonder neither speaks. No wonder that Betty unpacks her bag of food and cooks them a meal, a simple meal and they wander round the cottage staring at the white sofas and studio and the jars of white objects and the lake beyond: trembling with the realisation that being there brings.

And by the time they flop, drained, into Raphaella's bed, neither is strong enough to resist sleep.

*   *   *

Early morning in the sandworld. Richard rises early, unable to sleep. Unlike Adam and Josh for whom the water has been a revival, he finds himself troubled by his surroundings, and the people in it. For here they are: seven very different people all linked by a ridiculous common cause. They are each waiting for a woman to return. A woman who couldn't care about them, but who has let an enigmatic sign – candles lit around the outside of the structure – give them hope. Teasing them. And hanging on to this tenuous thread of hope, they all remain. They have tried to tolerate each other, shared their food, their wine, their words, their polite smiles but the tensions have not been dissolved in the lake. Maybe, Richard tells himself, it is too many years of goodness and courtesy spilling from him and he is now bursting. Husband, father, son, farmer: there has been too much duty and now it is time for truth. Maybe the water has empowered him (concentrated rather than diluted) for he feels himself not only angrier daily but bolder. More able to feel and say what it is he feels. Tired of serving and wanting to be served.

Julian is the next to wake this morning: his mind busy and excited by the new profit margin, he has risen to check his e-mails and faxes and to tot up some figures. Business is thriving. The irony is not lost on him and he's relishing it: that the daughter who caused him so much trouble in her presence has brought him enormous wealth in her absence. It is justice for the judge, after all. And why not? He sowed plenty: now it's time for him to reap.

"Good morning." Julian has just seen the figures for the gallery for the previous day and feels cheerful.

"I want to know something." Once again, Richard is surprised by the strength of his own words, his voice.

"Certainly." Julian finds himself feeling strangely nervous. Internally, he reprimands himself. What; are you, one of the country's top judges turned successful art dealer, afraid of a common farmer? "What do you want to know?"

"How you managed to persuade Martha to have a child for you?"

Julian sighs, sits down on the sofa. Not that same issue again. "That was a long time ago, Richard. Why don't you let –"

"It may seem a long time to you, but my wife has never recovered from it. It is because of that that our marriage suffered. It is because of that that her sons all suffered. It is because of that that we are all here now waiting for her to return. Have you any idea what effect that has had on her?"

"I wasn't to know that, was I? How could I have predicted that, Richard?"

"You have not answered my question. I want to know why she agreed to it? Was it rape?"

"Of course not. How dare you?"

Richard is towering over Julian now, his eyes a few inches from the older man's. Julian feels oddly afraid. This man is aggressive, rough, untamed. He could do damage. Why did Lucius allow him to stay?

"Well, you're not moving until I've had an answer." Richard has stretched his arm over Julian's head and is holding the sofa, cornering Julian. "Why? How?"

"Gertrude and I had been married several years and had been trying for a child. Gertrude had the idea that we should ask Martha, who cleaned the cottage for us, to carry a child."

"So you persuaded this young girl to sleep with you, knowing that the child would be taken away from her as soon as it was born?"

"That's right. Can I go now? I've got some work to – "

"And what was in it for her? Why would a seventeen-year-old girl agree to do that? For money? For a promise of some kind? Or because for some mad reason she loved you?"

266

"None of those. She just agreed."

"Yes." Richard's face has hardened, turned red. "Yes, and that would suit you, wouldn't it, you bastard? Your class, that's all you do, just take and grab and rape and steal, never thinking about anyone else or how what you do ruins other people's lives. You, you have got us all into this mess and I am going to get you into a mess. Do you understand me?" His face is so close to Julian's now that their noses nearly touch, their eyes are an inch away. The spit from his words falls on Julian's chin. "You will not get away with this. I will see to that myself. You have finally met your match."

For ten minutes after Richard has swum slowly away, Julian shakes with terror.

Chapter
XLVI

The atmosphere in the sandworld has changed. The air, the water seems unstill, unsettled as if disturbed by the new animosity. Julian sits on the sofa, sulking. When Lucius comes in with that morning's latest figures of soaring sales, he finds his business partner fuming.

"Good news," says Lucius, brightly. "Sales are higher than ever." Pause. "What's wrong?"

"Oh, it's just that farmer chap. I wish he'd leave. Everything's soured since he arrived."

"How so? I find him perfectly pleasant."

"He's irritating."

"Been through a hard time, hasn't he? Lost his wife. Doesn't know where she is."

"Yes, I suppose so, but he just irritates me."

"What did he say to you?"

Julian looks at Lucius. Why spoil a good working relationship?

"I'm just being silly," he says. "It's nothing. Nothing at all. Now, where are those delicious figures?"

Richard goes to find Gertrude. He sees her threading shells on to rope, smiling. She has a contentedness about her which is full, genuine. Richard feels a moment of guilt, that he is about to shatter it. She looks up at him warmly. He sits down near her, does not return the smile.

"How are you today, Richard?" she says. Her mock-motherly concerned tone angers Richard.

"Hypocritical bitch," he mutters.

"Pardon. What did you say?"

"This isn't a friendly visit. I've come to ask you some questions."

Gertrude puts down the shells. Sighs. She can tell from his tone that these questions will not be welcome ones. Which questions ever are?

"There are many things about Martha's past that I am unclear about. I knew when I married her that she had had a child, a daughter, who now turns out to be Raphaella. But I didn't ever question her about this. She had been through so much pain even though she was young, and I left her secrets alone out of respect. Maybe I was too passive in those days, as well. Anyway, little did I know that that birth would basically ruin her life and certainly our marriage. It clouded everything. That loss. It stopped her from enjoying her own sons, even from loving them, and it never left her mind. It was an obsession. And you and Julian caused that."

"We didn't know, Richard, that it would have that effect."

Richard's laugh is sardonic. Sadistic, Gertrude thinks. "What effect do you think it will have, if people ask someone else to have a child for them?"

"It wasn't like that, Richard."

"Well, how was it, then? Julian won't tell me. Will you? Why did she agree to do that for you?"

"It benefited her."

"How?" Richard is shouting. Gertrude feels unsafe with him. He will not leave her alone until he has the answer he wants. He is dangerous. There is insanity in his eyes. "Why would anyone agree to have a child for someone else? To just hand it over?"

"For money."

"I see. You bought the child."

"Don't put it like that."

"How should I put it? Black market? Slavery? Prostitution?"

"No, no." Gertrude is crying out. "It was a contract. An agreement. She needed money to help her parents on the farm. We wanted – couldn't have – a baby. No one was forced. Richard, you must believe me. We never intended her to suffer."

Richard's face is close to hers now. His nose almost touching hers. She is shaking. Terrified.

"Intend to or not, you destroyed her life. And you destroyed mine." Pause. "And I promise you. I will destroy yours."

After he has left, Gertrude sobs and sobs. It is true that the reality of what has happened has never hit her until today. The impact. The consequences. And suddenly the story seems implausible to her. Even after all these years. Yes, she can understand why Richard is not convinced. She is not convinced herself even though she was involved. Would a young girl – and Martha was no fool – agree to have a baby when she knew the disgrace it would bring to her parents? Maybe, there is more. Was more to it. She will ask Julian later. When she has stopped crying. When her body has stopped convulsing. Later.

Julian sits in the sandworld watching through the window, the figures of Lucius, Adam and Josh messing about in the water beyond the building. They splash each other, catch each other's feet in their hands so that they stumble, throw algae into hair, tickle each other with underwater greenery. They are generally laddish, almost hooligans, thinks Julian, drinking white wine and thinking it is overcooled, and he does not approve of them. He has no objections to men having fun but this, this male nonsense is repugnant to him. Is there something sexual in it?

Gertrude comes up to him, puts her hand on his arm. He turns to look at her, sees she is pale.

"What's the matter?" he asks, pleased for some female company even though there is little variety here.

"It's Richard."

"Oh, he's interrogated you as well, has he? Thoroughly unpleasant man, isn't he? He should go back to his pigs and sheep. He's more suited to them than to human company."

"Yes, he's unpleasant and aggressive, but in a way I do feel sorry for him."

"You do?"

"Yes. He says that what we did affected his life and Martha's very badly."

"What tripe. She had a choice in the matter. She agreed to it."

"That's what I said. But he didn't seem convinced she would have done it just for money."

"Oh, you told him about the payment, then?"

"I had to. He kept asking. I was frightened of him. Still am. But I don't think he's satisfied with my answer." Pause. "And nor am I."

"*You* aren't satisfied with your own answer? Now you're losing me. I'm out of touch with legal language."

"What I mean is, Julian, would she really have agreed to do that for us for payment?"

"She needed the money for her parents' —"

"Yes, I know. That's the pat answer. But what about the truth, Julian? It's time you told me. Yes, I know you've had flings. I know that. But what about Martha? Was she your mistress? Is that why she agreed to do it? Not for money but because she loved you? Maybe believed that you would even leave me and marry her? Is that the truth?"

Julian has turned his back to his wife and is watching the antics of the men outside. They are in a real mess: lacustine

271

plants and bits of shreds of shell on their naked bodies, their hair. They are laughing and squealing with delight. Lucius seems drunk with it all, delighted with his new life: business success, constant lover to Oliver, general laddy layabout in the day.

"Well?" He has almost forgotten that Gertrude is there. Waiting for an answer. "Was Martha your lover anyway?"

Julian has found it harder to lie in the lake. Is it the water or his age, he wonders? He used to be so good at it: the deceit, the cover-ups, both in work and at home were almost effortless. But since coming down here, it's been easier to relax, harder to lie. Maybe the water washes one clean. Maybe it dissolves disguises. Maybe it is purifying. Whatever it is, Julian cannot reply. The neat answer, the smooth response, does not come. He turns round to face Gertrude. His eyes – and his silence – confirm the truth.

She slips away, tears yet again forming in her eyes, and Julian watches the boys for longer. They have linked arms now, are trying to force each other playfully on to the sand bed. Watching their frolics, it occurs to Julian: this is why Lucius does not want father and sons to leave. Not for any supposed kindness to Richard but because he likes playing.

From a nearby window, Oliver is watching the men, too. He has noticed this new camaraderie forming: day after day they play and tussle with each other more and more. It is as if something has been released in the three of them. Yes, he knows Lucius genuinely loves him. Yes, he knows that Lucius would let him – indeed, has invited him to – join in, but it doesn't feel comfortable to him. Oliver isn't into these silly male games. So he feels – is – excluded. But there's more to it than that. It's as if there is some slight malice in Lucius lately, as if he's trying to get back at, take revenge on, Oliver. For what? He's done nothing wrong, hasn't betrayed him. Though maybe it's about Raphaella. For in spite of

272

Oliver's denials, he feels that Lucius knows. And he knows he knows. Yet they both go on pretending that all is fine.

Oliver goes to bed. So do Julian and Gertrude, with backs to each other. Richard and Joe have gone to sleep as well.

None of them is awake long enough to see the way the jollity turns into gravity as Lucius discusses, with Josh and Adam his new plan.

Chapter XLVII

"You know," says Betty after breakfast. "I don't really feel comfortable here." Nick nods his agreement. She does not add that the way it has made her feel towards Nick is more negative than she had anticipated. The way he tried to burn the house down. After killing her mother. The way that Miss Turner kicked her out. The way that Mr Turner abused and mistreated Betty. Why, thinks Betty, have I never been loved the way that I love others? Her thoughts turn to Richard: he was the first person ever to have valued her – and she let him slip away. Where are you, Richard, she thinks, looking out to the lake. And do you think of me still?

"I'm ready to leave," says Nick.

Although his voice is quiet and he still looks pale, Betty can see an improvement in him. She has tried to care for him the last few weeks, listened when he talks of Jesus and God even though he does not even understand any of the concepts he is expounding, fed him well and even hugged him. She has treated him with compassion as she might a stray dog, but her old love for him has not come back. She has waited but it has not returned. Still, he has improved. He speaks now, eats quite well, reads, and sits quietly. He is a man diminished, but at least with that reduction, the temper and aggression seem to have gone.

"Yes," says Betty, speaking quietly to him as if he were a child rather than a former drug addict, arsonist and convict. "I'm ready to go as well."

So together they pack their few belongings and head out to the sand. Then they see Matt and Micky smoking, their cameras ready on tripods, as if they had never been away. In fact they have. While Betty and Nick were in Lemon Cottage, the cameramen returned home only to be sent back there again. Things could get exciting soon, their editor says. And so they're back again, poised, ready to shoot.

"So where are you two off to, then?" asks Matt.

"We're looking for some people," says Betty tentatively. She's always been suspicious of the media.

"Ah yes," says Micky. "Like everyone else then."

"Sorry?"

"Well, everyone who comes here is looking for that loony painter woman and the farmer's wife. Is that right?"

Betty nods.

"Right then. You two pose for us for a couple of snaps and then we'll point you in the right direction. Deal?"

Betty smiles nervously. Her days of deals are over – but still. Perhaps if they find where these two women are, she'll find Richard, too.

So she and Nick stand awkwardly together, with the lake and cedar trees as the backdrop to their uneasy smiles.

"And one more, darlin'," says Matt, chewing gum. "Lovely. You can relax now."

Then he points out the sand dome visible in the distance and the sand tunnel which leads to it and Betty and Nick thank the two men and, belongings in hand, set out to meet the others.

Raphaella is sitting holding the baby. She is beautiful: more lovely than Raphaella could have imagined. Her name is right, Sky – for her eyes are as clear and blue as the canopy above the water. She, a mother; who could have believed it? A daughter and a mother. Martha arranges a baby blessing ceremony and plaits shells and lake lilies round her head and they celebrate her. Martha adores them both – Raffy and

Sophie. As my mother helped me, she thinks, so I will help you. This little girl, this dear little girl, has made Martha relive her own past: her mother, the birth of her daughter, how she gave her away, how she found her and now her grand-daughter. She cradles the child and plants kisses on her moist tiny forehead. If she could breastfeed her, she would do so. Do anything for her. Raphaella does that happily; breastfeeds Sky and the baby slurps at her mother's balloon breast. It is an act of nourishment and warmth, the baby nuzzling up to the mother's breast for love as well as milk. And the three of them make a beautiful sight: grandmother, mother and daughter: a trio, a family.

Raphaella is content: for the first time ever she feels satisfied. Yes, she yearns to paint again. Yes, she wants to return to Lemon Cottage, but there has been a completion, a filling in. She looks from Martha to Sky: mothers and daughters are here, beneath the water, and that is happiness. A future. A reason.

"You seemed to be having fun last night – you and the boys." Oliver is lying in bed, his voice tart, his body taut.

Lucius puts his hand on Oliver's shoulder. He shrugs it off. "Come on, Oliver. It's harmless fun, that's all. It would do you good to join in."

"And what does that mean?"

"Well, you're so serious and grave these days. If we're all going to be stuck here by a lake waiting for the bloody Messiah to come, we might as well enjoy ourselves. I don't know why you're so angry."

"I'm not enjoying it here, OK? I'm sick of the water, always being drenched, never getting my hair dry for a second. I'm beginning to feel soggy and soaking wet all through. I'm fed up with it. I don't know where Raphaella is. And the whole atmosphere in here has really gone sour."

"Yes. I know what you mean."

"It's all happened since Richard came. Before that, the four of us were fine. Two of us even better, yet I don't mind Julian and Gertrude. But since Richard's come, he's fallen out with those two and I sense some tension between Julian and Gertrude as well, so he's obviously stirred something up there, and then you never spend time with me any more. Can't you tell Richard and his boys to go?"

"No, I can't. They're waiting for their mother, remember? And besides, I've got a business venture that I'm going to start with them. D'you want to join in?"

"What's it going to be? An underwater art gallery?"

"No, something else. It will distract them while they're waiting and give me something to do. I'm restless here."

"She won't come. They're wasting their time."

"I'm not so sure. You remember that sign? The candles? That was pure Raphaella. Wherever she is, I'm sure her mother is too."

"Why don't they show up, then?"

"I don't know, but I'm sure they will soon. And therefore I think we should all go on waiting."

Or perhaps, thinks Oliver, you don't want to leave your new friends.

What's up, thinks Lucius: don't you want to see your female lover again?

The next morning. And the air and water are full of hatred and resentment. The sweetness of the water has turned acidic. Even the gorgeous blue sheen on the lake has dulled. And reflecting the lake, the sky is disapproving, stern.

Inside the sham sandworld, Julian and Gertrude barely speak. Joe is sullen and subdued. His father is angry. Oliver is cross with Lucius. Lucius is angry with Oliver. Meals are no longer communal. The community has been splintered.

277

 *   *   *

In the middle of the lake, by the algae, a meeting is going on.

"So," says Lucius, "the idea is that the three of us will run a trout farm. It will give us something to do while we're waiting and we can all eat the trout. What do you think?"

Josh and Adam raise their eyebrows at each other.

"I dunno." Josh. "I don't know anything about trout."

"Nor do I," says Lucius. His cheeks are pink with excitement. Something to do. Something to run. "But I've managed a successful business and you two have run a farm. How hard can it be?"

Adam and Josh smile. Maybe?

And it is into this tense atmosphere that Betty and Nick arrive.

Chapter
XLVIII

"What do you mean, no progress? I am not paying you a top salary so that you can stand there and say (imitates his voice but exaggerates its feebleness) 'no progress'."

Inspector Bloor looks down at his shiny shoes, back up at the boss again.

"I'm sorry, sir. What more can I do or say? All the witnesses keep disappearing."

"Oh, do they indeed?" The boss rises and puts his face into Bloor's. "Well, you listen to me, Inspector. You have two weeks left in which to solve this case and if you don't, you'll wish you'd disappeared by the time I've finished with you. Do I make myself absolutely clear?"

Detective Inspector Bloor leaves the office and walks down the high street. He opens his tablet box and knocks four down – double dose. He must solve this case. He must. Now, let's think. The painter, the farmer's wife, the farmer and his sons, the judge and his wife, and now the former maid and the arsonist have all gone. They must have gone to the same place. But where? He must find it. He will find it. He will go to Lemon Cottage in the morning and start out where they did. For an instant, the lake flashes large and wide in his eyes. He tries to dismiss it. Water. Again that vision which he has tried so hard to suppress, re-emerges. Uninvited.

They're by the pool: class 3C with Mr Roxborough, the teacher everyone hates. And he's shouting at them: "Get in the water. What's the matter with you?" And the pool is wide and grinning – an evil gaping blue mouth. Most of the children jump in, deciding it might be better to do it on thier own than be pushed by him. Bloor freezes to the spot, feet stuck on to the wet surface. Refusing to move.

"Get on with it, Bloor. Feeble little worm," and the child feels the man's bent knees in his back and a big push and Bloor's in, and he's underwater and he can't see and he feels like he's dying and it seems an hour or two until he resurfaces, wet and terrified.

The first sight he sees is Roxborough's smiling face.

"Good," he says, his evil grin widening so that it seems as large as the pool. "Next Thursday you'll do it again."

Bloor gulps hard and rubs his eyes. Deep within him, he knows where the missing people have gone to. And it's somewhere he does not want to follow them.

Bloor is not the only person to be reprimanded on this gorgeous summer's day. Pink-footed geese fly over the lake. A cormorant perches on a rock.

Matt and Micky are shifting nervously on the sand. Their boss is on the phone to them and they hold the mobile between them, each with one ear glued to the receiver.

"Do you think I've got money to pay you so that you can send me pictures of a bloody lake? I want action and I want it fast."

"Yes, sir." They're feeling five years old. First-year infants.

"The public is waiting. For news. For pictures. This is a hot story. And you're cooling it down. D'you get my drift?"

"Yes, sir."

"Now you get me some good piccies or you're unemployed. Right?"

The dialling tone replaces his voice before they have another chance to say "Yes, sir."

"What about him?" Matt points to Inspector Bloor, walking uneasily along the sand. He avoids the lake to his right. Stares at his feet making imprints.

Matt and Micky smile nervously at him. They know who he is, have seen him here before, asking questions, although they've felt he should have been here a lot more. What the hell has the man been doing?

"Hiya, Inspector." Unusually, Micky speaks first. "You alright?"

"Not really." The inspector looks more glum than anxious today. "Not so great really, gentlemen. The boss is on at me to solve this wretched case and I don't seem to be making any progress. What about you?"

"The same," says Matt. "Tell ya what. Let's have a picture of you looking out to the lake and at least that'll keep your boss happy. And ours."

The inspector complies, but points his body only diagonally to the lake and more towards Lemon Cottage. That expanse of blue. Good God.

"Nah," urges Matt. "More at the lake. That's where they've all gone to. Either drowned or changed into bleedin' mermaids or something odd."

The inspector moves his body towards the lake but averts his eyes so that the picture printed in the evening edition makes him look like a recalcitrant child, told to eat his bowl of cabbage.

"Bloody idiot," says the boss back at Head Office as he unfolds that evening's paper and sees a picture of Bloor, body pointing towards the water, eyes shooting sideways. "Stupid little arse."

*   *   *

Betty and Nick hover by the entrance to the sandworld and listen.

"I don't think so," Richard is saying. "I don't think that anyone would sleep with you, payment or not." Betty thrills at the sound of Richard's voice but is surprised by the harshness and anger within it. It's not like Richard at all. Maybe the water is distorting the sound.

"Yes, do carry on insulting me," says Julian, "but none of this will bring your wife or my daughter back."

"Huh!" snorts Richard. " 'My daughter,' all of a sudden. You're happy to exploit her work and make money out of reproducing her paintings when you know how much she would hate it. That's how much you care for your daughter."

"She couldn't stand you, anyway." Joe. Quietly-spoken.

"He's right." Oliver. "You're happy to betray what Raphaella wanted and yet now you pretend to be concerned for her welfare."

"Well, that's ripe." Julian's voice is sarcastic now. "You defend your lover doing it, but not me. That doesn't seem at all just."

"What doesn't seem just?" Lucius has come in from his work with Adam and Josh. It's going well. Lucius clutches a trout. Its brown-silver skin glints in the water, its eyes bulbous. "Oliver?"

"This whole business of reproducing Raphaella's work. You know how she felt – feels – about originals and copies. And you're going against that."

"Oh come off it, Oliver. You're not still going on about all that, surely? She'll be getting her share of the profits, you know. It's all above board."

Gertrude has kept quiet throughout the conversation, partly aware that she's the only woman there and partly because she feels torn between Julian and Oliver. Yes, Julian has let her down badly, but he is her husband. And Oliver. She feels protective towards him, likes the way he lies his head in her lap in the evenings and lets her stroke his hair; but he is also removed from her. Mother and son. A world away. Today, she feels alienated from these men and their bickering, from the gay boys out there, larking around, from the water and the algae and the salmon and the sand. In a way, she longs for home. But can she go on living with Julian when they return? Oliver feels much the same about Lucius. At first, the water seemed to unite them. Now, it has divided them, made reflections of their differences and projected them on to every stone, every shell.

"What the hell are we all doing here anyway?" asks Oliver.

"Getting on each other's nerves." Richard.

"We're waiting," says Lucius. "For Martha and for Raphaella. We all know that."

"And how long are we going to wait?" Gertrude.

"As long as it takes." Lucius. Confident.

"What? For you and Julian to make enough money and for you and my sons to build up your business?" Richard. Cynical.

For a moment, Betty wonders whether to grab Nick's arm and lure him back down the sand tunnel and to dry land again. But she hesitates, sees the change in Nick's face. The water has refreshed him, brought colour to his cheeks. His eyes are gleaming. He seems alive again. He is smiling, watching Adam and Josh, their hands full of trout. To Betty's surprise, she hears Nick chuckle.

Chapter
XLIX

Betty and Nick are not the only eavesdroppers that evening.

On the other side of the sandworld, Raphaella floats in the water and listens, too. Listens to the way her family and colleagues are fighting about her. Does she matter that much to them? Has she caused that conflict? She thought it would please her, the deceit, the trickery involved, but if anything it has made her feel more isolated. There they all are and, in spite of the fighting, they are all living together encased. Enclosed. She has caused unhappiness to others while she has her mother and her baby. So why has she come here? Thought for a mad moment that she would just turn up at the sham sandworld and say, "Hi everyone. Guess who's here?" And how would she be received? Delighted to see her again, darling or would they kill her for all the trouble she had caused? And how would she know if their response was genuine or fake?

Raphaella hears the fighting within and decides against it. Instead, she takes her candles in glass jars and lights them around the sandworld again. As her logo. Her sign.

In the morning, the sandworld is still. The sun drips gold into the water. Twirls it into spirals. Each group has retreated to its own unit. Julian and Gertrude sleep in their elegant quarters. Lucius and Oliver have retired to their black-leathered, modern prints apartment. Richard and Joe have made their corner into a farmhouse, floral curtained residence, window-boxes filled with geraniums. Adam and Josh have made their own mark on their space: inflatable

284

chairs, plastic plants, mock fish which stare disdainfully at their real relations, water beds for the two of them.

When they awake, there will be two surprises awaiting them: another one of Raphaella's signs and two newcomers.

Betty and Nick have scooped themselves beds in the sand in the middle of the sandworld and settled down for the night. Nick has had his best night's sleep in years. Soothed by the softness of the sand and the water lapping outside, he has dreamt and is feeling free, never waking nor stirring to question his surroundings, but as he has never done before – not in their attic flat nor in his crummy childhood home and certainly not in the jail (Nick in the nick) – now that he has arrived home. Betty has barely slept at all; feeling shivery and cold, unused to the sound of liquid nearby, preferring the smell of dry land. And she is worried, scared at the reception that her former employers are going to give her, that her former friend, Richard is going to give her, and what about all those who care for Raphaella and who work out that Nick burnt Lemon Cottage down? In her strong moments, she has thought that she could handle all this, come out triumphant, if anything, teach them all a lesson. But now, in this lakeside cavern, she wonders what it has all been about. How could she single-handedly have won? And what if Richard rejects her and the Turners reject her and Nick decides to join this strange commune and she is left alone, with nowhere to go to? Why has she come here, anyway?

At one point, Betty drifts off into a dream: she and Richard are living in a cottage. It is a cross between Lemon Cottage and the farmhouse and it is idyllic: chickens pecking at grain in the yard, a honeysuckle twisting its sweet-scented way up the brickwork, a cloudless sky, and, to Betty's amazement, on awakening, four little red-cheeked children running around the yard, chasing the chickens, threading

285

daisy-chains, laughing. She starts; what the hell is she doing here anyway? She looks across to Nick. Dawn is gently caressing his face; he sleeps soundly. Why has she brought him here? And is she still responsible for him?

Inspector Bloor fingers the paintings in the studio at Lemon Cottage. He is leading himself on a search – another one – to find some clues about Miss Turner and her strange vanishing. He has been here before, carried out investigations – basic and advanced and more advanced still – and found no hints at all. And yet, he has come here again. In his heart, deeper than he cares to venture, he knows that the reason is avoiding what he knows he has to do, but he can justify this to himself: not delaying tactics but routine, necessary searchings. All part of his work, you see. Even though his boss is on to him for results. Even though Matt and Micky, who have been watching it all, have told him. Still, he avoids the water and stays on dry land. Indoors.

"Interesting. I see," he mutters to himself even though he has found nothing and does not expect to. He speaks to no one. No one answers him. Except a tiny voice within him which implores him: go out, Bloor. Go out to the water. Out to and into it.

And the voice leads him. Almost without thinking, he opens the door to the cottage and walks along the sand, past Matt and Mickey, to where the sand becomes the lake. He stands at the edge of safety and stares.

Martha is holding Sophie and smiling at her.

"You're a darling," she coos, and is rewarded with smiles and a dribble of saliva which drops like clear syrup from the child's mouth and is lost in the water. She cuddles the child, in the absence of her mother. "Mummy will be here soon," she says. "She's gone to do something."

286

To Martha this child is everything: the daughter she had and lost and found and lost again. The mother who she took for granted. The baby son who she neglected. This child is the justification for all those losses. Embodied in her is all that is good, and all that has been lost has been restored within her. And who else does that child have besides Martha? The two women will look after Sophie. Martha has let one baby go; she is not prepared to lose another.

Raphaella returns from her night-time travels. She has lit her candles and placed them round the structure; she has swum and thought and played with the idea of running away and never returning. And yet the milk hangs heavy in her breasts and overfull, makes white rivers down her skin. She wants to feed Sky. Her body aches for her. She holds her now and feeds her, Martha stroking Raffy's hair. The baby slurps. Tiny fingers curl on the breast, and the sucks and gurgles the child makes against her nipple comfort her.

You will care for her, thinks Martha, and I will care for you.

Bloor stands by the water and closes his eyes. Big mistake. Roxborough seems so alive to him he could be standing there now. How Bloor hated and dreaded Thursdays. Chucking in the water time. Made to sink or swim time. How he would wake on Wednesday night, sweating at the thought of being submerged, hoping to God that Thursday would be cancelled or that the school would burn down or that Roxborough would have retired or something. But Thursday came always and so did the dread and the humiliation as Roxborough's knees would bend in the small boy's back and force him in. And the struggle to float and rise to the surface never seemed to get any better. He never learned to swim. It remained a nightmare and an anxiety, even long after he'd moved on from Roxborough's class to kind Mrs Carmichael who was gentle with the nervous boy and didn't take them swimming. But each time Bloor would pass Roxborough in the corridor, the teacher would smile slyly at him and with triumph: you never learned to swim. I made sure of that. And the boy's skin would break into a sweat and he would not be calm until he reached Mrs Carmichael's classroom where they grew mustard and cress on window-sills and did crayon rubbings of tree bark and got sticky gold stars if they did good work and never, never, thank God, went swimming.

And yet, here it is, fifty years later and it's as vivid as the water which tries to reach his shoes. Bloor can see the dome jutting out on the far side of the lake. He knows what he has to do. Matt and Micky are waiting. He is waiting. His boss is waiting. But there is no bent knee in his back to force him in and so Bloor stands. Stands and waits for the courage that he needs to come.

Chapter
L

Julian is the first to wake. To spot the new intruders. Betty's eyes open before he has even spoken.

"Well, look what the cat dragged in. Or should I say the fish have brought in?"

Betty smiles faintly. " 'ullo, Mr Turner. Alright?" She knows it's a ridiculous greeting but how else do you re-introduce yourself to your former employer, whom you also blackmailed, when you do finally bump into him in a sand temple beside a lake?

Julian smiles sardonically. Betty shudders. She had forgotten how nasty he actually was. "What are you doing here? Haven't we got enough problems already without you showing up?"

"So I 'eard last night. We was listening outside the walls."

"Oh, so snooping as well as trespassing. We'll have you on several counts then."

Gertrude stirs next. "What the – what are you doing here, Betty?" Betty feels quite flattered that at least the woman has remembered her name. Considering how many maids they get through. Or Julian, in particular, gets through. Gets into. And through.

"I simply can't believe it. Why is everyone flocking here?"

"Yes." Unusually, Julian echoes his wife. "What are you doing here? And are you going to introduce us to your charming friend?"

If you think he looks bad now, thinks Betty, you should have seen him in the nick before the water got splashed on his cheeks. Of course. The Turners never met him. Indirectly, they've been connected. Paid her so she could support him. Made sure he got put in jail for arson but have never had the actual pleasure of his disappointing company.

"This is Nick," she says simply. Let's keep it to first names only, shall we? "And we've come to see what's going on. It's not a private show, is it?"

"You've come to make trouble," hisses Julian. "Now get out before I throw you out!"

Lucius has woken as have most of the others. Intrigued by the newcomers, the tension seems to have dissipated.

"Ah, more gatecrashers! Welcome!"

All we need, thinks Julian. Lucius the great philanthropist. Introductions are made and then Richard enters. Betty smiles nervously at him; he looks cold. She feels disappointed. Even Richard has turned against her now.

"I think we've just about got room for you, if you'd like to stay," says Lucius, ever the host. "There's just one section of the building available."

"Hang on," says Julian. "Is your surname Fletcher by any chance?" Nick doesn't answer. "Yes, I thought so. I always assumed Betty was behind it all. Lucius, this man," (pointing) "is a convicted criminal and arsonist and she, she was our former maid and blackmailer."

"Blackmailer!" Gertrude is aghast. What more is there about Julian that she doesn't yet know? In fact, does she know him at all?

"I'll explain later, Gertrude. The point is that they're dangerous and we cannot have them living with us. None of us will be safe in our beds."

"Sand beds," whispers Joe, now awake and bemused by it all. Get me back to the farm, he thinks. Simpler life by far.

"You're right," said Betty. "None of us is safe wiv 'im 'ere." She points a rigid finger at Julian. "He's a molester. You ask any of the maids what's worked for him. He's evil, he is. I'm sorry, Mrs Turner, but that's the truth." Gertrude has gone wan. "Even his own daughter was not safe in her bed, you know. And that's the truth an' all." Gertrude collapses on to a sofa. Oliver sits by her and strokes her hand. Like a son. The one she never had.

"Look," says Lucius firmly. "There's a lot of bad feeling here and we need to talk about how we all feel. What our grievances are."

First a philanthropist, now a bloody counsellor, thinks Julian. What's the matter with the man?

And they all sit speechless and angry in the dull morning light, until Oliver points out the candle ring around the structure. "Look," he says, excited. "It's another sign from Raphaella," and somehow the tiny flames in a hundred glass funnels and the deep hostility they feel render them all still. And silent.

I have to do it, thinks Bloor. He turns to look at Matt and Micky. They're making thumbs-up signs, egging him on with their smiles. They have promised that once he has been and returned they will do all they can to help. They'd go themselves but the cameras underwater. Bad idea. But when all the vanished have been returned, what great pictures they'll take with Inspector Bloor at the centre. The hero. The solver. And they'll all be able to retire early.

Go on, then. Go on, Inspector. Deep breath, eh?

Bloor looks out to the expansive lake. Why does it have to be so big? He unscrews the pill bottle, swallows five tablets. What does it matter if he overdoses now? Who's going to care? He tries to push a foot forward but it does not slip. Simply wedges itself deeper into the sand.

*   *   *

"Right," says Lucius. "now that we're all calm, I'd like to say two things. First, this is the second sign we've had from Raphaella that she is near and that she wants to return to us. It will not be very long now before she does so and we need to be ready to welcome her. Secondly, if we are all to live together in harmony, we need to explain how we feel. There is clearly anger here and we need to express that. I propose this evening that we all sit together and share a meal – I'm happy to cook – and then we each have a turn to say what we wish to. This might even be the evening on which Raphaella returns. And Martha too. This evening, then."

They all disperse. The anger and hostility between them is electric, charges up the water until it's pulsating.

Tonight, thinks Lucius, shelling snails, I shall create harmony amongst us.

Tonight, thinks Bloor, looking into the velvety sky and rich stars for strength. Tonight, I will enter that lake.

Tonight, thinks Raphaella. Tonight I am a mother. I have found the answer.

And so, as night falls, at the edge of the lake and within its swollen belly, everyone waits.

Chapter
LI

All eyes turn to look at Lucius who has entered the main room of the sandworld carrying his best creation ever. He makes a mock fanfare to which no one responds. He has found the largest shell available and has lined it with fillets of trout (from his new venture) and salmon, pink-fleshed and shiny; shrimps still tight within their shells; snails as brown and hard as bullets, and all of it garnished with silky ribbons of water-weed. All there are tempted to gasp or clap or exclaim but the tension is too bad. How can you celebrate when there is such loathing, tangible in the water?

As each person goes up to be fed, however, they mutter appreciations, thank yous, as he serves them, parent to them all. Glasses of wine are poured. Cutlery, even implements for eating snails, are handed out. Portions are taken and eaten. The food and the gorgeous taste of it goes some way to calming the atmosphere but no one can dispel the bad feeling – just as no one can dispute that Lucius has excelled himself.

Finding himself seated by Adam and Josh, who tuck in as if they've never been fed before – a greedy sight which annoys Richard – Lucius chats to them. He has new plans for the trout farm, ideas for expansion. From across the way, Oliver eyes him uneasily. Gertrude talks quietly to Oliver, understanding, without him articulating it, his jealousy and alienation. Richard eats quietly on his own, watched by Betty. Joe sits nearby. Julian tries to talk to Gertrude, but she turns away. Nick speaks to no one although Betty sits loyally by his side. She tries to catch Richard's eye but to no avail. She feels her body go out to him. In spite of the food and wine, and the water lapping round them as they eat, the anger cuts deep. It blackens the water.

Julian clears his throat. "I think we should all thank Lucius for this delicious meal," he says. All agree and there are polite echoes but Julian's breaking of the collective silence is dangerous. Maybe he knew it would be.

"Yes, you always say the right thing, don't you, Julian?" Richard, of course is the first to be riled. "Even your wife doesn't defend you any longer. Even she has seen through you."

Julian looks to Gertrude for support. He receives none. Her heart is thumping; the food has stuck in her throat.

"Come, come." Lucius is determined to play the *bon viveur*, the host. "There's no need for –"

"I'm sorry." Richard's cheeks are burning. "I know you've gone to a lot of trouble, Lucius, but even good food cannot disguise the fact that people here have treated my wife and her daughter very badly. And Julian is guilty on both counts. He has destroyed my life, Martha's life, those of our boys."

"You don't know anything about what happened. You weren't there. You were on your little farm shagging sheep or something."

Richard jumps up, his face on Julian's face. "You corrupt little turd. After all you've done to destroy people's lives you can still sit there and sound like some pompous oaf who's learned nothing from his mistakes."

Julian laughs arrogantly. Too loudly. "What mistakes are those then?"

"Ruining Martha's life by forcing her into sleeping with you to have a child which you then took away and it nearly killed her. She could never be happy again."

"With you, I'm not surprised."

"Richard's right." Betty is standing up now, has found courage from somewhere – the wine, the food, Richard's presence. "Julian has treated me and the other maids very bad. He used to make us sleep with 'im and he abused his own daughter as well. If we resisted, 'e'd sack us." Gertrude has begun to cry. Oliver puts his arm on her shoulder to comfort her. "He's a crook with money and with women."

"Crook? Me?" Julian laughs again, but it is a laugh of terror. Richard, Betty and Nick are crowding in on him. "Look who we have here. A convicted arsonist, and you dare to call me a crook."

But before Julian knows what is happening, the three of them are on top of him and there is fighting, a riot. Julian howls in pain. Richard is holding him now but it is Betty who digs her knife in, as if it has been arranged. Nick stands beside Betty but does not kill. He is reformed now. Gertrude looks away but when she looks back she sees blood spiral in ribbons through the water. She screams. Adam and Josh are in there too. Julian falls to the sand bed but to everyone's horror, the fighting continues. Lucius has joined in, trying to break it up, and Oliver.

The sand bed of the lake becomes a place of murky water and blood and cries and bodies writhing and touching, some in anger, some in an attempt to make peace. Gertrude looks to Betty as the other woman there, to be a pacifier, but Betty is fighting too. Harder than the men.

Gertrude is shocked by her own passiveness. Her husband is dead and she has done nothing. She runs towards Betty now, more out of duty than desire and Betty digs the knife in her too.

"Yes," spits Betty, the saliva from her angry mouth forming strands in the water. "Your class, you think you can rule everything. You own everything, you do whatever you want, you control us all but not any longer. I control you."

And with that and another stab at Gertrude, the older woman, elegant even as she dies, flops, her body a curve in the lake.

"Stop," shouts Lucius. "Enough. This has gone too far. This is no solution."

"Huh!" shouts Oliver bitterly. "Mr Justice, helping everyone out. But have you noticed how miserable, how bloody miserable I've been while you've been running your little trout farm with your new business colleagues and ignoring me?"

"Don't be stupid, Oli – "

"Oh, stupid, am I?"

"Well, I invited you to get involved but no, you would rather sit there, moaning and whining. My attitude is to do something. Get off my backside and take action. And these boys have helped me."

"Oh I bet they have. All hours of the day and night and who knows what you do on your trout farm."

"What's that supposed to mean? Oh, you're jealous, are you? Rubbish. There's nothing going on. You have my commitment – "

"Yes, and you have mine," says Oliver, grabbing Lucius by the neck and strangling him, clutching at him, till the man's face goes red and then his neck snaps and his head falls on to his lovely fish platter.

"There," sneers Oliver, laughing sardonically, "I took some action, got off my backside. What do you think of that?"

Adam and Josh have run towards Lucius. "What have you done?" Josh, turning to Oliver. "He was our friend."

"I bet he was." Oliver, face red, hands shaking at their own strength. What would his mother make of that, eh?

"You fucking idiot." Adam. "Just 'cos you're a screwed-up failure. Lucius was fed up with you. He wanted to be with us. Said you got on his nerves."

Failure? Oliver? Even now, after all he has achieved, the words comes back to haunt him.

Oliver runs towards the boys now, but the two of them are stronger than him. Adam sticks the knife in, Josh snaps Oliver's neck and the man falls limp to the sand bed.

Richard runs towards them.

"Adam! Josh! My God, what have you done?"

He looks at the dead bodies strewn about him, blood mixed with algae and plankton, and the whole lake has become a horrible mess. Not what Lucius had intended at all.

Joe is horrified. "You idiots, getting involved with someone like that in the first place. You are mad, you wasters, you've destroyed Dad's life," and the three strong boys are wrestling and they still hold their cutlery and no one knows who stabs whom but all Richard sees are his three boys falling to the sand bed and the strands of blood that trail from them.

"No," he wails, "my wife has gone. Now my sons." He turns to Betty. She holds him.

Nick shouts. "She's mine. Alright? Leave 'er."

"Stay with me, Betty," whispers Richard. "I need you. I love you."

"What d'ya say to that, Betty? 'im or me?" Nick's face is angry now, his old face, the way he used to be.

Betty snorts. "I thought you were reformed, Nick. But you know what they say, once a criminal – I want to be with Richard. I knew I loved him but I tried to deny it."

"No," shouts Nick, running at Richard and punching him over and over until Richard is beaten and buried and cannot breathe. And Betty is screaming and crying and she takes her knife, the one she used to kill Julian and Gertrude, and now Nick. Why not? These are the ones who have manipulated her and ruined her and yes, she tried forgiveness but this feels so much better. She stabs Nick and his eyes bulge and he falls.

And Betty's body is convulsing. Death is no discriminator. There, on the sand bed, lie those who have maimed her and twisted the life and soul out of her and there, there lies Richard whom she loved and those boys. Those lovely strong boys who were as sturdy and robust as the cattle on the farm which Richard ran, which she could have run with him.

What has her life been? She wonders, as she sits looking at the debris and damage around her. It has been pain and suffering, interspersed by a few glimpses of nature: a kingfisher skimming a lake; primroses scattered on a bank; blossom frothing on trees. Pleasurable but not enough. Not enough to make the misery worth it – and with this thought, Betty takes the knife, the knife which has killed Julian and Gertrude and Nick and she turns it on herself.

All the inhabitants of the sham sandworld are dead. They lie strewn over the lake floor, some bodies touching, others aside. Blood continues to twist through the water even after the last human breath. The walls of the sandworld have collapsed, the sand in piles upon the corpses, the windows no longer distinguishable. Here and there, a bit of decorated sand wall remains but it is a jigsaw unfinished, an incomplete mosaic. Nothing stirs on the surface of the lake. There are barely any fish or living creatures left after Lucius's raid on them for his meal, the last supper. Feeding the dead to the soon-to-be dead. For the first time in weeks, the lake is quiet.

Or this part of the lake anyway.

Not very far away, a discussion is taking place between Martha and her daughter.

298

"Mother," she says. "I have been thinking." Slurps from Sky. Raffy slips her off one breast and attaches her at the other. "Much as I love our home here, I would like us to return to Lemon Cottage. The three of us. I want to paint again. I want to bring Sky up there. What do you think?"

Martha hugs her agreement. I lost my daughter once, she thinks. I will not lose her again. I have found happiness. This is it.

This is it, thinks Bloor, by the edge of the lake. It's now or never. Now.

And closing his eyes he walks into the lake, counting in his head, praying, anything to get him in. The water's cold but by the time it is over his head, he has ceased to feel chilled by it. It becomes the norm. He finds the sand tunnel and creeps along it, the walls and direction a help to him. At the end of the tunnel is a mass of sand and blood and debris. Good God, he thinks. Some party's gone on here. He has forgotten his fear of the water in the face of chaos. He looks at the pile of dead bodies, heaped. He turns one over. Shudders when he sees the face of Betty, a trail of blood stretching from her mouth. He stands and watches, aghast.

Apart from Bloor, there seems to be nothing living in the lake at all. Not a fish nor human ruffles the water, the surface or below. Bloor is the only one to breathe and suck and blow and move. And although the sight of death in front of him is not pleasant, it makes himself feel strangely soothed to be living among the inanimate. He sits on one of the sofas (an unoccupied, non-stained one) and closes his eyes. The water covers his eyelids, his face. He can feel it on his lips, his arms, his feet. It is not frightening at all: a friend, rather than foe. A protector rather than a danger. It is like discovering that the person who you thought despises you has been rooting for you all along.

Bloor smiles, then opens his tablet bottle and chucks out all his pills. They dissolve and effervesce all around him and it liberates him.

He has found the bodies.

He has closed the case – mass suicide. (Probably a religious cult, he reckons. Look at all those candles.)

He has come to trust water.

He will not take medication again.

Bloor takes one more look at the bodies, makes a few notes and then turns back to swim through the tunnel. Then he will report back to the boss and tell Matt and Micky where they can get some really good photos. If they hurry, they might be developed in time for the next day's papers.

Chapter
LII

"Eh up. Look who's here." Matt pulls Micky by the sleeve and points to Bloor.

Emerging from the sand tunnel near the edge of the lake, Bloor looks a changed man. Drenched from head to toe, he carries files of notes and bags of evidence.

"Mission successful?" asks Micky.

Bloor nods, happily. Then he checks himself: he has just discovered ten dead bodies and still two missing. Maybe he shouldn't be too self-congratulatory. What's the boss going to say? He sits on the sand with the two cameramen and tells them more. They reward him with whisky to warm him up, towels to dry his hair with.

"But you two have got to get over there – now. You will get the most amazing snaps."

Matt and Micky look at each other reluctantly. Theirs was never meant to be an underwater mission: there are others to do that. Dry land men, them. But it would certainly please the editor and put an end to it all. As soon as they've said goodbye to the inspector, the men take deep breaths and underwater cameras and head into the lake.

"Yes, I see. So there are still two people – the key players if you like – who are undiscovered. But you have traced the other ten. You've done well, Bloor. Any explanation as to what the heck they were all doing there?"

"Yes, sir. I think I can say conclusively that they were all involved in two ways: business links and a religious cult. To take the business deal first, here" (he spreads out the contents of his bag on the desk) "are faxes, e-mails and accounts which show that the prints made from Miss Turner's work were fetching in a fair fortune. Miss Turner did not approve of her work being made into prints. She was an obstacle to them, so I suspect she has been done away with, as well as her natural mother who would have been her defendant, a troublemaker in the business partners' eyes."

"Go on."

"So this business was taking place underwater, surreptitiously, but also I've a belief that there was a cult-like dimension to it, as well. Evidence of this" (again he produces items from his bag) "is plentiful – wine, hundreds of candles in glass containers, shells, a kind of water-worship taking place, I suspect. Also some samples of drugs which I found on the bodies of the younger men."

"Bloody weird. So how do you explain the mass-deaths, then, Bloor?"

"Definitely struggles and fights. Maybe over money or beliefs, who knows? But certainly things went wrong that night. Two pressmen are in the lake right now, taking photographs."

"This is a big story and a big case and you've solved it well, Bloor. I'd like to have seen the actual bodies of mother and daughter also, but it seems most likely to me that they are no longer alive. Not that the others were, either, if you know what I mean. And what about you, Bloor? How do we reward your patience and hard work?"

"Well, sir," Bloor feels himself blushing. "Now that you mention it, I don't suppose early retirement –"

"Say no more about it." The boss rises and thumps Bloor so hard on his shoulders that he nearly loses his balance. "It shall be done. Going to tend your begonias, are you? Buy yourself a greenhouse?"

"No, sir. I hadn't realised until I went into the lake how I've missed the water. I'd like to start swimming, maybe take up other watersports. Surfing?" The physical adventure of it all makes Bloor blush again. Shaking the boss's hand, he turns and walks away.

"Well, if isn't the bloody Beach Boys," says the editor. "I thought you men were going to spend the rest of your days beside that lake." He laughs loudly, too loudly, Matt and Micky think. Even when he's smiling, he seems really nasty. More nasty, perhaps, when he's smiling.

Matt and Micky hand the pictures over. They are gruesome sights: mounds of bodies underwater, sand and debris around them. The editor flicks through them, without flinching.

"These are excellent," he says. "Tomorrow's front page without a shred of doubt. BODIES DISCOVERED – UNDERWATER CULT. You've done well."

The men smile, suddenly bashful. Maybe they've become rather reclusive, on their own all this time. No women, no company.

"Now," says the editor, "as of today you're both on leave for a while. Get yourselves bathed and shaved again. Then I've got rather a nice project lined up for you."

Matt and Micky half-smile. Curious.

"Yeah. Moon mission. Space rocket going up. Thought you might want to go too."

Matt and Micky smile weakly. Great, they both think without speaking. Months beside a lake. Now up in the bloody sky.

They shake hands with the editor and leave.

"Yes, yes," says Bloor's boss the following morning when he picks up the papers his secretary has spread over his desk.

"Fan-bloody-tastic." He looks close-up at the clear pictures of a heap of corpses, sand and bits of shell and clothing strewn about them. "Brilliant." Scans the columns for Bloor's name. Yes, and there again. Acclaim has rightly gone to Bloor – and to him. Another case neatly stitched up. He picks up the phone to ring Bloor to congratulate him. He's not at home.

Bloor has enrolled on a ten week swimming course for beginners at his local baths. And today is lesson number one. Breast stroke.

Chapter
LIII

Raphaella is a bird tonight.

After months of not changing and exploring, she has spread her white-down wings and flown through the clouds, till white is swallowed by white. Her beak is sharp and long, her eyes tiny and bright. And as she flies, she sees beneath her the lake shrunk to a puddle, her cottage just visible, the landscape a picture postcard of itself. She will go home and paint again. Originals. Originally. Nothing which is a sham or fake or copy of itself. Nothing will reproduce here.

Uncurling to her human shape again, she re-enters Lemon Cottage. Martha and Sophie Sky are asleep. Her cottage smells of baby and paint and flowers and the lake. Raffy did not know such happiness existed or, if it did, it was for others, not her. Now it is hers. Theirs.

In the living room, candles on the floor. Jars on the shelf with white buttons, shells, feathers. On the table, *shabbat* candles from the previous evening.

She goes into her studio and begins painting. How good it feels to dip brush in paint again. Blue. Her arm lifts, sweeps the brush against canvas. Hears the brushstroke. And she continues, the painting returns to her as if it had never gone away.

Here, she will spend the rest of her life with her paintings and her mother and her daughter and the lake and her home – all of them, her shapes.

Photo: Emma Findley

Tamar Hodes was born in Israel in 1961 and came to the
UK aged five. She grew up in North London, then read
English at Homerton College, Cambridge and has spent
the past twenty years teaching in schools, universities and
prisons. Many of her short stories have been broadcast on
Radio 4. Tamar is married with two teenage children.

THE BOY I LOVE
By Marion Husband

"Compelling & Sensual. Well written..."

Set in the aftermath of World War One. Paul Harris, still frail after shellshock, returns to his father's home and to the arms of his secret lover, Adam. He discovers that Margot, the fiancée of his dead brother, is pregnant and marries her through a sense of loyalty. Through Adam he finds work as a schoolteacher; while setting up a home with Margot he continues to see Adam.

Pat Morgan, who was a sergeant in Paul's platoon, runs a butcher's shop in town and cares for his twin brother Mick, who lost both legs in the war. Pat yearns for the closeness he experienced with Paul in the trenches.

Set in a time when homosexuality was 'the love that dare not speak its name' the story develops against the backdrop of the strict moral code of the period. Paul has to decide where his loyalty and his heart lies as all the characters search hungrily for the love and security denied them during the war.

ISBN 1905170009   Price £6.99

PAPER MOON
By Marion Husband

"This is an extraordinary novel. Beautifully controlled pacy prose carefully orchestrates the relationships of many well drawn characters and elegantly captures the atmosphere of England in 1946...This novel is perfect."
Margaret Wilkinson, novelist.

The passionate love affair between Spitfire pilot Bobby Harris and photographer's model Nina Tate lasts through the turmoil of World War Two, but is tested when his plane is shot down. Disfigured and wanting to hide from the world, Bobby retreats from Bohemian Soho to the empty house his grandfather has left him, a house haunted by the secrets of Bobby's childhood, where the mysteries of his past are gradually unravelled and he discovers that love is more than skin deep.

Following on from *The Boy I Love*, Marion Husband's highly acclaimed debut novel, *Paper Moon* explores the complexities of love and loyalty against a backdrop of a world transformed by war.

ISBN 1905170149   Price £6.99

THE CORRUPTED
By Dennis Lewis

Taff Motley is a disgraced Iraq war veteran who returns to his home city of Cardiff. He accepts without qualms a job as a drug dealer - which soon involves him in a murderous 'turf war' against a corrupt police force. Motley's uncertain destiny is decided for him by his abiding love for a woman.

There are no heroes and no villains between these covers. There are only people; ordinary people, struggling to forget their pasts, hoping to find forgiveness, or revealing their dangerous weaknesses, their potent evils. At its heart, *The Corrupted* is a story about love. Its pages lift a poignant mask on the questions of why men love and what love does to men.

The story is a heady cocktail sensualism and moral degeneracy, violence and ferocity - shockingly realistic.

ISBN 190517036X   Price £7.99

REMEBERING JUDITH
By Ruth Joseph

A true story of shattered childhoods...

"Elegantly written, atmospheric, nostalgic and full of trapped emotion. One of those books that manages to be both harrowing & elegant."
Phil Rickman, BBC Radio Wales.

Following her escape from Nazi Germany and the loss of her family Judith searches for unconditional love and acceptance. In a bleak boarding house she meets her future husband – another Jewish refugee who cares for her when she is ill. Tragically she associates illness with love and a pattern is set. Judith's behaviour eventually spirals into anorexia – a disease little known or understood in 1950's Britain.

While she starves herself, Judith forces Ruth, her daughter, to eat. She makes elaborate meals and watches her consume them. She gives her a pint of custard before bed each night. As the disease progresses roles are reversed. Ruth must care for her mother and loses any hope of a normal childhood. The generation gap is tragically bridged by loss and extreme self-loathing, in this moving true story of a family's fight to survive.

ISBN 1905170017   Price £7.99

RED STILETTOS
By Ruth Joseph

An intriguing and provocative collection of short stories by Cardiff based Jewish writer, Ruth Joseph.

"An astonishingly honest, real and utterly moving collection of short stories that haunt you long after reading."
Western Mail

Snapshots of family life contrast with dark tales of suffering in this multifaceted and startling collection. Ruth Joseph's unique voice reverberates with honesty and passion. She has live trapped with these stories and memories. Now they must be heard...

A sensational collection of quality short stories. The writing style is deft and stylish but accessible on many levels making it attractive to those buying for book groups and readers who enjoy quality short fiction.

ISBN 0954489977   Price £7.99

Name	Name
Fielding	